THE BOY FROM

ZION STREET

by

Geoffrey Seed

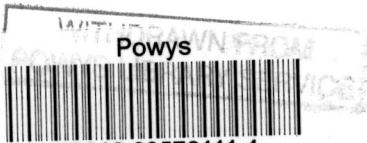

D1745245

Powys

37218 00576111 4

First published in 2016 by CreateSpace Independent Publishing Platform

Copyright © 2016 Geoffrey Seed
All rights reserved.

This book is sold subject to the condition that it shall not, by way of trade or otherwise, be lent, resold, hired out or otherwise circulated without the publisher's prior consent in any form of binding or cover other than in which it is published and without a similar condition including this condition being imposed on the subsequent purchaser.

This is a work of fiction set against actual events.

ISBN : 1530890837
ISBN-13: 978-1530890835

www.geoffreyseed.com

Geoffrey Seed is a former newspaper journalist and TV producer who worked for every leading British current affairs programme - BBC Panorama, Granada's World in Action and the ITV series, Real Crime, which re-examined controversial murder cases.

He specialised in producing major investigations - cocaine smuggling in South America, repression in the Soviet Union, political murders in the Balkans, torture in Africa, corruption in football and the British Army's covert role in terrorism in Northern Ireland.

The Boy From Zion Street is his third political thriller. The Kindle edition of his acclaimed debut novel, *A Place of Strangers*, topped an Amazon chart for months and the follow-up, *The Convenience of Lies*, was a best-seller, too.

Reader reviews of *A Place of Strangers*

"Nothing is what it seems in this beautifully written spy story, morally complex, multi-layered and intelligent."
Alan P. Wilson

"A wonderful first novel... a joy to read."
Patricia Manners

"Geoffrey Seed certainly has a place in the line of successors to le Carré while at the same time being completely unique."
Karen Bryant Doering

Praise for *The Convenience of Lies*

"Geoffrey Seed has the capacity for writing prose of a haunting quality that whispers and lingers long in one's memory."
Judy Bryan

Reaction to *The Boy From Zion Street*

"...beautifully vivid scene-setting and a plot with real depth... a seriously un-put-downable book."
Pauline Bradshaw

"I was gripped from the start... a beautifully written page-turner."
Annik Lamotte

"More than a thriller, more than a memoir, this is Geoffrey Seed's best book so far. Deftly plotted and springing some satisfying surprises, it digs deep into the hidden life of a judge who himself must face the inescapability of justice."
Patrick Malahide, star of Game of Thrones, Indian Summers, The Singing Detective etc

Dedicated to John Rodney, the best of brothers, and
to those whose hour upon the stage we shared.

*

*...there is no-one on earth
who is righteous, no-one who does
what is right and never sins.*

Ecclesiastes 7.20
New International Version

Prologue

The Lincolnshire coast, Monday 10th November 2014

The ageing judge stepped down from the causeway with care then into the wilderness of the marsh, through its pale bearded reeds and by the arteries of sly black water wherein a man might fall and never be seen again.

He made for where the soft earth gave out to the swelling sea and it was too perilous to go further. There he stood, leaning on his stick, a man like any other, rendered insignificant beneath a massing caul of gun-grey clouds.

The collar of his long black ulster was turned up against a wind bending through the dying sedge around him. He took something from an inside pocket and stooped down by the ebbing waters of a narrow creek.

His chauffeur watched from the official Jaguar, bemused. This wasn't a judge he had driven before. They'd been heading to Lincoln for a murder trial but he'd insisted on leaving their planned route to cut across the fens to this desolate place with no name.

'Is there a particular reason, your Honour?'

The judge did not answer immediately. He stared at the treeless plough lands thereabouts then caught his driver's eyes in the rear view mirror.

'I've some tidying up to do before I retire, matters I mustn't forget to remember.'

'Personal matters, you mean?'

'Yes... personal matters.'

Watery sleet began sliding down the Jaguar's windscreen. The chauffeur fetched an umbrella from the boot. The only landmark - a ruined building far out across the marsh - almost vanished in a whitened sky filled with the cries and calls of unseen birds. He found the judge amid clumps of sedge and rushes, his left arm oddly stiff by his side. But what he saw, he couldn't readily explain.

He was putting letters in the creek, maybe twenty of them, each with a blue stamp on the envelope showing the head of the wartime king and addressed in black ink or pencil to a person whose name was too small to read. They were not being discarded but placed almost reverentially, like an offering to the gods to spin and twist their way to the sea. The chauffeur knew better than to ask questions though he would have thought fire a more certain way to dispose of written evidence, not water.

'I hope you haven't got too wet, Sir.'

'No, I'm all right, thank-you. But time is pressing so we must leave.'

The judge's cheeks were pinched purple with cold and seemed damp as if the sleet had melted on whatever warmth came from within - either that or he'd been weeping.

'Don't worry, your Honour, I'll get you there. We can't have justice delayed, can we?'

'Quite so. And my little pilgrimage... that can stay between ourselves, yes?'

They shook hands on this understanding and got back into the Jaguar. The matter need not be mentioned again. A few minutes into their resumed journey, the judge made a note in his diary. *It's done; the circle is finally being closed.*

For his chauffeur, the reverse was true. He had retrieved one of the judge's letters without being noticed. Once a policeman, always a policeman - and what he'd just witnessed intrigued him.

One

Number 3 Zion Street, Fallowfield, Manchester, Saturday 23rd July 1955

Joan smoked her last Woodbine beneath a pewter figure of Jesus, hanging in perpetual agony on an ebonised crucifix above a school photograph of Spence, her quizzical, changeling of a child who was also worshipped.

He was the son the doctors said would never be fit enough to fight or die in another war. And that, as she'd recalled the earth shaking beneath her feet from the bombs of the last one, seemed like a deal worth doing with her God.

But as she looked through the kitchen window at him kicking a ball in the whitewashed yard, she felt less sure. He remained underweight for a boy coming eleven, however much nourishing food and cod liver oil she spooned into him every day. Still, you didn't get rats from mice. That's what her aunties said. Joan had only a small frame and John Henry was stocky but not big.

And when all was said and done, they had to give thanks. Many children didn't survive Spence's cruel disease. She told the hospital people that he never caught it at home. You could eat your dinner off her floors. Cleaning all day, she was – if not in her house, then at someone else's. But the polio took him down all the same. They said he'd been lucky.

It got into his arm, the left one, but it could have been far worse so that was a blessing. That's what she prayed for now - another blessing, if not a miracle.

Joan glanced again at the flat brown paper package on the table. Here was deceit and wickedness tied up in string. But what choice did she have when her belly betrayed her a little more each day?

She put on the court shoes she'd bought from a catalogue and the navy coat kept for best and funerals then set a beret amid her cropped black curls. They always said her sister might have the brains but Joan had the looks.

'I'm just going into town, Spence.'

'Shall I come with you?'

'No, I don't know how long I'll be and you'll not want to miss the circus later.'

Joan cut through the builder's yard behind the house to avoid those who kept watch from behind the curtains of Zion Street. For them, nothing went unnoticed.

She caught a bus from the stop across from the Friendship Inn and sought an empty seat. Her mind was too full of worry to share with strangers that day. Right or wrong, good or evil - nothing seemed simple any more.

The bus went by the university where Miss Arbib taught. They'd become good friends over the years. She treated Joan as an equal, not a skivvy, and said she should call her Zilla but that seemed too familiar, not respectful enough.

Miss Arbib was cultured and clever and thought Spence should go to grammar school then university, maybe even Oxford or Cambridge. John Henry said this was a damn fool idea to put in the head of a kid who'd need to get his hands dirty once schooling was done.

Yet how could a boy who'd had polio do manual work? John Henry didn't think about that - or a lot else, if truth were told. That was why she'd not tell him about the baby. He'd want to keep it.

But that'd mean money being even scarcer and Spence condemned to a future in a factory. Joan wasn't going to let that happen.

*

Spence hated school, loathed the chanted prayers and the enforced physical jerks in the hall where they only wore underpants so everyone could see he'd a skinny, polio arm. *Skellington, skellington, Spencer's a skellington.*

It was the same chant most afternoons as the others tumbled into the street to jest and fight and goad the weakest amongst them. But today, none of that mattered for he'd be at the circus - the vulgar, clowning, out-of-his-world circus, all paid for by Auntie Kitty's bookie.

He was a little round man with wetted-down hair who hired a coach from Finglands every year to take the kids of his punters to Belle Vue to see the jugglers and bareback riders and the tigers that could bite off a man's head.

Auntie Kitty said it was Spence's reward for carrying her bets to the bookie's runner, Birdie Gill, who hid in an old air raid shelter by Zion Street. Spence only ever saw his hand reaching out from the darkness to take Auntie Kitty's shillings, wrapped in a piece of paper with her horse's name on it - that and a code word showing it was her bet. And if it won or was placed, she'd tip him sixpence and say it was his wages.

'But don't ever let a policeman catch you feeding the Birdie,' she said. 'Spoil all our fun, do those buggers.'

So Spence pretended to be a secret agent, keeping to the shadows to get to the Birdie's nest without being seen. That was the game. And how he loved living in his head, for there no one tried to knock him to the ground or call him the *cripple boy*.

11

Auntie Kitty said people's words didn't hurt and she should know. She went into pubs dressed in suits like a man with a cravat and smoked cigarettes in a holder and made her lips into a Cupid's bow with bright red lipstick. And she was always dyeing her hair a different colour - ginger one week, lemon the next.

'I don't mind if people laugh at me,' she said. 'I cheer up their day and God knows, we all need that.'

Auntie Kitty waved at Queen Victoria once. She and Frances and Emily were young then and watched the old queen open the Manchester Ship Canal.

All three sisters still lived in the same house but Auntie Frances wasn't very well with her heart and sat by the fire with her hands in a tea cosy to keep them warm. She couldn't always get her breath and seemed tired and sometimes spat on a piece of paper so Spence looked away whenever she did.

His Mum's clever sister, Vron, lived with them, too. She slept in the attic and they all made a fuss of Spence and said he'd the head of a professor and would show the world a thing or two when he grew up.

But Spence's favourite was Uncle Edgar - Frances's husband, who took him to see adventure films at the Odeon *...so we can get away from all these chattering bloody jackdaws at home*.

Spence felt safe in their chaotic, kettle-whistling house - safe and loved by its cussing cast of grown-ups, ruffling his hair, giving him toffees and kisses he pretended he didn't want and where everyone knew it just as '35' because that was its number on Grenville Road.

*

Joan's bus passed houses beyond counting, all lost in a yellowish haze of coal smoke and full of women like her, forever trying to make ends meet and never quite succeeding.

Vron and their Dad went to live in a street near there after Mother died. Joan's first memories were from that time - a glass-sided hearse and two big horses snorting the cold air. She'd understood nothing, not the plumes of black feathers or the man who wept or why they had to move to a different house.

Joan couldn't go with them. She was only three years old but her sister, Vron, was already at school and needed less looking after. So Joan was given to her aunties like a present and put in their care.

They were kindness itself but nothing compensated for not having a real mother. Still, everyone made the best of a sad job and in this way, her Dad kept his responsible position at the Labour Exchange.

Such a gentle and considerate man, her Dad. He didn't drink or smoke and when she was older, took Joan to the music hall every Friday. Lovely nights, they were... all singing and gaiety then he'd put her on a tram home to 35.

Her bus nudged between cars and cabs and lorries loaded with baled cotton or huge reels of newsprint for the presses in Withy Grove or Deansgate.

Here and there were great gaps between the sooty-black offices and department stores where buildings once stood before the German bombers terrorised the night. Faint zigzags of burnt-out stairs were visible on the ends of buildings still standing. Even a few metal fire grates somehow clung to the bare brickwork, all open to the wind and rain and the restless, dirty pigeons circling the ruins.

Joan got off near Albert Square and hurried with her package through a shuffling blur of shoppers till she found the art gallery she'd heard about in Cross Street.

The decor was stark white, modern and unsettling. The pictures displayed were daubs, not proper paintings that Joan would've hung on her walls.

A man emerged and took in all that she was - and was not - in a single, refrigerated glance.

'May I help you?'

'I've got some paintings... they're very good, they're family heirlooms.'

The man sighed from experience.

'But a crisis has cropped up and you need to sell them. Is that it?'

Joan could only nod. He ripped off the paper wrapping to reveal two pictures behind glass in slightly chipped but matching gilt frames and mounted within gold board surrounds. One showed a fisherman kneeling to offer his catch to a woman on the seashore. The second was of an old fashioned Dutch house and a windmill with two men rowing on a mere nearby.

The gallery owner's small magnifying glass swung on a ribbon over the waistcoat of his fawn check suit. But the naked eye told him everything he needed to know. He noted down Joan's name and address. His nostrils crimped as she told him.

'And you think these pictures have some value, Mrs White?'

'Yes, they were a present from someone I helped during the war and he said they were valuable because they were painted by an artist who was quite well known.'

'Unfortunately for you, that isn't the case.'

'No, that's what he said,' Joan said. 'He was a picture restorer himself so he knew what he was talking about.'

'He wouldn't have needed to be in the trade to know that these are only prints.'

'But look, it's painted there in the corner... the artist's name, *Alex Lawson*.'

'As I could paint my name but these would still be mass produced, Edwardian prints.'

'But he told me - '

' - it doesn't matter what he told you. Apart from that signature, there are no actual brush strokes on the paper as there would be if these were original works of art.'

Joan's face reddened. So the old devil had lied to her. She looked and felt stupid and didn't know where next to turn for help.

'A pawn broker might give you half a crown against them... if you're that hard up.'

The dealer watched her walk away, her ignorance tucked under her arm. It started to rain. He returned to his office and picked up the telephone to dial the city's police headquarters in Bootle Street.

'I want to be put through to Detective Inspector Challis.'

'Who's calling?'

'A contact of his. I've got some information that might interest him.'

Two

In the night when he could not forget and in the day when he could not be sure, it seemed to Edgar Sydenham that the stench of the unburied blew about him still and even now, half a lifetime later, he struggled to believe he was ever in those places or witnessed what he had.

Sometimes, he wished he'd fallen on one of those long, steady walks towards the guns, fallen with all those others who'd cobbled the earth with their skulls. That would've been quicker, more humane.

He shut the front door of 35 Grenville Road and walked down its black and white tiled path then turned right. It was four hundred and thirty six paces to the main road where he went left at the Post Office sorting depot and crossed over. The Friendship Inn was a quarter mile further on.

Edgar was advancing through the no-man's land of the time remaining to him, a big slab of a man, slightly stooped but five eleven and fourteen stones. Some of that was shrapnel, little tumours of metal it was safer to leave in than take out.

He wore a long gabardine coat and a brown trilby. His shoes were brown, too – stout, spirally patterned brogues, shined each morning in a ritual of polishing. He soled and heeled them himself, sitting in an armchair with a mouthful of tacks, hammering at an iron last on a stool between his knees.

Edgar got through forty Park Drive a day. The palm of his right hand was nicotine stained from the unlearned habit of cupping cigarettes against snipers. A goods train clattered beneath the road bridge just beyond the

Friendship Inn sending bomb-bursts of smoke over the blackened stone parapets.

The old soldier's step didn't falter. Edgar went up the steps and into the bar and ordered a pint of mild in a straight glass. He saw an unoccupied table under the best room's tall window and put his trilby on the seat by it. His silvery hair was combed thinly over a high-domed pate. The flesh of his face had an industrial pallor in the sunshine filtering through the layers of smoke from the cigarettes of others. He lit one of his own with a match he broke in half to extinguish.

Another Tommy once told him that of all the world's creatures, only men and a type of ant waged war on their own kind. That's what they must have looked like from the spotter planes... a multitude of expendable, khaki-coloured ants, yawing across a moonscape of mud.

He'd known them well, those other ranks - the carpenters and plumbers and factory hands like him. But to close his eyes now, to try and remember their grins and voices was to see only the grotesque, an indistinguishable litter of trepanned strangers slipping beneath memory. Yet he survived and felt only guilt at doing so.

Edgar drank methodically until his glass was empty then dabbed the corners of his mouth with a pressed white handkerchief and left as discreetly as he came.

From the Friendship Inn, he turned right, crossed the railway bridge then left at Martins Bank and into Sherwood Grove. Another thirty paces took him by Davis's second hand furniture lock-up on an embankment swaying with tall pink lupins.

He reached Hay Street, passed the tiny cat-pissed gardens of a terrace on his right and a bomb site on the left. The Blitz took five families from there, the old, the young, the unready. Not much was found to bury. The rubble was cleared and kids held bonfire nights there now.

Edgar entered the corner shop at the start of Meadow Street where he was known. He pushed a shilling and sixpence across the counter to the woman who'd left her preparations for Sunday dinner to serve him. She weighed a quarter pound of chocolate-covered Brazil nuts into a paper bag and handed it to him. He lifted his trilby in farewell. The doorbell chimed behind him.

Meadow Street was eight houses long. Its doorsteps were dirty but each would be mopped and stoned yellow next morning after the week's washing was done. The last house was rented by Heaney, a feckless labourer with a carrot-haired wife and seven kids but not a stick of furniture in the front room or even curtains to hide their shame.

Zion Street was just around the next corner. Edgar knocked the door of number 3, painted green for luck which never came. He was looking forward to his roast beef, now... that, and to seeing his little lad.

*

By all that was decent in the world, the most odious tip-off merchant on Detective Inspector Challis's books shouldn't have been walking the streets. His fancy was for young boys.

But a greater public good - and the cop's self-interest - were served by the pederast spying on who and what he saw in the sewers where he swam.

Challis had skewered him in an Anderson shelter with a kid who should've been in bed with his teddy. A gentleman's agreement was quickly reached, for the offending party realised that the cells of Strangeways were no place for a nonce. He called himself an art dealer these days, wore a half decent suit and moved in more polite society than a detective ever could.

The café at London Road Station was crowded. It was best to meet informants in public places. People come, people go. They saw nothing and remembered less. He'd rung in with a nickel and dime tip about a nervy woman trying to palm off a couple of cheap prints as original paintings.

Challis wasn't interested till he heard mention of an artist whose name was forged on both - *Alex Lawson*.

Suddenly, he was back in the burning height of the Blitz, called out to a death he'd known in his water was most likely a murder but his over-wrought boss deemed a casualty of yet another air raid.

Fifteen years on and a pair of worthless pictures might prove Challis right after all. This wasn't just unfinished business. Professional pride and honour were at stake. He looked up and saw the pederast heading towards him.

Twisted smile, twisted bastard. But he was coming in useful - just as Challis always knew he would.

*

No two Sunday dinner times were ever the same with John Henry. Sometimes, he'd come back laughing and joking from the pub, pretending he was a tenor like Richard Tauber and singing a babble of made-up Italian words from the wireless or his records.

He'd put his arms around Joan and try to kiss her or sing *You Are My Heart's Delight* because that was their special song from when they first met. She'd push him away with a smile, but it wasn't a happy smile and Spence could tell. His Dad never cared for being brushed off like that or told what to do by anyone. He'd had enough orders in the army and wasn't taking any more.

There was always something to fear about him, something unpredictable, like those buildings in town that'd looked safe but were so weakened by bomb blasts they just collapsed without warning.

His sister, Evelyn, owned all five houses in Zion Street. She lived on the other side of England and had done well for herself. So had his brothers. Auntie Emily said Dad was a black sheep and it was a good job he'd found Joan or else who knew where he would've ended up?

It was better when Uncle Edgar came for dinner. He always gave Spence a shilling spends and they didn't row as much, either. Everyone at 35 thought Dad funny and nice. Mum said he could be but they didn't know the other side of him. When Spence was supposed to be asleep, he heard them arguing downstairs. She said he was no good with money. Once, she said he was no good at anything then they didn't see him for days.

Uncle Edgar was like a giant. He was in the war, not Dad's war but the first one, the Great War. Mum said he saw hundreds of men shot to pieces or blown up by the enemy's bombs.

Spence wanted to know what fighting in the trenches was like.

'No, you don't, son,' he said. 'Believe me... you really don't.'

Sometimes, Spence worried that his questions might be upsetting.

'What's the matter, Uncle Edgar? You're not crying, are you?'

'No, it's just my eyes... just a bit of gas from Wipers."

'What's *wipers*?'

'Another damned place you're best not knowing about.'

20

There was hardly room to turn round in the kitchen in Zion Street, not with the table pulled out and everyone trying to find a seat. Dad was singing and Mum didn't look pleased. When they finished, Uncle Edgar said he wanted to take them to Platt Fields and the boating lake.

Dad turned awkward to get his own back on Mum and said Spence had been cheeky so couldn't go out which meant she couldn't, either. He wanted his Mum to stick up for him but it didn't always seem like she was really with them these days so Spence had to speak out himself.

'Who was I cheeky to, Dad?'

'Never you mind.'

'Why can't I go with Uncle Edgar?'

'If you know what's good for you, you won't argue.'

'But that's not fair – it's not bloody fair.'

Dad pushed his seat back and stood up. So did Uncle Edgar. The kitchen was hot with cooking and anger. Dad's hands were straight down by his sides, fingers twitching. That was a bad sign. Someone would pay for this later. He banged out of the back door. Uncle Edgar touched Mum's arm. She looked so miserable.

They set off for Platt Fields and left the dishes in the sink, unwashed. That wasn't like Mum. Uncle Edgar hired a skiff and let Spence pull the oars. He wasn't quite strong enough and they drifted but Uncle Edgar worked the tiller so no harm was done.

The sun caught on Mum's wavy black hair. She'd put on make-up and her eyes were less red. Spence could see children buying lemonade and ice creams at a kiosk near the bandstand and boys lying on their fronts, trying to catch sticklebacks in jam jars.

Mum and Uncle Edgar talked quietly so he couldn't hear. He didn't care and sat facing the other way, like an explorer alone on the high seas, peering into the future to where the new world must start.

They said good-bye to Uncle Edgar later and set off home. Mum was still very quiet. The blinds were down at Mr Dean's shop where she used to take their ration books for groceries. Nothing stirred in the grid of narrow streets.

Those confined within would be slicing sandwiches of salmon paste for tea or clucking over the scandals of others in the newspapers. The houses of Zion Street were all in shadow. Spence imagined other places, golden cities in far-off lands beyond the green ocean's edge and willed himself to fly across the world to bathe in their colours and make himself whole.

His mother paused outside number 3, key in hand. She looked down at him in her hopeless, adoring way and he didn't need to be told something was wrong.

'What is it, Mum? Is it Dad's fault, him being nasty?'

'No, it's nothing you can help with.'

'But you aren't happy, are you?'

'Not all the time, no.'

'Why's that, Mum?'

'No-one ever is, Spence. No one ever is.'

'But why, why not?'

'You'll understand one day, love... when you're older.'

But he didn't need to wait till then to know life was unfair and people were weak and their hopes rarely fulfilled. Yet something in her eyes made him feel nervous and unsure.

'You're not going to go and leave us, are you?'

She drew back slightly at this. He knew he shouldn't have said that. If sad things weren't put into words, they couldn't happen and no one got hurt. But it was too late and the question hung between them as they entered the empty house.

Three

Whenever he felt miserable at home, Spence wished he lived at Miss Arbib's. It was disloyal to think this but it was true. Her house on Egerton Road was called *Arundel*. The heavy front door was painted dark blue and the steps up were lined with terracotta pots full of geraniums.

'Spence - how lovely to see you,' Miss Arbib said. 'Come in, tea's nearly ready.'

Miss Arbib had soft, olive skin which creased round her eyes when she smiled. Spence thought her very old but Mum said she was not even forty-five and that was hardly any age at all.

Arundel was as quiet as Withington Library and with just as many books, piled from floor to ceiling and on chairs, too. Every room held treasures which his Mum was paid to dust and polish - a baby grand piano, a dark oak tridarn from Tudor times and an Oriental grandfather clock inlaid with mother of pearl dragons and serpents.

He had started visiting to watch children's television. Miss Arbib would cook him scrambled egg on toast to eat from a plate on his knee.

But when the programme finished, she made him read her Manchester Guardian. Then they would discuss the news though he wasn't always sure he understood what she was telling him. According to Miss Arbib, a famous atom scientist who gave secrets about the British nuclear bomb to the communists in Russia was a hero, not the traitor that newspapers like Dad's Daily Express always kept reporting.

'His name was Klaus Fuchs,' she said. 'The world is safer for what he did because the powerful countries will all have the same weapons now so one country can't blackmail another.'

'So there won't be any more wars?'

'That's what we have to hope for and work towards, isn't it, Spence?'

'But people still go and kill each other, don't they?'

'Well, I'm afraid for all our sophistication, there are times when we human beings can still act in violent and dreadful ways.'

'On the wireless this morning, the man reading the news said a lady had just been hanged in prison because she'd murdered a man who'd been her friend.'

'Yes, she was called Ruth Ellis,' Miss Arbib said. 'It was a terrible thing to do.'

'Do you mean it was terrible that she murdered someone or that she was hanged?'

'Those are good questions, Spence. What do you think? Is hanging right or wrong?'

'Well, it says in the Bible that you can take an eye for an eye,' he said. 'But isn't it a kind of murder for a country to kill a prisoner, whatever they've done?'

'Yes, I believe that, too. You think deeply for a boy of your age, don't you?'

Spence wasn't just her cleaner's intuitively clever son but Miss Arbib's protégé. She always told Joan he was a gift from God to be cherished and nurtured in every way. It hadn't mattered that he was damaged by polio, that the muscle from his elbow to his left shoulder was wasted away and only skin and bone remained. Spence had lived when others hadn't.

And as time passed, the teacher in Miss Arbib saw within him a diamond on the beach of pebbles where the Fates had seen fit to place them both.

*

25

The Kardomah was noisy with lunchtime shoppers, the air hot from steam folding out of coffee machines and big steel catering kettles. Joan paid for a pot of tea and sat waiting for Vron.

It was worth a special trip into town. Vron was her last hope. That damned old rogue, Freddie. He'd sworn the pictures would be worth a packet one day.

'Believe one who knows, Joan,' he'd said. 'I can't give you any wages but these are better than money in the bank.'

Joan should have realised the nature of the man. His children had. They'd cut him adrift long since... all except John Henry, of course. But with him away in the army, she'd felt a duty to care for his ailing father. She'd walked through the blackout to nurse Freddie's chronic chest. Time and again she went to cook and clean for him. Only now did she realise what a fool he'd taken her for.

Joan would be too ashamed to ask Miss Arbib for an advance against her wages. And whatever John Henry earned - plus the little she got for cleaning - always had its hat and coat on. As for money lenders, she'd never be able to afford to even pay back the interest.

Vron came in, shaking rain from her brolly and looking smart in a new grey skirt and top. She'd rather pointy, bird-like features with a high colour and thinnish black hair pulled back in a bun. She had never married and seemed content with older gentleman friends from the rag trade like her.

They hugged then Vron ordered a ham salad and offered Joan the same but she felt more sick than hungry. Vron looked at her, head to one side like a robin on a wall, curious and sensing something wasn't quite right.

Joan fought an urge to break down. She mustn't, not in front of business people Vron might know. The waitress came with Vron's order. Joan went to the ladies to compose herself and only when she returned did she share her secret.

'Congratulations, that's wonderful news.'

'No, it's not. It's the worst possible news and that's why I've not told John Henry.'

'Why ever not? It's as much his baby as yours.'

'Because we can barely manage as it is and I just don't want another baby.'

'Come on, you're only saying that for now. Everyone knows you're a great mother, you'll manage. You always do.'

'No, not this time. I have to get rid of it.'

'Keep your voice down, Joan. That's a most dreadful thing to be saying.'

'But it's true and I've been told about this man in Moss Side - '

' - you don't mean a back street abortionist, please say you don't.'

'Call him what you like but I'm at my wit's end.'

'I'm finding it hard to believe that my sister is actually talking this way.'

'It's easy for you. You don't know what my life's like, not really you don't.'

'But what you're suggesting is against the law and all the teachings of our Church.'

'Do you think I care about any of that?'

'Then what about the risks you'd be taking? All those horror stories about women dying from infections and worse and where would that leave little Spence?'

'It's because of Spence I'm doing this.'

'You could've fooled me. You don't appear to be giving him a moment's thought.'

'That's where you're wrong. I just need a little help from you.'

'If it's money you're after, Joan, I'll not give a penny piece towards the murder of an unborn child.'

*

On the bus home, Joan had no wish to catch the eye of anyone she might know, anyone who might glimpse the fear in her own. It wasn't meant to be like this. John Henry had promised her only happiness.

He'd been the shy boy working for the decorator painting the salon where she washed hair and swept up. He asked her out and they went to the Odeon.

The weather was awful that night, all swishing rain and the pavements shimmering with light from shop windows. They sat close together, warm and safe. The film was *Boys' Town* with Spencer Tracy. That's how Spence later came to have his name - to remind them of their first perfect night together.

Miss Arbib was right. Spence *was* a gift. But he was so self-contained and different that Joan worried she'd left hospital with the wrong baby - a clever one. His real parents would turn up before long and demand she give him back. It'd all be Joan's fault, of course. She wasn't a confident person. And John Henry was another insecure soul without a mother.

Joan had kept the letters he'd sent after he'd been called up into the army, little notes of love and affection scribbled in a train or a truck on the way to God alone knew where. He'd so many plans for their life after the war. They'd run a chicken farm, a roadside café, a country pub. Everything would be roses-round-the-door. But nothing came from anything save disappointment and resentment.

Since the army and whatever happened to him during the war, the gentle John Henry she'd known had slipped from her and she'd not the guile to summon him back.

The bus stopped by the Friendship Inn and she got off. So did the man in the dark raincoat who'd been reading the Evening News across from where she sat.

Had Joan noticed him - which she did not - she would have put him at around forty with hair like iron swarf and an unsmiling face that suffered boils but not fools. She crossed over to Sherwood Grove, passed by Martins Bank and Davis's used furniture lock-up and made for Zion Street. Had Joan looked round - which she did not - she would have realised she wasn't alone. But she was too pre-occupied.

It was cruel of Vron to say Spence wasn't on her mind. He was never out of it, nor his innocence or his wisdom or the hopes he carried for them all. At that moment, though, she was concerned only with her other child, the one growing inside her - the one that must be sacrificed.

Four

Judges' Lodgings, Lincoln, Tuesday 9th December 2014

It had been an exhausting day, an exhausting trial. The accused woman was never a murderer. The Crown accepted a revised plea to manslaughter late on in the case and Judge White gave her a suspended sentence. She could now be with her children at Christmas but sans the man who'd so wickedly oppressed them all.

It was a satisfying outcome to a tragic affair and one on which he was content to end his legal career.

By next spring, he'd be free to spend more time with his boat - and maybe some with Elspeth. But that wasn't a given. He began packing for tomorrow's journey home. The chauffeur was due soon after breakfast. His mobile rang, not the one used for work but the birthday present from Elspeth - her de facto direct line, whatever the hour.

'Is that his Honour, Spencer White?'

It wasn't Elspeth but a man. He sounded young, educated, professional.

'Yes, who is this?'

'My name is Dan Luston, Sir. I'm a special adviser at the Ministry of Justice.'

'This is my private number. Where did you get it from?'

'From the people who sent me up to see you. There's something I'd like to discuss with you on their behalf, if I may.'

'With me? You had better explain what you mean.'

'That would be easier done face to face,' Luston said. 'There's a pub called the Magna Carta just by the entrance to the cathedral. Maybe we could meet outside at six.'

There was frost in the early evening air. It glinted on the lace-like stonework of the cathedral's carved west front, arc-lit and golden above the red pantiles of the houses clustered at its holy feet.

White's breath condensed in little white puffs as he walked up the steep, cobbled approach to the pub. A figure approached out of the darkness.

'Judge White? Thank you for coming, Sir. I'm Luston.' He was in his mid-thirties with an eager, political apostle's face, meant to inspire immediate confidence in those who didn't know better. White's handshake was no warmer than the weather.

'Sorry it's all a bit on the discreet side,' Luston said. 'But there's no dagger in the cloak, I promise.'

White would withhold judgement. Luston led the way through to the Minster Yard and into the cathedral. Choristers were practising for Christmas. Their pious voices echoed round the ribbed and vaulted ceilings, bell clear and angel high, just as others had for nine hundred years.

'Utterly majestic, isn't it?' Luston said.

White nodded and wondered when he'd get to the point. Then Luston asked if he'd read press reports about the recent rioting in Manchester.

'About some deaths in police custody, wasn't it?'

'Three men in the space of eighteen months and involving officers based at the same police station.'

'Not a happy state of affairs.'

'No, and one which is going to get much worse. The far Left have now hijacked what they call a campaign for justice and are threatening more violent action on the streets because they say these deaths are being covered up.'

31

'And are they?'

'No, definitely not.'

'But there must surely have been an official investigation into what happened,' White said. 'Hasn't any police officer been held to account?'

'I'm afraid the Independent Police Complaints Commission didn't find the evidence to even justify a disciplinary charge, still less one of a criminal nature.'

'That is a surprise but why does any of this concern me?'

'We're in the early stages of a general election, Sir. But even if we weren't, doing nothing is not an option for this or any government. The boil has to be lanced.'

'Kicked into the long grass, you mean?'

'No, we intend holding a very transparent tribunal of inquiry,' Luston said. 'And the people who matter in our world want you to be the judge to chair it.'

White was genuinely taken aback. He was a circuit judge with an unspectacular record, a clean nose but no powerful patrons that he knew of. So why whisper him into this role? Had all the other judges they must have approached been savvy enough to sniff some poison in the chalice?

'I'm flattered to have been considered worthy, Mr Luston,' White said. 'But I must decline this singular honour. I'm coming up to seventy and about to retire. I believe I've paid my dues to Queen and country and the laws of this land.'

'With respect, Sir, this tribunal is going to be very high profile and before reaching a final decision, might you wish to talk the matter over with your wife, for instance?'

'My wife? But this is a professional matter, not a personal one.'

'Well, it has to be a question for you but you should be aware that if handled in the appropriate way, the tribunal's chair will, in all probability, receive ample recognition for services rendered.'

'What exactly do you mean?'

'Do you wish me to spell it out?'

'Judges are not encouraged to have imagination, Mr Luston.'

'Then I'm told that a knighthood or even a peerage wouldn't be considered an unreasonable expectation. Isn't this something Mrs White might wish to hear?'

'Forgive me, but you give the impression of already knowing the answer to that.'

'Well, I couldn't possibly comment as they say, but I am instructed to tell you that whatever you decide, you and your wife are invited to a special drinks party on Boxing Day. There's a formal invitation already in the post.'

'Really? And who is giving this drinks party?'

'One of your fellow-residents down in Cambridgeshire... our esteemed former prime minister, Sir John Major.'

Five

Arundel, Egerton Road, Fallowfield, Saturday 30th July 1955

Zilla Arbib spread newspaper across the bare boards of the kitchen table and set out her silverware in readiness for Joan to clean when she arrived.

This was a fortnightly task, polishing the cruets and wine goblets and the elaborate picture frames wherein the distant dead still smiled. The largest piece was her family menorah, a treasure carried to England by Zilla's maternal grandparents after a pogrom in a place that was no more.

They were old people when she was a young girl and her enduring memory was of candles burning in its nine branches on the Feast of Lights '...*so we shall always know who we are and who we can be.*'

For Jews like Zilla, the menorah represented inner divinity. Its ninth candle was called the *shammes,* meaning servant. This candle lit the remaining eight and symbolised how love and light could be given to others without any loss of one's own radiance.

Joan arrived looking drawn and pre-occupied. She folded her headscarf into a triangle and tied it around her head like women did in factories during the war. Zilla said they could have coffee before Joan began.

'No, I better make a start on all this but thank-you all the same.'

This wasn't like Joan. She was usually chatty and full of gossip about the goings-on of her neighbours which Zilla filed away in her head for a paper she planned to write on working class social attitudes.

Those who lived in that little enclave might have withstood Hitler but the day was coming when Zion

34

Street and its stories would be lost to the town hall's vision of progress.

'Joan, forgive me for saying so but you don't look very well.'

'I'm just a bit off colour, that's all.'

'Maybe you should see the doctor.'

'No, I don't think he can help me.'

'Why, what's wrong, Joan?'

'Nothing... no, I'm sorry. I can't tell you - '

' - come on, we've known each other long enough not to have any secrets.'

Zilla admired Joan's uncomplicated honesty and fierce pride, even if her actions were those of someone forever on the defensive but ready to risk everything to fight for her own. Beyond this instinctive urge, Joan displayed scant ability to plan for whatever random events tomorrow might bring. She simply prayed they'd be bearable.

Zilla was fixed on showing her that this need not always be the case - and certainly not when it came to Spence and *his* future.

'I'm sorry, Miss Arbib... really I am. I've got a lot on my mind at the moment.'

'There's no need to keep apologising. Look, this cleaning can wait. Let me take you home.'

In all the time they'd known each other, Zilla hadn't ever crossed the invisible line between them by actually entering Joan's house. But something was clearly upsetting her. Their friendship required Zilla to find out what it was.

Her Sunbeam convertible looked ostentatious and out of place in Zion Street. Boys playing football on the bomb site near the corner shop came to inspect a car they guessed cost lots more than a thousand pounds to buy.

Zilla and Joan passed through her chill front room, barely six paces square yet somehow containing a three-piece suite, radiogram and a sideboard with two gilt-framed pictures on the wall above. She sat Joan in the kitchen's only upholstered chair, close by the black-leaded range on which stews and puddings were cooked.

'I'll make us some tea,' Zilla said. 'You just take it easy.'

She heated the kettle on Joan's gas stove and looked into a small yard with a tin bath hanging from a nail above a mangle for wringing out wet washing. Beyond the wall, topped with broken glass set in cement, was the saw-toothed roof of a warehouse. No trees or bushes were visible, no colour save that of slate and weathered brick.

Zilla put two spoons of sugar into Joan's tea. Her hands shook as she held the cup and saucer. Amid the cheap ornaments on the mantelpiece was a thrift tin with slots for coins towards her coal and electric bills, and a scatter of half-smoked cigarettes she called *dimps* and put by for Thursdays and Fridays when money was even tighter.

In the centre where a clock might have stood was a photograph of Spence, posed at a desk with him smiling to order and writing in an exercise book with a pencil.

'This is a lovely picture, Joan. I haven't seen it before.'

'It's him in class last year.'

'Your aunts are right, he *has* got the head of a professor.'

She'd badgered Joan into agreeing for them to take Spence for an interview at Manchester Grammar - a school where Zilla knew his talents would be recognised and encouraged. But John Henry thought Spence was doing well enough where he was.

'What if your husband puts his foot down and won't let him change schools?'

'Then Uncle Edgar will back me up. It's Spence's life that's important, no-one else's.'

Zilla would've asked Joan what else was troubling her but Spence came in through the back door. His face, knees and shirt needed washing. The smile died in his eyes as he saw Miss Arbib out of context and his mother looking unwell.

'There's nothing to fret about,' Zilla said. 'Your Mum felt a little poorly this morning so I brought her home.'

Spence shot glances between them, sensing a threat but not knowing what it was.

'I'm all right love, really,' Joan said. 'Why don't you show Miss Arbib what your Dad brought home for you last night?'

He seemed reluctant but went to his bedroom and came back with a violin, scratched and scuffed and with only two strings across the damaged bridge. It wouldn't have made a table at a jumble sale.

'Goodness, that's a challenge to take on, Spence.'

'I know, but Dad says I could buy some new strings for the price of a few comics.'

'And what about having some lessons?'

'He didn't say anything about that.'

'So how are you going to learn to play?'

'He says I can listen to his records and get the hang of it and then I'd be another Fritz Kreisler if I kept at it.'

Zilla despaired. Poverty wasn't solely a matter of economics but it was better to leave before she said so. She drove away, reflecting on the lives of those in this cramped little ghetto who were unable to see a route out, even when shown one.

As Engels witnessed - and Zilla could still see - they remained oppressed by landlords and exploitative capitalists, purblind victims of a system they could change if only they recognised their power.

Yet these same people were waving the flag even as they were cut down like flowers in Flanders. And now they'd just voted Churchill's Conservatives back into Parliament. Would it ever change? Zilla Arbib doubted it, however much her comrades in the Party claimed that revolution was inevitable and on its way.

Six

Spence saw Robert Heaney waiting near the Friendship Inn as they'd planned. Robert only ever wore black smelly wellingtons.

Girls at school ran away if he came near at play time. He pretended this was a funny game but he wasn't laughing, not inside. Robert had six brothers and sisters and the teachers were always caning him for fighting or drawing rude pictures on the lav walls but he didn't seem to care.

He was still in short trousers though he looked older than twelve. Spence wasn't allowed to make friends with Robert. His Dad said the Heaneys were common so better class families like theirs shouldn't have anything to do with them. Miss Arbib laughed when Spence told her this.

Her scorn somehow added to his suspicion that Dad was to blame for whatever was wrong with Mum. Spence had an urge to pay him back for this and for everything else he resented but hadn't yet the words to express. He would defy him and be secret friends with Robert. And for once, Spence might feel ordinary, might be accepted and not picked on for his cleverness or his polio arm.

'All right, let's get going, Spence... if you're sure you won't be shitting yourself.'

'I won't be... honest, I won't.'

'I still don't believe you 'cos you don't get what really happens where we're going.'

'Yes, I do. It's experiments... they do experiments there.'

'Yeah, on animals and such like so if we're caught, you know what'll happen?'

'Nothing'll happen. We'll get told off, that's all.'
'That's where you're wrong, *skellington*.'
'Don't call me that - '
' - they'll cut you up, too.'
'Stop trying to scare me because you won't.'

*

Edgar Sydenham had a pair of working boots to mend for the man next door. He rolled back his sleeves and set up the last. The worn leather soles curled away under his short-bladed assassin's knife and he lost himself in the monotony of shaping and trimming the new.

Frances wouldn't be out of bed till Emily arrived back from the chemist's with her medicine. Kitty was putting bets on the Saturday afternoon card. What a sight she was sometimes, striding into pubs dressed in a man's suit and never giving a damn for what anyone thought.

It wasn't that Kitty hadn't ever married. She'd out-lived a couple of husbands but always wanted to wear the trousers - and the trilby and tie when she felt like it. Deep down, she was a good sort, always tipping Spence a shilling or two from her winnings and that gave her top marks in Edgar's book.

The neighbour's boots needed only polishing to finish. Spit, polish, spit, buff, polish till a man who should be dead stared up from the toe caps. They stopped bawling out soldiers for dirty boots back then. There was no point... not when they were ankle-deep in slurry and sewage and bits of blokes they'd known not a day before.

But what was the point of any of it? The generals said there was a bigger picture. That was a laugh if your world was a scrape of earth to be kissed and fucked like it was the end of days and all you wanted was to

40

crawl through the carnage and burrow back into your trench like the animal you'd become.

The fire needed more coal. He brought up a shovel of slack from the cellar then leaned both hands against the mantelpiece and watched the smoke and flames spiral up the chimney to nothingness.

Emily's key turned in the front door. She went straight to Frances in the front room. Her heart was giving out and that was the unalterable fact of the matter.

Edgar headed upstairs for the solitude of the cubicle by the bathroom. He bolted the door, unbuttoned his trousers and sat, human and vulnerable. The flesh of his bare arms and his once-strong legs was no longer firm.

It looked yellow in the light of the naked bulb above him and the blue tracery of his veins ran like rivers on a sapper's map.

After a minute more, he stood and opened the small window by the cistern. And there, in the stink beneath him, memory came alive again - the sight of liquid earth shot through with the vivid, poppy-redness of life and death.

He pulled the chain. It'd be nothing. On Monday, he'd be back at Dunlop's and the first aid woman could give him something from her cabinet. Frances was the one to worry about.

*

'Listen, *skellington* - '

' - stop calling me that.'

'I'll call you what I want till I can trust you to keep a secret.'

'You *can* trust me. I won't tell anyone anything.'

'You better not 'cos if you do, you'll be more than sorry.'

41

Robert said the experiment place was tucked away so no-one could see what was going on. It was at the end of a cul-de-sac with overhanging trees and big houses on one side facing the railway embankment on the other.

'There's no way out at the bottom,' he said. 'That's how they trap you.'

'Won't we be seen from the houses?'

'Not if we stick to the embankment till we get to where we want to be.'

Barbed wire and spiked railings were meant to stop kids trespassing on the tracks but Robert knew where to squeeze through. They set off on a crouching run, ducking through the long grass and lupins till Robert signalled for them to lie flat on the ground.

Spence felt his heart thumping. This was real, not a story or a game he'd made up. They crawled the last fifty yards on their bellies. A train of loaded coal wagons rumbled by and the earth shuddered beneath them. Robert helped Spence climb over the railings opposite the laboratory. Then they hid under the canopy of laurel bushes in its front garden. The building seemed locked up but it was weekend so it would be.

They couldn't hear any cats or dogs crying out in pain and the very silence added to Spence's sense of danger. Robert ran round to the back and Spence followed. Wooden sheds occupied what was once a garden.

Nearby were three metal baths covered with wire netting, each half full of water swimming with frogs which couldn't climb out.

'I told you they cut things up,' Robert said.

'But why would they cut up frogs?'

'To see what's inside them, stupid.'

Robert started scooping them out. Spence did, too. They were cold and slippy to the touch. They set them on the ground to hop away to freedom. Spence felt a sort of liberation, too. He was doing something forbidden with a boy whose approval he craved. And all the while, his Dad didn't know.

He kept laughing as each creature escaped because he was a child and happy and no longer afraid. Then Robert did something awful. He stamped on a frog. He just raised his foot and brought it down and squashed it into the gravel.

Bits of blood and custardy stuff oozed out from its fat belly. But it wasn't quite dead. The legs were still moving. The skin under its mouth bubbled into a pouch. Robert stamped on it again. Its guts and slime stuck to the heel of his wellington. Spence had never seen anything killed like that before. Here was violence without rage or reason.

'Why did you do that?'

'Because I can.'

Robert turned away and ran up a metal fire escape to the first floor of the main building. Spence followed, but slowly. He heard a window being broken and saw Robert leaning through it to open a door.

'Hurry up, *skellington* - or are you getting scared?'

They entered a room smelling of chemicals. The long wooden bench before them had gas taps with Bunsen burners and rows of big glass jars.

'This is where the cats and dogs get cut up.'

'Then why aren't there any here?'

'Cos they'll have used them all up so they're out stealing some more.'

'Come on, let's go now, Robert.'

'Why? You're shitting yourself, aren't you? Just like I said you would.'

43

'No I'm not. I just want to go, that's all.'

But Robert stood by the door and wouldn't let him out. Spence didn't like how Robert was looking at him or the malice and indifference on his face.

'OK, *skellington*, let's see your willy.'

'No, stop it. You can't.'

'I'm getting hairs down there. Let's see if you've got any.'

'No, get away. Leave me alone.'

'Have you ever seen a girl's?'

'A girl's what?'

'A girl's willy, stupid.'

''Course I have.'

'No you haven't. You're a liar.'

'I want to go. You've got to let me go.'

'Why don't you ask our Brigit? She'd show you hers and she'd tell you something you didn't know, too.'

'Tell me what?'

'About how babies come... 'cos you don't know that either, do you - *skellington*?'

'Stop calling me that.'

'You don't know that your Dad puts his willy in your Mum's willy.'

'What are you talking about? Why would they do that?'

'My Mum says that's what your Dad's just done so your Mum's having a baby.'

'No, she's not. She's just not very well, that's all.'

'Is that a fact? Well, you're not as clever as they say, are you?'

Such a consuming anger took hold of Spence, a desire to crush Robert's leering face, to see it bubble with blood and snot like the harmless creature he'd just done to death. He felt his fingers twitching as his Dad's did and in that instant of blind rage, he'd no

44

thought to the consequence of what he was about to do.

He seized a bottle by the neck and threw it at Robert, threw it with force and venom. But it just missed his head and shattered against a shelf of test tubes, which smashed across the floor. Robert made a grab for him but Spence pushed past and ran - ran from where they chopped up cats and dogs and frogs and it all stank of gas and pain and nothing added up.

*

Zilla Arbib was a valued account holder at Kendal Milne, the upmarket department store on Deansgate.

No one challenged her as she strode through the din of the *Goods Out* bay where the firm's green and gold delivery trucks were loaded. A supervisor pointed out John Henry.

In all the time she'd employed Joan, there had been no reason to meet her husband. He was sitting on a wooden crate eating sandwiches from greaseproof paper, which had once wrapped a loaf.

'Mr White?'

John Henry looked up at her and in those uncertain eyes and in that unfulfilled face, Zilla could see his son - and all that might yet befall his future.

She smiled and introduced herself. He wiped his fingers on his brown overalls and they shook hands.

'Joan's always talking about you... and Spence does, too.'

'You must know how fond of them I am,' Zilla said. 'That's why I'm here.'

'Nothing's wrong, is there?'

He was handsome in a rough-and-ready sort of way, black hair swept back and glossy with brilliantine. She could see the scar on his upper lip, which Spence claimed came from fighting with the Desert Rats in

45

North Africa. But Joan said was more likely a shaving cut after a night drinking.

'I'm afraid there is. Joan isn't at all well at the moment and I'm worried about her.'

He stood up and Zilla knew she mustn't trespass on what was his or appear to be interfering or offering charity.

'Well, I only came to say that if you'd like to borrow my car any weekend, you could take Joan and Spence for a drive in the country. A bit of fresh air would do her good.'

'That's most kind, thank-you but I've got a part-time job on Sundays.'

'Take them out on a Saturday, then.'

'I'm not sure about that. Saturdays are my half day.'

And Zilla had a good idea where he spent them.

'Well, it's probably none of my business, Mr White, but Joan works as hard as anyone and I'd have thought she deserved a half day, too.'

Driving home, Zilla thought of the photograph Joan once showed her of John Henry, smiling in a morning suit in the sunshine of his sister's wedding before the war. Back then, he'd had plans for all their tomorrows. But that's all they ever were.

Yet for all his inconsiderate, working man's ways, Zilla felt only pity for him - Joan, too. They were prisoners of circumstances over which they had no control and neither would Spence unless he was helped to escape.

*

Spence sat hidden amid the tall pinkish flowers, which Uncle Edgar said were called Rose Bay Willow Herbs. Butterflies wafted between the stalks - just ordinary white ones, not like those in hot countries, which were

46

all brightly coloured and bigger than a man's hand. He'd been happy earlier but not any more.

Still, the train would come soon. It would sound like thunder in hell which was what Mum said Uncle Edgar heard, marching towards the enemy's guns. He hadn't been scared then so Spence wouldn't be now.

His Mum and Dad hadn't done what Robert said and they weren't going to have a baby. And he didn't care if Robert wasn't his friend. He didn't need friends. They only ended up hurting you or calling you names.

Spence moved off the embankment and onto the flinty brown ballast by the track. He'd show Robert. It was then the train exploded out of the tunnel beneath the main road, black and snarling. He lay by the wooden sleepers close enough to touch the rail. He *did* dare do it, he *did* dare do it.

Then the engine was by him – pistons hammering, wheels pounding, the air hot with oily steam and flying cinders. He didn't move, couldn't move, not until the deafening, clanking iron wagons passed, the smoke cleared and all went quiet again.

Never had he felt so light-headed, so alive and happy. He was as brave as any other kid and ran back onto the embankment, pushing through the waving grasses which dusted his bare legs with pollen.

If only Robert had been watching. But no one was. What he'd done, he'd done unseen. Yet even as he regretted this, another thought stole up on him, a gathering sense that he wasn't entirely alone. Someone else was with him, someone he'd not known until that day but who must always have been close by.

Then he realised who it was. The stranger was the boy within, the boy he never noticed in the mirror, the one with all that anger who'd wanted nothing else but to kill Robert.

47

Seven

Joan hoped she'd given a good account of herself at Manchester Grammar School. She'd not wanted to go at first. But Uncle Edgar said she must or she'd be letting Spence down.

The teacher who met them was such a gentleman. He made her feel at ease - and so proud of her son, too. Miss Arbib knew him, of course. Lots of boys from Jewish families went to Manchester Grammar. She and Miss Arbib waited while the teacher interviewed Spence in another room. Miss Arbib said they'd quickly realise how bright he was.

He'd sail through the entrance exam and get a scholarship, maybe one with a bursary. But if he didn't, she would pay his fees. And Joan wasn't to worry about other kids picking on him because of his polio arm. Passing exams was more important at this school than doing physical jerks in a vest and shorts.

Joan's sense of achievement, of it being recognised that she'd brought someone special into the world, took her mind off more immediate concerns. But it'd all been a mental and physical effort. She sent Spence round to Miss Arbib's to say she wasn't feeling well enough to clean her house next day.

Her last hope had been Frances, not necessarily for a loan but the understanding and forgiveness she sought. Of her three aunts, only Frances was maternal. Emily would be returned to heaven unopened by choice and though Kitty was kindness itself, she was too waywardly eccentric ever to have charge of a pram.

After Miss Arbib dropped her and Spence in Zion Street, it'd taken all Joan's resolve to walk round to see Frances and confess what it was in her mind to do - and why. She risked the old lady's Catholic disapproval but far worse would be the pain of unwittingly stirring up a great sadness from their family's past. Yet she had a crying need to talk to the one who was her mother in all but name.

Frances had been asleep. Her hands were crossed chastely over a heart beating only softly now. Joan saw how thin the gold ring on her wedding finger had worn, how defined by her skeleton she was becoming. She leaned over and kissed her forehead. Frances stirred then smiled.

'Joan, love... how nice to wake up and see you.'

Frances propped herself up against her pillows and sipped water from the glass on the bedside cabinet. She put on her spectacles and looked into Joan's anxious face.

'Something's wrong, isn't it?' Frances said. 'Your Uncle Edgar told me you're not quite yourself. What is it, love? What's bothering you?'

Joan shifted in her seat and flattened out the pleats in her skirt.

'Come on... if you can't tell your Auntie Frances, who can you tell?'

Joan began to weep in her confusion, quietly at first, then allowing herself to be rocked and shushed in Frances's arms and to have her hair stroked as she gabbled out the sin she wanted to commit against God's teachings.

'I can't cope in my head, Auntie Frances,' Joan said. 'I know it's an awful thing to say to you of all people but I want shut of this baby.'

'It'll pass, Joan love. Everything does... it'll pass like everything else in this world.'

'You must hate me. I'm so bad and ungrateful.'

'No, Joan... you're not bad, you haven't a bad bone in your body.'

'Then tell me what I should do.'

Frances gave her the weakest of smiles. She lay back on her pillows once more and closed her tired eyes.

'All I'd say is if whatever you do is for Spence, then that's not a sin in my mind.'

'Everything's for him, Auntie Frances... you know it is.'

'I'm glad to hear it, love. He's all we've got... any of us.'

And in her head, Frances could hear another child playing, far away and long ago and she wanted more than life itself to bring him safe home. But that wasn't to be so all that remained was for Frances to go to him.

*

Spies and danger were everywhere. They'd poisoned Mum and were coming for Spence. He dodged through the traffic, skirted the Friendship Inn and ran like a four-minute miler to Miss Arbib's house.

His arms pumped, his chest heaved but he had to show the other kids that he wasn't a cripple. *Arundel* was not a hundred yards away and he was still panting for breath as Miss Arbib opened her door.

'Spence – what's the matter?'

'It's my Mum. Says sorry but can't come tomorrow, keeps being sick.'

'Dear me, that's not good, is it? Is your father with her?'

'No, doing his job at the pub. I'm going to 35 to tell them.'

He set off for Grenville Road, climbing walls and trespassing through gardens to evade the merciless foreign agents. Yet his heart wasn't in the story. Not that day, not when it wasn't make-believe.

Auntie Kitty would know what to do. She could be sensible - but not always. Spence didn't like Auntie

Emily. She'd been a teacher and ordered him about, making him go to the shops for cigarettes. She was forever croaking into her hankie but said *it's not the cough that carries you off but the coffin they carry you off in*.

They all got dressed up on Fridays and Saturdays and went out singing and drinking at the Friendship Inn. Auntie Emily wore a dead fox around her neck. Its eyes were made of glass but it still had teeth so she said it was best to count your fingers if you stroked it.

Everyone was in the living room at 35 which was full of steam and cooking smells from the scullery. He told them about Mum.

'She's not well, you say?' Auntie Emily said. 'But she was here not an hour ago and she seemed all right then.'

'You go play outside for a bit,' Uncle Edgar said. 'Then I'll walk you back home and we'll see how your mother is.'

Spence knew they wanted him out of the way. The garden was long and narrow and split in two by a trellis of roses.

Beyond the back gate was a tennis club where he'd watched games and thrown back balls that came over the wire. He'd seen a dragonfly there once, darting above him like something from dinosaur times. It had four wings and was strangely beautiful - and *iridescent*. That was a word he'd learned from the dictionary at Miss Arbib's.

His Mum was sitting in the comfy chair in the kitchen when they arrived. Uncle Edgar asked if she'd like something to eat but she didn't want any fuss. She looked grey and exhausted. Spence was sent outside while Uncle Edgar talked to her.

Dad came home soon after, smelling of the pub. He opened a new pack of Players, which he could only afford at weekends. Then he started singing his made-up Italian songs that were stupid and embarrassing. He tried to put his arm around Spence but he ducked away.

'Stop mucking about.'

'Don't you want a kiss from your old Dad?'

'No, I don't.'

'You'll be sorry when I'm dead and gone.'

'All I want is to know what's wrong with Mum.'

'Whatever it is, you're not to worry. She'll be as right as ninepence tomorrow.'

But tomorrow never comes. Everyone knew that.

Eight

The man in civvies at Zilla Arbib's door could only have been a police officer. The evil they saw men do calcified as suspicion in their faces. This she recognised even before he told her he was a detective and his name was Challis. Zilla immediately thought Spence was in trouble but Challis just wanted a private word. She took him into the kitchen where he refused tea and didn't engage in any small talk.

'Your cleaning woman, Joan White... worked for you long, has she?'

Challis's delivery was flat and nasal and owed much to the damp Manchester air.

'Since the war. Why do you want to know?'

'You seem very friendly with her.'

'Why shouldn't I be?'

'Even more so with her lad.'

'So what if I am? I don't see the point you're making.'

'Do you find yourself counting the spoons every time they leave?'

'What are you suggesting - that they're thieves?'

'The way it works, love, is that I ask the questions and you answer them.'

'This is disgraceful, you come into my home - '

' - we can talk in *my* police station, if you'd prefer.'

Zilla checked her rising temper, but only for the sake of Joan and Spence.

'Let's try again,' Challis said. 'The kid's a ragamuffin yet he's round at your house all the time. Why is that?'

'It's none of your business but he's going to Manchester Grammar School soon so he might look like a ragamuffin but he's a clever one and he'll go places in this life.'

'But only if he gets a leg up from you, eh?'

'His family are just ordinary people.'

'Dad drives a van for Kendal Milne, yes?'

'You clearly know already so why are you asking? Where's all this leading?'

Challis fixed her with a belligerent stare and said he was investigating a serious matter so anyone who refused to help with his enquiries could be in trouble.

'What do you mean? What *serious matter*?'

'I can't say. I'm not at liberty to tell you any more at this stage.'

'Then you'd better leave because I'm not at liberty to be your spy.'

He nodded as if he'd expected her reaction. Challis paused on Zilla's front step and took a moment to button up the jacket of his chalk stripe suit, as crumpled as him in the service of the law.

'My information is that you inherited a lot of money from your father's business.'

'What on earth has that got to do with you?'

'So you're a very wealthy woman.'

'The audacity of you people.'

'And you're a big donor to the Communist Party of Great Britain - '

'This is outrageous.'

' - on the quiet, of course. You'd not want the university knowing, would you?'

'The police have absolutely no right to know what I do with my money.'

'You're wrong there, love,' Challis said. 'Still, your sort were all Russians once upon a time, weren't you?'

His smile, such as it was, mutated into a sneer then he drove away in a blue Wolseley. His questions made him more than a workaday detective. Zilla wasn't paranoiac but he'd be Special Branch - a nasty secret policeman trying to unnerve her for reasons she couldn't fathom.

The very smell of the man was like something dead behind the skirting boards. She telephoned her solicitor, Malcolm Feingold. He was a Mason and they'd eyes and ears everywhere.

Malcolm listened and said he'd sniff the air for Challis's spraints. Zilla ran a deep bath. She needed to feel clean again.

Nine

Should he tell him? Should he answer the lad's questions so he might know and could explain to his children and they to theirs? But who in the future would believe, who would understand? Edgar was there. He was one of those shadows in the silent newsreels - crawling, falling, killing in the narrow, unstopped graves they had dug for themselves. He couldn't work it out then so why will those yet unborn?

But to say nothing, to leave the words in his head unspoken and the wound in his heart unhealed, was to deny himself the release of the confessional and his guilt would remain, as black as the bits of shrapnel within him.

He sat with Spence eating ice cream cornets on a bench in Platt Fields, appearing for all the world to be the grandfather he wished he could've been with the grandson he wished he could've had.

The warm, cloudless air was full of children's playful shouts and the creak of oars from the boating lake skiffs. Spence deserved a treat. He didn't understand why his Mum wasn't well. And John Henry needed to sober up. The man was a damned fool. Never learned, never would - not until it was too late.

God might fit the back for the burden but Joan wouldn't take too much more on hers.

'Was it always raining, Uncle Edgar?'

'When do you mean, son?'

'In your war because in the pictures in Miss Arbib's books, it looks like it never stopped raining where you were, it was all just mud as far as you could see.'

'There was mud, all right. But some days, it could be sunny like this one.'

56

'Like holiday time?'

'Some bloody holiday, that's for sure.'

'You couldn't take a holiday from the fighting, could you?'

'No. Not unless you copped a bullet.'

Municipal decree required the skiffs to be rowed clockwise round the thick copse of beech, sycamore and rhododendrons on the island in the middle of the lake. Edgar remembered other woods... Mametz, Montauban, Sanctuary, Polygon, and all that marching with blood in their boots and exhausted men dropping at the side of the road as if rehearsing their roles in what was to come.

'Mum says you were at the battle of the Somme.'

'Yes... that's right. In 1916, that was.'

'Lots of the soldiers were killed, weren't they?'

'More than you could count, young Spence. Tommies and officers, rich, poor. Didn't make any difference. Everyone... just slaughtered.'

'But you got out alive.'

'Yes, most of me did, I suppose.'

'Miss Arbib's let me see some books of poems about it.'

'And did you understand what they were saying?'

'Not always but Miss Arbib says you've got to read between the words and look for other meanings and ideas in them.'

At this, Edgar took a fold of paper from his wallet. On it was a verse he'd copied out himself. He handed it to Spence and the child read what the man could never forget.

Merry it was to laugh there –
Where death becomes absurd and life absurder.
For power was on us as we slashed bones bare
Not to feel sickness or remorse of murder.

'Does it mean *you* were a murderer, Uncle Edgar?'

'That's what it felt like at times though they told us God was on our side so that made everything all right.'

'Did you take any Germans prisoner?'

The boy looked into his face and waited for an answer. How could he tell him?

'Some blokes thought we took too many prisoners, we should've shot the lot.'

'Did they hate the Germans because they'd killed their friends?'

'All of us probably did... but I let one go once.'

'Why was that?'

'On his knees, he was, a much older man... begging me for his life.'

'Why didn't you shoot him if you'd shot some others?'

'In those times, if you lived or died, it was all just chance,' Edgar said. 'But I'll tell you this for nothing, son... by not pulling the trigger that day, I felt a better man, almost like a decent human being again.'

He heard his own words and it was as if the bandages were starting to uncoil from around a gangrenous old wound. What he'd said was the truth - but not the whole truth. Edgar Sydenham wasn't ready for that just yet.

*

They left Platt Fields and walked back towards Zion Street. Uncle Edgar said he was really pleased that Spence might be going to a new and better school.

'My Dad's not happy about it,' Spence said. 'But Mum told him that he'd not get his way on this because there was more to life than slaving in a factory and drinking beer.'

'Good for her... and don't you worry, I'll have a word with your Dad.'

58

Quite by coincidence, they saw him coming towards them. He'd left Joan sleeping and said that was the best thing for her. Uncle Edgar took Dad's arm and said they needed to talk. Spence went home on his own.

He tried to open the back door from the yard but something was stuck behind it. However much he pushed, it hardly budged. Then he heard a faint moan. He leant hard against the door till he could just about squeeze through the narrow gaps.

As he did, he almost stepped on his mother, lying crumpled at the bottom of the stairs. The lino was slippy with blood. It was on her hands and her face and in her hair and smeared on her dressing gown so it looked like a butcher's apron. And when he touched her face, she didn't move.

Ten

Hartford, Cambridgeshire, Wednesday 10th December 2014

White hadn't slept well during his final night at the judges' lodgings in Lincoln. The meeting with Luston unsettled him. It could be that he was simply asking him to delay retirement for the duration of one more case. This would be business as usual - sifting evidence, having witnesses questioned and reaching a judgement based on matters of fact. But this time, he could be knighted for his verdict or made a member of the House of Lords. As Miss Arbib would've said, w*hat's not to like?*

Yet the unorthodox nature of the approach somehow offended White's lawyerly mind. It had come out of the shadows - almost literally - and not through the Lord Chancellor's office, as he would have expected.

Luston was obviously a man for all reasons, one of those behind the political curtains without whom the show didn't go on. But whatever the tune - and whatever the motive for it being played to White - why should he agree to dance to it when he'd already retired, if only in his head?

A note on the kitchen table said Elspeth had gone Christmas shopping in Cambridge and then for lunch with her daughter, Celia. He rang Hartford Marina to confirm they'd finished servicing his narrow boat, *Zion*.

Elspeth thought her husband an atheistic, closet communist so to give his boat a name with religious overtones puzzled her. He said it was a memory from Sunday school and she'd taken him at his word. After all, he was a judge.

White changed into his civilian disguise - cord pants, thick shirt, jumper, boots - and made for where the garden sloped down to the River Great Ouse.

Here was the refuge of his summerhouse, a place without books, phones, obligations or responsibilities, just a view over to the water meadows across the river, to the grazing cattle and pollarded willows and the leafless poplars swaying in the low afternoon sun.

To his left, swans and grebe swam the river's tidal reaches. To his right, the stub stone tower of All Saints, the church built where the Romans once had a lookout post.

There was something yearned-for about this bucolic fen countryside. It touched a subconscious desire to retreat into his own dreamtime, to steer *Zion* between both banks and all their inherent complexities, never to land, never to arrive.

An element of this fed into his reason for not wanting to return to Manchester. He'd no more funerals to attend there and was finally ridding himself of the physical remains and reminders of times he wished he might forget but never could.

By chance, it was the chauffeur who'd been present on the marshes of The Wash three weeks before who had driven him from Lincoln that morning. White had not wanted to talk on the way back but the hint wasn't taken.

'Forgive me, your Honour, but do you have any connection to Manchester?'

White looked up from a report in The Times about the case he'd just tried.

'I'm sorry, what were you saying?'

'I was wondering if you were from the north of England because sometimes I think I can detect a trace of a Manchester accent in the way you speak.'

'Is that where you come from, then?'

'Originally, yes. But I left years ago. What about you?'

'I was at Manchester Grammar School for six years so maybe that explains it.'

'So that's where your family lived is it, where you were brought up?'

'As I said, I attended Manchester Grammar then I moved away.'

He returned to his newspaper. If the past was a foreign country, White hadn't even taken Elspeth there so an inquisitive chauffeur wasn't about to make the journey.

It was dark by the time she arrived home. He'd lit a fire of logs and Irish peat in the lounge. Its flames shone in miniature in the blue plates on the oak dresser Elspeth brought from her failed first marriage. White saved only himself from his.

She told him - in some detail - why shopping in Cambridge was hell and that Celia expected them for Christmas lunch. White feigned a smile but knew her children would be there - and so, too, their tedious accountant of a father.

'And you'll never believe it but we've had an invitation to a drinks party at the home of John Major.'

'On Boxing Day, yes,' White said. 'I heard we'd be getting one.'

'Really? But we've never been favoured like this before so why now?'

White explained about Luston and being asked to chair the deaths in police custody inquiry in Manchester.

'He said there was a gong in it for me... or maybe even a bit of ermine.'

'That's wonderful news. Marvellous, some recognition after all these years.'

'Not really, I've told him I'm not interested.'

'You've done what?' Elspeth said. 'I don't believe it. Spencer, you've got to tell them you've changed your mind. The job wouldn't take long then you can retire and toddle off on your damned boat for as long as you want.'

'And you'd be happy to be left at home as Lady White, I suppose?'

Elspeth was still a handsome woman, bus pass and arthritic knee aside. She shook her steely grey head and left the room. Nearly thirty years into the convenient arrangement that was their marriage, he knew it would've been wiser to have kept quiet about Luston's proposal. But maybe some tiny part of him also responded to the idea of being *Sir* Spencer White... or even Lord White of Hartford. Wisdom might yet fall to vanity. It had been known to happen.

Eleven

Wilbraham Road Synagogue, Fallowfield, Tuesday 2nd August 1955

Those around Zion Street who prayed for better times didn't lack for places to bend the knee. Catholics, Methodists, Baptists, Jews – all were provided for. Zilla Arbib, forty-three and unmarried, left a social event at the white stone shul on Wilbraham Road, barely five hundred yards from where Spence lived.

Hers was a solitary life, fulfilled yet incomplete. She'd felt this more painfully than usual some weeks before during *Shavuot*, the festival to celebrate the ripening of fruit and crops still to be harvested.

There had been men in her life - especially one before the war - yet her way to the *chuppah* was barred and the joyous anticipation of motherhood denied. But all happiness was transient. Jews were taught never to forget that - or their suffering.

And was this ever greater than in that archipelago of camps where fire consumed so much of European Jewry not so long ago?

Zilla's family escaped only because they'd fled an earlier persecution and made it to the mercantile greatness of Victorian England. They prospered in the garment business and achieved much. Then came the time of Hitler. When survivors finally spoke and cameras bore witness, some demanded to know where God had been during this crime of all history.

For Zilla Arbib, the assimilated rationalist, the answer was as shocking as the events provoking the question. She came to believe that God had also suffered in the ghetto. He, too, was whipped into the gas chambers, burned in the ovens of the crematoria. Not to accept this was to deny all hope.

For the first time, she experienced the primitive need for the tribe's protection and approval. She drew comfort from religious ritual and thereby affirmed against those who would have expunged her from the human record.

But in the cruellest of twists, at the very moment she found God, He turned His back on her. Zilla's blood ceased to flow. Doctors in Harley Street concluded she'd suffered a premature menopause. She knew that in all of life, no less in mind and body, nothing was without a reason. Rightly or wrongly, she believed that becoming barren was a reaction to the cataclysm of the Holocaust, a form of survivor's guilt.

The condition was her own yellow star, a badge of difference but which conjoined her to the collective suffering of her kind - those of smoke and memory whose voices had been stilled and whose blood no longer flowed, either.

Her car was parked outside the synagogue, close by the grassy croft of wasteland, half the size of a football pitch, where children from Zion Street and beyond played their games. She looked for Spence as she always did. And she saw him, not acting out one of his made-up adventures but sitting in a broken armchair someone had dumped. He looked lost and vacant, almost as if in shock. She hurried across to him.

'Spence? What is it? Whatever is the matter?'

He took a moment to realise who she was. Then he reached up and put his arms around her neck without saying a word and let her carry him away.

*

Zilla set a bowl of chicken soup before Spence and urged him to eat. It concerned her that he looked listless and neglected but any explanation could wait. He was still hungry and ate the bread and the apple she gave him next. She suggested as tactfully as she could that he needed a bath.

They went upstairs and she helped him off with his white canvas pumps and unbuttoned his pants and shirt. He offered no resistance, showed no embarrassment at his nakedness or exposing his polio arm. This she'd known from Joan was unheard of.

Spence stood in the big roll top tub while Zilla washed his straggling, curly hair with Vosene then soaped him front and back and in each dip of his afflicted body. She did this gently and with infinite care like a holy woman tending her saviour. For Zilla, it was an act of supplication, for Spence it was human contact, natural and warm and without any shame.

They went down to Zilla's sitting room. She put a record on her radiogram - a nocturne by Debussy, which Spence always liked. He sat on her chesterfield, small and silent. Zilla joined him and took his hand.

'So what's been happening to you, Spence... what's making you unhappy?'

'Mum's in hospital,' he said. 'I found her at the bottom of the stairs. She was covered in blood, didn't move or say anything.'

He'd run next door to Dolly Thomas and shouted through her letterbox for her to help. They dragged Mum onto the rug by the fireplace.

Dolly said he must go to the telephone box outside the Friendship Inn and dial 999 for an ambulance. He did exactly as he was told. Dolly tried to clear up the mess. When Spence got back he saw something folded in newspaper on the draining board, bleeding like a small joint of meat.

His Mum was moaning and saying she hurt all over. Dolly ordered him outside so the ambulance men would know where to come. He didn't want to leave her but Dolly insisted.

As he opened the front door, a policeman was crossing the street towards him. Other doors opened and curtains twitched for uniforms disturbed the peace in streets like theirs.

'You're Spencer White, aren't you?'

'Yes, but you're not the ambulance man. There's been an accident.'

'I'm not here about any accident, I'm here about you trespassing on the railway. You were seen playing near the railway line.'

Spence felt knotted up inside. He couldn't help it but he was sick. Some of it splashed on the policeman's polished boots. Zilla asked if he really had been trespassing.

'Yes... but that's not all.'

'You mean it gets worse?'

He told her about breaking into the experiment place with Robert and smashing some of the equipment.

'Spence, this is shocking behaviour, criminal even,' Zilla said. 'It's serious enough to make Manchester Grammar School think twice about accepting you if they ever found out.'

'Yes, but what if it's the policeman who finds out and they put me in prison?'

'You should have thought about that at the time,' Zilla said. 'Your poor mother will be so worried if she gets to hear about this.'

'The ambulance took her away.'

'And what did the policeman say?'

'That I'd better not do it again or else I'd be in big trouble.'

'Did he say anything else?'

'Only that it looked like a murder had taken place in our kitchen.'

Twelve

'I'm a good girl, aren't I?'

Joan's words drifted back to her as if spoken by someone far away and a hundred years before. Her eyes were closed but there was a fierce brightness beyond, like she was staring at the sun.

She could hear footsteps, the squeak of trolley wheels over a polished floor, coughs and voices and bird song from an open window. Each sound wafted over her like a breeze from a distant land. She felt calm but empty, drained of all lifeblood, a sacrifice offered to the gods of old.

What did she know? What did she care? She was not in heaven or on earth but floating in some feathery in-between place where she might see her mother again and be held forever in that love she had lost.

'I'm a good girl, aren't I, Dad? Tell me you want me… please, Dad.'

*

The two sisters sat with their own thoughts on the bus to the hospital. Whatever had happened, Emily blamed John Henry. She'd always deemed him inadequate and selfish, lacking all ambition. Kitty worried about Spence and what was to become of the child. Edgar shared their concerns but he had to stay at 35 to look after Frances till they got back.

The matron was a kind, considerate woman from Dublin. They were all Catholics together. Whatever had overtaken Joan might have been God's will but didn't He make them all suffer?

'She's bruised and battered and very weak,' she said. 'Sleep's probably best for her.'

'But she'll get better before long, won't she?' Kitty said.

'Our bodies heal quicker than our minds is what I've found over the years.'

'Has her husband been in to see her?'

'Oh, yes, and her sister... and a policeman came, too.'

'A policeman? Why would a policeman come?'

'I can't tell you that, dear. It's enough for me to know that she's lost her baby, poor soul.'

Kitty continued to stroke the back of Joan's hand. Once the matron had gone about her other duties, the waspish, worldly Emily lit another Craven A and offered a reason for the policeman's visit.

'Stands out a mile,' she said. 'They'll want to know if she tripped or if she jumped or if she was pushed.'

*

Spence found the last of the butter and made it into five balls, each the size of a marble. He rolled them in the sugar bowl till they sparkled then ate them. Mum gave him butterballs and sugar to suck overnight as a comfort when he'd a sore throat.

The house was empty. He didn't know where his Dad was or when he'd be home. Dolly Thomas had washed and ironed the sheets that'd been soaked in blood.

Spence took them upstairs to leave on Mum and Dad's bed in the back room. He didn't normally go in there. One of the pillows was darker where Dad's Brylcreem rubbed off. The walls had no pictures or photographs, not even from their wedding. They'd had to sell Dad's little Austin Ruby for £8 to pay for it so that left nothing over for a photographer.

Their brown wood wardrobe contained his grey demob suit and skirts Auntie Vron no longer wanted. At the back, behind some shoes, was a tin document box. Spence knew he shouldn't but he opened it. Inside

70

were the love letters Dad had written to Mum during the war and a few he'd managed to save from her.

Spence sat on their marriage bed and read what he was never meant to see. It felt wrong for reasons he didn't understand but ignored all the same. Most of them were scrawled thank-you notes for the cakes and cigarettes she'd sent or the Postal Orders when he'd no money, which was most of the time. Dad hated army life.

Until I actually handled a machine gun, I never realised what a terrible thing war is but now I do and it's quite upsetting having to spend two hours a day having it drummed into me how to use it, to learn the correct range to fire fast and straight and be able to cut a man in half. After the machine gun practice, we stand in line, each with a rifle and a wicked-looking bayonet and are taught how to slice into a man's belly with one end or smash his head in with the other. I guess I'll get used to all this eventually but at the moment, I don't like it one little bit.

He read more. Dad was asked to sing at a concert party. He told of seeing a German bomber shot down in a field. His unit was forever training, marching and always shifting base.

He prayed for the war to end. Spence could hardly believe it was his Dad writing, expressing himself tenderly with words he'd never heard him use before.

I adore you, always have, and always will, with all the love that's in me. It may not be much but what there is, is all yours. I'd die for you in one hour's time if need be. When this bloody lot's over, we'll be the happiest little family in the whole world and the richest, too, if love is counted as wealth.

Mum was just as daft about Dad.

I'm just waiting as patiently as I can for the next time you're home. I love everything about you, all the kindnesses you do for me and even your changeable ways. It all makes me love you more and want you home. We haven't had the best of starts to our married life but there are plenty worse off than us. Keep smiling, John Henry. I'd not know what to do if anything happened to you.

As the months passed, the angrier Dad seemed to get. His news was only of drinking bouts with other soldiers to relieve the misery of separation from their wives and girlfriends and getting rotten jobs like guard duty.

They've got it in for me in this damned place and I've been to see the sergeant but he's no use. I swear to God I'll kill some bugger round here before I've finished.

The war dragged on and Dad's letters became rude. He wrote words that Robert used and drew pictures of ladies without clothes that boys got caned for at school. He described what he and Mum would do when he got his next leave. It was what Robert said they did.

If the good Lord's invented anything better to do with a dick then he's kept it to himself.

Spence didn't like this. He threw the box of letters into the wardrobe, back into the dark from where they came. But something else upset him, too. It was there in black and white in Dad's own handwriting – Private 4130410 John Henry White, nobody important, nobody brave, just an ordinary soldier who drove trucks and motorbikes. He'd never been to any foreign countries, only places like Kent and Dorset and North Wales.

He was not a commando and hadn't fired a single bullet at a German like Uncle Edgar had. This wasn't the daring warrior he'd told other kids about, a man with a chest full of medals for fighting and killing. Yet he'd so wanted to be proud of him and put his good arm around the shoulders of the hero he needed him to be.

But this was just another of Spence's playground stories - a lie dressed up in its Sunday best to hide the nakedness beneath.

*

'I can see you, Dad.'

'I never left your side, Joan love. How did all this happen to you?'

'You know the answer... you don't need me to explain.'

'Can I detect John Henry's hand in all this?'

'I've always tried to be a good wife to him.'

'You wouldn't listen, Joan, would you?'

'He was a good man, once.'

'All good men have a bad man inside them.'

'Do you, Dad? Do you have a bad man inside you?'

'I'm no different to the rest.'

'Is that why you didn't choose me?'

'There wasn't a choice to be made... you know that, Joan.'

'But it was Vron who went with you, not me.'

'I'm with you now.'

'And will you stay with me?'

'For always, yes.'

Visitors started to arrive. She heard the scrape of chairs being pulled closer to the beds of other patients. It was time for Dad to leave. He was such a private person. She needed to rest anyway, to get her strength back. But as her eyes closed, she started to fear she might fall again... tumbling blind and bleeding and her womb on fire. Dad took both her hands and she felt his lips gently kiss her forehead.

'You didn't ever want the baby, did you?'

'No, I didn't. That's true... I didn't.'

'Then why are you mourning?'

'Because I held it, Dad. It was only little, just a poor little thing.'

'But it was dead, love.'

'Like I wanted it to be and that was wicked of me.'

'You should sleep now, Joan.'

'I love you, Dad.'

His voice faded from her ears and the scent of his hair oil from her nostrils. The matron drew back the curtains and plumped up her pillows.

'Who was that you were talking to, Joan?'

'Only my father... he came to see me.'

'That's nice for you. I'm sorry to have missed him.'

'That's all right... he'll come again. He'll not leave me this time.'

Thirteen

Zilla's supper was steamed fish, two boiled potatoes and a single floret of broccoli. She'd no desire to fill out any further as her mother had. The telephone rang while she cleared the table. It was Malcolm, her lawyer, still at his desk despite the hour.

'That policeman you asked me about - '

' - Challis?'

'Yes, Vincent Challis. I've picked up a bit of gossip.'

'And he's the rat I told you he was?'

'More of a terrier, I think,' Malcolm said. 'Got a reputation for never letting go.'

'Has he, now? So why are he and the Special Branch interested in my cleaner?'

'He's not in the Special Branch, Zilla. He's an everyday detective officer from CID.'

'Really? Are you sure?'

'Completely sure, yes. But he's a hard and determined man, wasn't called up during the war and worked all through it as a detective and they say he's sent more than one murderer to the gallows.'

'I can believe that, all right. But why's he making enquiries about Joan?'

'That I don't know but there will be a reason. The police won't be wasting their time.'

'But she's no criminal, Malcolm. You'll never meet a more innocent person.'

'Maybe that's right but my advice would still be to steer well clear.'

'There speaks a lawyer - '

' - and a friend, I hope.'

'Of course you are but so is Joan,' she said. 'Something's not right about all this and on top of everything else, the poor woman's just suffered a miscarriage.'

'Then I'm sorry for her but face the facts, Zilla. You cannot know what's behind this police investigation but you can be absolutely certain that it's not in your personal or professional interest to get caught up in it.'

Yet how unjust would it be to heed this gypsy's warning and turn her back on Joan - and therefore, Spence - at the very time they might need help most? She would drive to Zion Street next morning - and visit Joan in hospital, too. Whatever Malcolm said, Challis wasn't the only one with questions demanding answers.

*

Not half a mile away, Edgar Sydenham lay holding hands with Frances on the bed they had shared for thirty-seven years. Her breathing came in rasping gulps and her head moved from side to side on a pillow dampened by the labour of staying alive.

On that evening in high summer, Edgar thought back to the Red Cross volunteer she once was, helping to heal that which couldn't be put into words. It was hard to believe but she'd taught him to embroider cushion covers - a wounded, foul-mouthed Tommy slowly stitching his mind back together with needle and thread.

But men driven to the edge knew the truth, knew the lies of those who sent him and his pals to compost the fields of a foreign land.

Frances was never a beauty but honest and kind and better than he'd a right to expect. They married before the Great War ended, even as all those letters of regret were still falling across the land like a blizzard of black snow.

And now, what had he left to repay her save for a little tenderness in this, the dying of her day? Edgar had seen enough of life to know when its burdens were being set down. Pray as priests might, the end would not be long in coming.

'Edgar?'

'Yes, love.'

'You do still remember him, don't you?'

'Of course I do.'

'Wasn't he just perfect?'

'That he was... a grand little fellow.'

'Just to hold him one more time... that wouldn't be too much to ask, would it?'

'No, it wouldn't, love. But you mustn't go upsetting yourself... we'll see him again soon enough.'

'You do believe that, don't you, Edgar... you do, don't you?'

And he said that he did for he'd not the heart to deny her the hope she'd need to sustain herself in what was to come.

*

The tiny kitchen Joan prided herself in keeping so neat was a mess of dirty plates and fish and chip papers left unburned in the cold grate. Zilla heated a kettle of water and began to clean up. She'd brought eggs, cheese and milk which Spence put in the food cupboard beneath the stairs.

He also fetched his shirts, pants and socks from his bedroom and these she washed by hand then pegged out on the line across the yard. Joan's neighbour, Dolly Thomas, watched from her side of the wall.

'I'd have done all this, you know.'

'I'm sure you would but it's no trouble.'

'John Henry's a very stubborn man, won't be accepting help from anyone.'

'I can understand that but Joan wouldn't want standards to slip, would she?'

'No, true enough. How is she, do you know?'

'I'm going into the hospital later so I'll find out then.'

She'd noticed Spence holding his jaw. He said he'd toothache. She looked inside his mouth and saw one new adult tooth already rotting. Two others were going the same way and would need pulling if he didn't get treatment.

'When did you last go to the dentist, young man?'

'I don't like dentists. They smother you with this rubber mask and it's like drowning.'

She gave him two Aspro tablets from her handbag and said she'd make him an appointment with her own private dentist when Joan came home.

'Dad says they won't let me visit her in hospital.'

'I suppose they think hospitals can be quite frightening for children.'

'I wouldn't be frightened and she's my Mum. I found her.'

'I know and you were very brave.'

'Where did all that blood come from, Miss Arbib?'

'Well, when she fell down the stairs, she must have cut herself inside, mustn't she?'

'And what was in the parcel?'

'What parcel?'

'Wrapped up in some newspaper on the draining board... that was bleeding, too.'

'I've no idea, Spence. You'll have to ask your father and see if he knows.'

'Auntie Emily said that a policeman has been at the hospital.'

'A policeman... at the hospital? Whatever did he want?'

'They're trying to find out what happened with Mum. That's what Auntie Emily told Uncle Edgar because I heard them talking.'

'Did your Auntie Emily say if it was a policeman in uniform or in plain clothes?'

'I don't know. I was sent outside. But why would a policeman be asking questions?'

*

Zilla arrived at Joan's ward just as other visitors were leaving. She told the Irish matron she'd only come to give Joan her prayer book.

'Be only a minute then, no more,' matron said. 'And as quiet as a mouse.'

Joan looked like a sleeping child. Her skin had a bloodless, ceramic purity about it. Zilla put the missal on the bedside cabinet. It'd been on the kitchen mantelpiece in Zion Street, page-marked with holy pictures and texts from Joan's teachers.

The sower set forth to sow his seed; some fell on good ground and grew and bore fruit even unto a hundredfold. From Mother Columba to dear Joan, 1927.

Matron coughed. Time was up. As she left, Zilla said she'd heard that a policeman had been making inquiries about Joan's accident.

'I'm sorry, that's official business,' matron said. 'I can't talk about matters like that.'

'But you can tell me when Joan might be coming home, can't you?'

'It's the doctors who'll decide but I dare say it won't be long, now.'

'Her family will be so pleased. I don't suppose they've missed a single visiting hour.'

'No, they haven't, but one of her aunties is quite poorly and they telephoned to say that's why they couldn't come today.'

'What's happened to Joan will have hit them all very hard,' Zilla said.

'Yes, but she didn't lack for a visitor this afternoon because her father came instead.'

'Joan's *father*?'

'That's right. Joan said he was here earlier but I didn't get to meet him.'

Zilla made no reply. Everyone yearned for a sign from their gods. But it would have taken a great miracle for Joan to be visited by her father. Soon after Spence was born, she'd asked Zilla to look after him for an afternoon.

Joan had a funeral to attend - that of her father. He'd lain in his grave in Southern Cemetery for almost ten years, unless he'd rolled back the stone and risen from the dead.

Fourteen

Fen Meadows Medical Centre, Cambridge, Friday 12th December 2014

Judges need confessors no less than those who appear before them. So it was with Spencer White. He couldn't ever have shared what was sometimes in his head or in his heart with anyone else in his calling. Signs of self-doubt or depression might be evidence of weakness and unreliability and find their way into the files which the Lord Chancellor kept on all judges.

But White's ability to appear to be what people assumed was learned long since. Fellow students reading law at Keble, those in the enviable freemasonry of the confident and the entitled, knew he was a grammar school boy - one of those they sneeringly dismissed as *stains* - but little else. By then, he'd consciously shed his northern accent and was loosening the ties that bound him.

Had he been asked who'd watched him with pride from the Sheldonian's steep wooden benches on graduation day, would he have introduced them to the frail old man from the Great War or the shuffling, shambling woman holding so tightly to Miss Arbib's arm? The answer shamed him but it was how it had to be.

Later, during pupilage and in chambers after taking silk, he still saw no merit in removing the dust covers from the past.

Yet every life had need of a priest once in a while. White's was a doctor, a man also obliged by oath to keep secrets. He'd taken an interest in White's infantile poliomyelitis and as with the law, context was everything in medicine, too. Over time, he would learn more about the boy from Zion Street than most ever would. White saw him next day for an annual check-up on his heart, lungs and blood pressure.

'Any chest pains, breathlessness, lumps anywhere?'

'No, just my duff arm being more painful than usual.'

'Post-polio syndrome,' the doctor said. 'Haven't got a pill for that. Anything else on your mind to bother you?'

White finished dressing and appreciated a moment to sit and talk through what he would never confess to his wife. He told the GP about being asked to chair the deaths in custody inquiry.

'Sounds like friends in high places think well of you.'

'Friends I never knew I had, you mean.'

'So when do you start?'

'I'm not going to do it,' White said.

'Really? I'd have thought it'd be a fine way for you to finish your career.'

'Elspeth would doubtless agree but she'd also say I've always lacked ambition.'

'So why don't you prove her wrong?'

'I suppose if it were not Manchester, I'd probably agree to take it on.'

'So what's the problem with Manchester? That's where you're from, isn't it?'

'Maybe that's the problem. It's a while since I've been back... forty years, I suppose.'

'Something to do with memories, then?'

'Probably... if you mean leaving the past where it lies and the dead in their graves.'

'But I still don't fully understand. Everything will have changed and it'll all be very different to how you remember it; it'll just be another city.'

'No, it can't ever be that... not for me, anyway. I've got these images in my head and it's as if I'm almost afraid of going back.'

'Then you must ask yourself what it is you're afraid of.'

Spencer White, a judge whose trade was the finding of facts, didn't answer... or preferred not to give one, even to his confessor.

Fifteen

35 Grenville Road, Fallowfield, Thursday 4th August 1955

Spence knew they were hiding the truth from him - his Dad, everyone at 35, even Miss Arbib who always said finding it out was important for only then could causes and consequences be understood.

Yet when he asked what was really wrong with Mum, they talked behind their hands or sent him out of the room. This annoyed him. Nothing was the same as before. The pictures behind his eyes wouldn't fade – Mum lying in all that blood, the policeman coming for him, the cell they might lock him in.

He couldn't make sense of it and this was worse than his toothache. Zion Street wasn't happy any more. He wanted to run away but to where, he didn't know. Robert Heaney shouldn't have said those rude things about what mums and dads got up to. Yet Dad's letters meant Robert was right after all.

But what about that parcel on the draining board? It wasn't there when he raced off to telephone for the ambulance so where had it come from? And why was it sopping red and if Mum had had a baby, where was it?

Spence was running and thinking, trying to work it all out, and found himself in a narrow service entry between the tennis club and the backs of the houses in Grenville Road. He pushed open the gate into the garden of 35 where the roses on the trellis were coming out, pinkish white like the cheeks of girls in old paintings.

Auntie Frances was asleep in a deck chair by the French windows where the sun caught each afternoon.

84

Her hair was coarse and grey, crinkly like the tail of the rag-and-bone man's horse.

She'd grey skin, too, with yellow-brown dabs around her eyes. Even with them closed, she looked sad enough to cry. He stood watching the rise and fall of her pale blue cardigan and listening to the bubbling rattle which went with it. Then she woke with a start, unsure of where she was.

'Is that you, Billy?'

'No, Auntie Frances. It's me, Spence.'

'Oh dear, of course it is. I must've dozed off.'

'Are you a bit better today, then?'

'Just enough to get out and feel the sun on my face.'

'Where are the others?'

'Your Uncle Edgar's at work and Kitty and Emily are away to Zion Street because your Mum's coming out of hospital and they want to welcome her home.'

'Is she, honestly? Dad didn't tell me.'

'We're going to have to look after her, aren't we, Spence? She's not been at all well.'

'I know, but no-one will tell me what's been the matter with her.'

'She's had a poorly tummy but she's on the mend, now.'

'So she's going to be all right?'

'Bound to be, love... if we all help her like I know you will.'

'Auntie Frances?'

'Yes, love.'

'Why did you just call me Billy?'

'Did I? Well, that's because of me only being half awake,' she said. 'Now, let's see if I've got some toffees in this handbag of mine.'

*

Joan sat at the front of the bus, wanting only to be quiet and still. It pulled away from the hospital stop on Nell Lane and passed by Wood's Family Butchers and Fletcher's Bakery.

A German bomb cratered the road near there during the Blitz. So many people died. She'd heard talk of a mass grave near Hulme. There hadn't been time to bury the victims properly.

Fear of those nights still made her tremble. Her insides felt like kneaded dough but there was nothing more to say about what happened. Out in the summer streets, women pushed prams and clean white nappies blew on washing lines in the warm breeze.

You too, my mother, read my rhymes
For love of unforgotten times,
And you may chance to hear once more
The little feet along the floor.

Her Dad adored poems and storybooks. He bought her Blackie's Children's Annual every Christmas and they'd always go to pantomimes together.

When the better weather came, they'd take a coach to the seaside and it'd be donkey rides and ice creams and treats all day till she fell asleep in his arms on the long journey home.

John Henry never knew such affection so how could he give it? What a dreadful childhood he'd had. Not that it was ever talked about.

She doubted there'd be any food in Zion Street or if he'd cleaned around the house. Yet none of this seemed to matter. Something would turn up. Others got by - owing the grocer, leaving the housework.

The hospital doctor said she should rest, take it easy. But it wasn't *her* body that worried her. She had held it, held that little creation she'd wanted dead. Any prayers she offered would be thrown back in her face.

Vron was right. She'd harboured wicked thoughts. No act of contrition could ever scrub away the sins she'd committed. John Henry was best left out of it. He wasn't a Catholic, anyway. Only Dad would understand.

She got off the bus opposite the Friendship Inn and walked to Zion Street. The house seemed familiar yet remote, as if this was where strangers lived.

Spence wasn't at home. She'd so wanted his arms around her, to know he didn't hate her like she'd begun to hate herself. But this was part of her punishment - this and the questions he'd ask and the answers she couldn't give. She sat under the crucifix and closed her eyes.

'You're at home now, Joan, love.'

'Hello, Dad.'

'Was it a girl or a boy?'

'I can't say for sure.... a little girl, I think. She was so tiny.'

'Daughters are so lovely.'

'Was I lovely, Dad?'

'Yes, you were. Like a lovely little doll.'

*

Kitty and Emily meant well but Joan was glad when they'd gone and left her to clear away the teacups. She was tired and needed to rest. The kitchen clock hadn't been wound up and she sat in silence.

All evidence of her crime had been cleaned away but she was consoled by having her Dad to talk to. He loved his cricket. She'd a picture of him somewhere, sitting in his pressed whites alongside other young fellows with those centre partings that were all the rage in Edwardian days. Handsome boys. Dead now, of course... Ypres, Arras, Passchendaele. It was strange to think, but Uncle Edgar could've gone into battle with some of Dad's cricket team and never known it.

Dad hadn't the best of health but he volunteered all the same. He didn't want the bloody bandages of a wounded soldier thrown at him, which is what they did to cowards.

He was never a big man, quite slight. Spence took after him. Dad wasn't sent to France but he saw his share of death and destruction during the Zeppelin raids. Mum was a beauty. Clever, too. That's where Spence got his brains. Only one photograph of her survived - pretty lips, determined chin, curly black hair. Joan began to sob.

'Don't upset yourself, love.'

'I can't help it, Dad. I've done wrong.'

'We all do wrong in this life but God forgives us.'

'He won't forgive me this time.'

'He forgives everyone or just think of the sorry state we'd all be in.'

There was a noise in the yard. The back door pushed open. It was Spence with that face which always needed a wash. He stood staring at her, half in, half out of the kitchen, as if unsure about staying. Then he spoke.

'I heard you talking to someone but there's no-one here.'

'Did you, love?'

'You've been crying.'

'Only because I've missed you so much.'

Then he came to her without another word and folded his arms around her neck as she prayed he would. His fragile body convulsed against hers and she knew there was nothing she could say, nothing she could do to make it right, not for him, not for her. She kissed his cheeks, his forehead and his eyes and their tears ran together.

He was no longer a child prodigy or the professor-in-the-making. Spencer White was just a little boy wanting to be found.

Sixteen

For all its certainty - and however foreshadowed by illness - death has the power to suck the air from those it touches but leaves behind. It was six thirty. Emily served shepherd's pie from the remains of the previous day's scrag end lamb.

Edgar moved a pile of ironing from a chair so Frances could sit to the table. Kitty poured their cups of tea. Vron would eat later. A small fire burned in the grate in case Frances wanted to stay up.

Beyond the back garden, a tournament was taking place at the tennis club. The shouts of players and the swipes of their racquets cut across the light orchestral music coming from next-door's wireless.

The meal was enjoyed, after a fashion. Frances went back to bed in the front room and Edgar cleared the table then washed their dirty plates in the scullery.

Emily lit a Craven A and set out the cards for a game of patience to the hypnotic rhythm of Kitty's sewing machine. She'd one of Vron's skirts to alter for Joan.

It was a pleasant summer evening of no consequence.

Around eight o'clock, Edgar took Frances a glass of water for her evening tablets. The room was silent and in semi-darkness. Edgar switched on the light.

Frances was not asleep in bed. He couldn't see her at first. But she was leaning against the bay window, only held upright by being twisted inside one of the curtains like an Indian woman wrapped round in a sari.

Edgar did not immediately get the others. He released her from the drapes and carried her gently to their bed as if she were his new bride. Then he allowed himself a moment of memory, a final kiss.

After this, he went to the kitchen. Death, like birth, was the work of women as it had been when streets thereabouts were country lanes.

Kitty and Emily knew their duty. Edgar was sent to call the doctor from the neighbours at number 15 who had a telephone. Clean towels were fetched from the airing cupboard. Water was boiled and brought in an enamel bowl with a bar of Frances's favourite Wright's Coal Tar Soap.

No words were spoken. They removed their sister's clothes and began to wash her with love and regard... the belly wherein a child once grew, the breasts where it had fed and the arms in which it was held so gently.

They stole glances at her in fright and wonder and knew that one day they, too, would be cleansed like this.

And when at last they finished, Frances was dressed in the best blue nightie she had, all silk and satin and fit for a queen.

Kitty applied a little lipstick and make-up. Yet however hard each tried with the artifice of cosmetics, it was impossible to bring any sense of ease or peace to the chill face of suffering and loss before them.

The front door bell rang. It would be the doctor. The outside lights were on at the tennis club pavilion. Young men and women chattered and flirted one with another in the balmy, moth-blown air. They made plans to meet again then went their separate ways.

It was still a pleasant summer evening of no consequence.

Seventeen

Sydenham: At home on 9th August, Frances Lillian of 35 Grenville Road, Manchester 14, beloved wife of Edgar, sister to Emily and Kitty, auntie to Veronica and Joan, devoted great auntie to Spencer William. Service at St Cuthbert's Church, Withington on Monday, 15th August at 9.30 am followed by interment in Southern Cemetery.

Spence had never read his name in a newspaper before nor seen a man crying. Uncle Edgar should have been at work like Dad but he arrived at Zion Street soon after breakfast.

He didn't give Spence his usual wink or pretend to twist off his nose and replace it with his thumb which always smelled of tobacco. He had just stood at the front door, forlorn and somehow smaller.

His shoulders began to shake and without a word being spoken, Mum understood what must have happened. Spence was sent out to play, unsure what he should do next. He'd seen Auntie Frances sleeping in the sunshine only the day before. Even then, she must have been dying.

This felt strange and scary but not as much as it did now, sitting in church across from her coffin, heaped with roses the colour of blood. Spence shivered at the idea of being nailed in a box, unable to get out. Light streamed in through the stained glass windows, through the smoke of candles and incense, over the priest's rainbow robes and the mourners in black, murmuring responses in that place of peace but little ease. Prayers were offered for Frances who was already in heaven. Uncle Edgar used to say he'd no idea where that was but knew where hell had been.

92

People stood as the pale pine coffin was carried out on the shoulders of the undertaker's men. Mum didn't seem to know where she was. She'd hardly followed the service. Dad shuffled in the pew. He didn't like being in Catholic churches.

They'd shouted at each other again that morning. Dad said he couldn't afford to take time off work, not with Mum still unable to go back to cleaning. But she'd never forgive him if he didn't attend the funeral, not after all the kindnesses Auntie Frances and Uncle Edgar had shown them down the years.

Anger was better than her not seeming to care about anything. That was how she'd been since coming out of hospital - staying in bed all morning, leaving Dad to get his own meal at night.

Everyone assembled near the porch. Spence saw Miss Arbib and some others standing on the pavement which blew about with confetti from a wedding days before. The family's funeral cars were waiting to leave for the cemetery so he didn't have the chance to speak to her.

He knew they were going to put Auntie Frances in the ground and throw soil on top. But he was frightened. He didn't want to see this happen. Yet Dad made him stand at the very edge of her grave, so close to the sheer clay sides that he could topple in and be buried himself. Holy water sprinkled onto the coffin by the priest rolled in tiny globes across its polished surface and pooled over the brass plate with Auntie Frances's name etched on it.

Final prayers were said then she was gently lowered into the earth on long canvas straps... down, down, down and into the darkness forever. Spence couldn't get his breath. He had a dread of enclosed spaces and fought for air as he did at the dentist's or as Auntie Frances had done at the end.

He wrenched his hand free from his mother's then turned and ran... ran from them all, ran as fast and hard as he could, just as he'd always wanted to do.

*

There were sandwiches and coffee on the bar with beer or sweet sherry if people preferred. Hatches, matches, despatches - whatever the occasion, the Friendship Inn always put on a decent spread. Joan calmed down after the funeral director told her Spence had gone off with Miss Arbib in her car. The poor lad was so upset.

John Henry said he'd teach him a lesson later as he'd no cause for behaving the way he did. Edgar quietly took him to one side and promised to break every bone in any hand laid on Spence from that day forward.

It came to something when such words had to be uttered on an occasion like that. But John Henry was a waste of rations who didn't deserve such a smashing kid. He soon cleared off back to work, very sheepish. All bullies were cowards.

Joan looked as if her spirit was finally breaking. She'd shed weight and couldn't be eating properly. Kitty thought losing the baby had taken more out of Joan than anyone realised. It would do that, all right. She would find it like being nailed to a cross for the rest of her life.

The wake began to thin out. Frances's women friends gave Edgar sad looks, touched the lapels of his suit jacket or adjusted his tie and said he'd always be welcome to eat with them if he ever wanted.

Edgar nodded and said he'd had the best wife a man could wish for. Then he backed away, knowing it'd all be over soon. But the old love would've smiled at so rare an expression of his affection.

Joan went to 35 with the others. Edgar paid his bill and wanted only to be on his own. It might be the way of life but the closer he got to the end of it, the more he wanted to return to the beginning. He sat upstairs on a bus into town, smoking and thinking. At Cambridge Street, he got off and walked the sunless terraces where he was born and raised, condemned now as slums and awaiting demolition.

His four brothers and two sisters were all dead. Their father was a cabinetmaker, his mother from Dublin. All sorts of people washed up around there - Poles, Russians, Austrians - each stuck on the same damned flypaper.

And above them, the iron-banded chimneys of factories where they were destined to work... mills of drudgery, Klaxons for shifts starting, shifts finishing and always the near certainty of never making old bones.

No wonder so many enlisted in the Manchester Pals. Here was a farewell to the humdrum, an adventure across the sea with blokes from down your street or where you worked – and just for a bit of valour with the bayonet. That's what they were told, that's what they believed.

From these crowded little cribs came all those laughing lads he had known, kitted out in temporary uniforms of tram guard blue then real khaki to march behind a bugle band as their families gathered with pride to watch Lord Kitchener take the salute in Albert Square.

One recruit's grandfather had survived the Charge of the Light Brigade. It'd not be long before the Pals would look upon that particular battle as a textbook lesson on military strategy.

For now, the streets he walked were empty. He heard only the sound of his own footsteps. And after today, he was even more alone. What had it all been for - any of it? But the Salutation was nearby. Some of his Dunlop mates might be in there having a drink. The towels would go on at two o'clock so he'd need to hurry. At such a time as this, there was only one way to deal with sorrows.

*

'Are you saying your Dad deliberately tried to scare you at the graveside, Spence?'

'That's how he is.'

'But why?' Zilla said. 'That sounds like a horrible thing to do.'

'He says he always gets the dirty end of the stick so then he takes it out on others or anyone weaker than him.'

They were driving through the narrow country lanes of Cheshire - all arching oaks, half-timbered farmhouses and fat brown cows. The car roof was open to the wind and Spence's untrimmed hair furled about like a girl's.

Zilla had caught hold of him as he ran through the cemetery gates in his best blazer and clumpy, ill-fitting shoes, afraid of something he couldn't put into words. It disturbed her to see him so anguished.

She sent a message to Joan that he was safe then got him in her car and headed south into the countryside. The further they went, the more absorbed Spence became in sights he rarely saw - hills and fields, stone cottages in gardens aflame with flowers, grand houses glimpsed between avenues of trees.

'It's like being in a calendar, isn't it?'

'Yes, but never forget where the wealth of these people comes from, Spence.'

'Do you mean they've stolen it?'

'In a manner of speaking, lots of them have, yes.'

They stopped at a café where he had a poached egg on toast. Zilla bought him a piece of chocolate cake, which he ate with his fingers, not the fork she offered. Only when he'd finished did she ask why he was running away.

'I wanted to be somewhere else.'

'Away from the funeral, the cemetery, your parents... what, exactly?'

'Just everything.'

'What can I do, Spence... what can I do to make you happy?'

He looked at her with unwavering brown eyes but had the wit to say nothing, which was an answer in itself.

'All right, I understand but you must promise me that you'll not run away again.'

He shook his head but not in a manner to put Zilla's fears to rest. The boy worried her, his mother, too. Losing a baby was awful but Joan seemed to have also lost her will to fight, that resolve that'd kept her going against the odds.

Zilla knew a private doctor who might help. But Joan's family might see this as interference in their affairs, especially if she offered to pay. It didn't take much to upset John Henry and Emily could be prickly, too. But the damage being done to Spence by those who loved him most was self-evident. It wasn't something Zilla could stand by and let happen, for Joan's sake as much as anyone else's.

On the drive back to Zion Street, she got Spence talking about Frances to get his child's eye view of the first person he'd known who had died.

'She and Uncle Edgar made me feel special, like I was important to them and not just by getting me toys or new clothes but the way they talked to me and looked at me.'

'It's called *love*, Spence,' Zilla said. 'You're going to miss her, aren't you?'

'Yes, but she'll always be at 35, won't she? They'll always be there... all of them.'

*

Joan wanted to be close to Frances and all that memory meant - the clothes she wore, the seaside ornaments she'd bought, her rings and brooches and jewels of paste which were treasured. The everyday and the mundane made death incomprehensible. That which was cheap and disposable endured while its owner perished. Joan had found it impossible to pray in church. She hadn't dared to. It felt as if everyone was looking at her and knew of her guilt – just as God did.

The others were out in the garden... Kitty, Emily. Vron, too. And some of Frances's friends. All drinking tea, nibbling biscuits and remembering her.

But they couldn't feel the loss of Frances as cruelly as her. Frances wasn't just her auntie. It was like losing her mother for a second time but now being old enough to understand and to know the pain of it all. Coming on top of everything else that had happened, it was getting ever harder for Joan to cope.

She sat in Frances's bedroom armchair, breathing in the last of her scent before it, too, faded. Dad was there with her.

'Lovely service, wasn't it?'

'Was it? Not for me, it wasn't.'

'You're troubled, Joan... it's not just the baby, is it?'

'No, not just her... no.'

'Then what, love? Tell me... tell me what's in your mind.'

98

'You know what's in my mind. It's always been there.'

'Yes, but none of that was your fault, love.'

'Wasn't it? I was with him, Dad... it was me. I was to blame.'

The door pushed open and Vron came in, her cheeks red from rouge and sun and the sherry she liked too much.

'Are you all right, Joan? They're all asking where you are.'

'Just thinking about Auntie Frances, that's all. I'll be out in a minute.'

'I thought someone was with you. I could've sworn I heard voices.'

*

Zilla got no reply at Zion Street. Spence knew where the key was hidden in the backyard but she didn't want to leave him in the house alone. Not that day.

They drove to Grenville Road. Joan would most likely be there and if not, his aunts could take care of him. They parked near 35 and got out. As they did, two men in dark overalls could be seen coming towards them dragging a third whose arms clung round their shoulders. It was Edgar Sydenham, bareheaded and borne by his friends like Christ between the thieves. His shoes scuffed and bumped along the pavement as if his ankles were broken. The mourning suit, pressed and cleaned in Frances's honour, was dirty and disarrayed with traces of vomit on the lapels and the waistcoat.

Here were eyes wet with sorrow, damned with remorse, for what they had witnessed was beyond bearing. Then he saw Spence. Each was transfixed by the other. A man reduced, a child bewildered.

Edgar fell to his knees and took the boy in his arms, stroking his hair and rocking back and forth. Those

99

watching on did not move, did not speak. There was no comfort to be had.

All that could be heard was Edgar whispering the name *Billy* over and over again.

Eighteen

Great Stukeley, Cambridgeshire, Friday 26th December 2014

A protection officer with a handgun holstered beneath his dark jacket inspected Judge White's invitation.

Elspeth smiled, as if being pleasant might save her were she ever in his sights. He handed the card back and the Whites were admitted to the home of Dame Norma and Sir John Major.

It was a detached, 1920s house hidden from the road by a strategic screen of trees and bushes and only accessed via heavy security gates. Plain and ordinary it might once have been but it'd been extended, gentrified, given a huge conservatory - and wired against assassins, though the owner no longer held high office.

A young man in black trousers, white shirt and a dickie bow, sashayed through the guests with a silver tray of champagne flutes. Another offered canapés.

Elspeth was tall enough to look over the heads of the assembled worthies for someone they might recognise and who'd make them feel less like outsiders. That was when Luston appeared at their side.

'Judge White, good to see you again,' he said. 'And Mrs White. I'm Dan Luston and I've really been looking forward to meeting you.'

He shook their hands warmly. Luston had the assured manner of a young army officer on leave - clipped fair hair, pale pink shirt, no tie, stone-coloured chinos and highly polished brown brogues.

'It's quieter in the kitchen,' he said. 'Let's edge in there if we can.'

He had their glasses refilled and was effortlessly charming. He admired Elspeth's long fringed skirt and top in black and white dog's tooth. Was it a Beatrix Ost? Who was her hair stylist? On what distant beach had she obtained such a deep tan?

White looked for a sick bag but knew Elspeth was already seeing in Luston something of the son they could never have had.

'Has your husband told you about the inquiry which the powers-that-be are still hoping he'll agree to chair?'

'He's mentioned it, yes, but he seems dead set on hanging up his wig.'

'But what's your view, Mrs White? Should he ride to hounds on this one or sit it out?'

Elspeth took another sip of champagne and deliberately avoiding White's eye, said she thought it a fitting way to end an honourable career.

'Deaths in police custody are a hugely important issue,' Elspeth said. 'I've read up about them and it all goes to the heart of public confidence in the authorities.'

'Couldn't agree more,' Luston said. 'What we have to do now is to convert the judge to our way of thinking and to that end, there's someone who wants to meet you.'

Their presence at such a gathering had always been a set-up. White knew it but was minded to enjoy the game a little longer. He saw Luston nod to an older man by the door. The Whites were then introduced to Sir Patrick Prentice, the senior civil servant overseeing the Manchester inquiry at the Ministry of Justice.

'Sorry if this seems like an ambush,' Sir Patrick said. 'But I've less than a fortnight to finalise all the arrangements that we need to announce when Parliament reassembles.'

'Or we'll have more allegations of a cover-up and more riots,' Luston said.

Sir Patrick nodded with some weariness and said that with a general election five months away, this couldn't be allowed to happen politically.

'How many other judges have turned you down, Sir Patrick?' White said.

'None, you're our first choice. You've the experience and the wisdom that's needed and Manchester's your home turf so that'd play well, too.'

'If you don't mind me saying, it all seems a bit on-the-hoof, a bit last minute.'

'Thank the blessed politicians,' Sir Patrick said. 'These deaths happened on their watch and suddenly, there's rioting and it's a crisis and they've got to be seen to be sorting it all out, not failing.'

White saw Elspeth looking at him hard. To her, his duty was clear. Deep down, maybe he knew he had no choice.

'Very well, Sir Patrick, I suppose we should meet again... more formally, perhaps?'

Nineteen

Sorrento Café, Withy Grove, Manchester, Wednesday 17th August 1955

For Vincent Challis, policing was akin to working for the sanitary department, dealing with rats and effluent and trying to ensure neither infected those above the sewers.

He'd no time for protesters at Ruth Ellis's execution. She'd aimed a gun at a lover and pulled the trigger. And not only the once, either.

It was said she'd recently miscarried so her mind was skewed. Nonsense. Ellis knew what she was doing. The law had to take its course and be blind - even if it sometimes needed a helping hand to avoid stumbling in the dark.

He knew of a man hanged for a murder he didn't commit. But he'd got away with a previous killing so the books balanced in the end. Challis himself had planted a piece of broken bottle from a murder scene in the trouser turn-ups of a suspect.

It was a little conjuring trick in case the jury wobbled over a partial thumbprint found on a door. Happily, they didn't and the day just got worse for chummy.

Challis knew how he felt. A marathon boozing session to celebrate the birth of his son had left him wanting to lie down on a mortician's slab. Breakfast at the Sorrento that day could only be coffee - and more of it. Becoming a first-time father aged forty-two proved yet again that life was no more neat and tidy than a burgled house.

Having a baby hadn't been in his script. Besides, most evenings he was rarely home early enough to perform the necessary acts preparatory. It must have happened around Christmas.

There were parties and nights he could no longer remember. His wife didn't let on till after Easter and even then, he didn't believe her. But he'd held the reality in his arms at the hospital. Each looked as bemused as the other. Challis quickly handed him back, unsure what to say or think, and sought refuge at The Abercromby next to Bootle Street nick.

Forty-eight hours later, he booked on for his shift. Maybe he'd feel better if someone had done as he'd asked and located a particular wartime file. Then he might finally get round to solving the murder that never was.

*

Spence was treated by Zilla's private dentist. Joan seemed too pre-occupied to object to her taking him. More distressingly, Zilla heard her acting out both sides of a conversation with her dead father when she arrived. So did Spence.

'I'll not be going to Mass any more, Dad.'

'Why ever not, love?'

'Because devils don't go to Mass, do they?'

'But you're not a devil, my lovely.'

'Am I not? Then why isn't my conscience clear? Tell me that, Dad.'

Zilla saw Spence wince. It was as if some invisible stranger had colonised his mother and taken over her mind. He felt threatened on every side. But for the moment, he rested - minus a tooth - in his Uncle Edgar's room at 35, reading a new *William Brown* book Zilla had bought him for being brave.

She sat in the kitchen with Edgar, Kitty and Emily and told them Joan's mental state was deteriorating. But she knew a psychiatrist who might help. Emily, who played bridge and talked politics with friends over tea and cakes in the Midland Hotel, had no wish for the taint of madness to attach to her.

'Don't you think you're taking a lot on yourself, Miss Arbib?'

'I'm very fond of Joan. I'm concerned about her.'

'I'm sure you are but Joan's our girl, you know.'

'Yes, but she's clearly unwell and needs help.'

'And we'll give her that help here. We'll look after her.'

'But with respect, I don't think you're able to do that.'

'Joan's run-down, nothing else.'

'No, I'm afraid it's far more serious,' Zilla said. 'She's become delusional since losing the baby; she's talking to her father as if he's with her. I've heard her and so has Spence and so did the matron at the hospital.'

'Well, I haven't and I think you should leave Joan to us, her family.'

'And what effect do you think seeing his mother in this state will have on Spence?'

'Spence is our business, too. Joan might be your cleaner but she's our kith and kin so she and her son are our responsibility.'

At this, Edgar, who'd just lost his wife and couldn't face losing Joan, got up from his chair and stood with his back to the fireplace.

'You take her to this doctor, Miss Arbib,' he said. 'You get her better for us because that's what Frances would've wanted and I'll hear no more about it.'

*

The file Challis had banged his desk to get for weeks was incomplete and dusty and so damp that the typescript tended to smudge if touched.

He settled back to read a crime report he wrote just after Manchester's infamous Christmas Blitz.

106

From Detective Constable Challis to Detective Superintendent Hayes. In the early hours of the 29th of December 1940, the body of a woman was found in the kitchen of her home, 24 Scott Street, Hulme, which had partially collapsed due to enemy action. As you know, the area has been damaged in the widespread bombing of the city during the past days.

She was identified as Maud Elizabeth Tester, a spinster, born on the 30th of April 1871. Her remains were conveyed to the Cavendish Road Mortuary and examined by the pathologist, Dr Reece.

In his opinion, what she had suffered was consistent with compression injuries occasioned by falling masonry in a bombing raid.

However, he noticed an injury to the nape of Miss Tester's neck which he said was consistent with a blow inflicted by a heavy object like a brick. On further examination, Dr Reece said he regarded this injury as the most probable cause of death and that the others most likely occurred after death.

Given the angle at which Dr Reece thinks the nape injury occurred, and as Miss Tester's body was found face up, it is hard to see how this injury was caused other than by a blow inflicted by human agency.

Enquiries were made locally by myself and revealed that Miss Tester had no known relatives. Her neighbour at number 22, a Mrs Turner, said she had carried out Miss Tester's housework and shopping for several years. Mrs Turner said Miss Tester was a cultured lady.

On being taken inside Miss Tester's house, Mrs Turner said several of the possessions normally on view were missing including a silver canteen of cutlery, a stamp collection, two pictures in identical gilt frames, one showing a seashore scene and the other a Dutch windmill, a collection of rare silver coins, a watercolour painting of Caernarfon Castle and a red leather handbag usually containing cash.

It is my belief, Sir, that in view of the pathologist's stated concerns and the fact that several items of valuable property are missing, we are not dealing with a case of death caused by enemy action but one of murder in the furtherance of theft.

The response of Challis's boss was short, like his temper.

You should guard against seeing things which are not there. You have no evidence of murder. This city has just experienced several days of bombardment in which nearly seven hundred of our fellow citizens were killed by, inter alia, flying or falling bricks. The missing property may or may not have been looted. You have established no connection between this property (still less recovered it), and the owner's death. The pathologist could be gainsaid in court at the outset, even if we had the luxury of a defendant, which we do not. No further action.

Challis allowed himself a smile. He might soon have enough to go upstairs and finally get permission to turn his suspicions into the murder investigation which Miss Tester's death should always have been.

*

Zilla took Joan to the psychiatrist she knew in St John Street. She hoped for the best but feared the worst. Looking back, she realised she'd sought approval for her intervention from Joan's uncle and aunts, not her husband. John Henry came across as a man afraid of what he didn't know - which was plenty. Edgar soon put him straight as he had done about Spence going to Manchester Grammar.

For all Emily's initial affront and Kitty's peculiar ways, their love for Joan was well meant and protective. These were women case-hardened by wars or widowhood and all the iniquities life laid against their class and kind. They only had Joan's best interests at heart - just as Zilla had.

*

'So, Mrs White, would you please tell me who is in this room?'

'Miss Arbib, you and me and that lady, the nurse.'

'Is there anyone else with us?'

'No, just us.'

The psychiatrist nodded and smiled and made notes with a fountain pen.

'What about your father, for instance? Is he with us?'

'No, he's not here.'

'Are you sure, Mrs White?'

'I am, yes. But he often comes to see me.'

'When did you last see him?'

'Yesterday. I saw him yesterday.'

'Describe to me how he looked, if you will. Physically, how was he?'

'Well enough, I suppose.'

'What did he say to you?'

'Oh, you know, the usual... that I should eat more.'

'And you could hear him all right?'

'Of course, yes.'

'Could you summon him here now?'

'No, not today. He's got a very important job at the Labour Exchange so he can't just leave his desk because I want to see him.'

'Mrs White, how did you come to lose your baby?'

'I don't think I should talk about that, if you don't mind.'

'Why is that? Do you believe you were responsible for the baby not going to term?'

'You'll have to ask my Dad. He knows all about it.'

'And what of your son, Spencer? Tell me about your feelings towards him.'

'How do you mean? I don't understand.'

'Well, have you perhaps started to feel as if you may wish to harm him in some way?'

Joan stared at him. The question confused her - and Zilla, too. Joan stood up.

'I want to go home, now. I'm not staying here.'

The nurse steered her to a side room. The consultant reviewed his notes. Joan was suffering from puerperal depression with psychotic features. It was commonly known as the *baby blues* and affected some women soon after giving birth.

'But she had a miscarriage,' Zilla said. 'She didn't give birth.'

'Not to a live child but the physical process is virtually identical and so are the irrational fears and emotions that can follow.'

Joan displayed signs of low self-esteem, appeared isolated socially and within her marriage - and hadn't wanted the baby.

'Cases like this can sometimes have quite sinister outcomes, Zilla.'

'In what way?'

'With these hallucinations and bizarre false beliefs she's having, it's not unknown for a woman to think she's possessed by devils,' the psychiatrist said. 'Some abandon their new baby, others even kill them, which is why her other child could be at risk.'

'No, it's unthinkable that she might hurt Spence.'

'I'm sorry, it simply isn't unthinkable. She might even kill herself.'

110

Faced with such danger, he advised putting Joan in an asylum for observation. Zilla was aghast and immediately overtaken by remorse for interfering.

The journey to Zion Street took them near the university. Joan became agitated and wanted to stop to find her father. She insisted he and her sister lived nearby.

The moment passed and Joan lapsed into silence once more. Zilla knew she'd exceeded her brief, wilfully blundered into the lives of decent people with good intent. But the law of unexpected consequences had been invoked - and she'd not be thanked, least of all by those she had sought to help.

*

Later, with Joan and Spence in bed, Zilla the socialist academic, cleaned and tidied the kitchen in a small act of reparation then kept vigil in their brick box of a house.

She sat in the firelight, awaiting John Henry's return. He could still be at work, doing overtime to make up for Joan's loss of earnings. Or he could be drinking in the pub. She didn't want to believe that.

But if he spent more time there than was good for any of them, it was a symptom of social conditioning. On his treadmill, who wouldn't seek escape, however temporary? Whatever the truth, Zilla was required to face the realities of working class life, not the idealised fiction in which her comrades indulged. She couldn't know how John Henry would take the news about Joan's failing mental state. But as Zilla had brought matters to a head, it was her responsibility to tell him, be he drunk or sober.

Twenty

Spence had the front bedroom with a view across Zion Street to the gable end of Robert Heaney's house. Before going to sleep, he'd try to imagine how Chagall might have painted this dullest of scenes.

His sky would be a brilliant blue, the stars would swirl and dazzle and he'd have magical figures flying through the midnight air.

Miss Arbib had books about Chagall's pictures. She said they were like folk memories of villages called shtetls, which didn't exist any more. The Germans killed everyone in them. She also had photographs of what happened. All the dead looked like they were wearing pyjamas. Those families the Germans bombed near Zion Street had been in their pyjamas, too.

Some of the shtetl people escaped and lived in the Holy Land. Miss Arbib had been on a plane to visit them and said she'd like to take Spence there. But he didn't think Mum would agree. It sometimes felt as if Miss Arbib wanted him all to herself.

But if he did go, who would care for Mum? Dad couldn't be trusted to do it. Spence wished only for everything to be back to how it'd been, for them all to be in their rightful places again - Mum cleaning at *Arundel* and Miss Arbib teaching at the university and not tidying up in the kitchen at Zion Street.

Miss Arbib was rich so she might get a new cleaner. Mum would feel really unwanted then. She said Miss Arbib could buy and sell Dad's snooty sister, Evelyn, ten times over. Evelyn thought Mum was *uncomplicated,* which meant not very clever.

But on happy days, Mum made him laugh. She couldn't speak French like Auntie Vron but said she'd always be able to get a cup of tea in Paris. Not that she'd ever go in a plane. The *more firmer, the less terror,* she'd say.

Miss Arbib smiled when she explained what Mum meant. Miss Arbib said we all had to find ways to compensate for what we know we'll never have or never do.

Spence couldn't settle his mind to sleep. Everyone at 35 was still sad about Auntie Frances. Auntie Kitty said Spence mustn't think badly of Uncle Edgar for getting tipsy. Losing Auntie Frances was like losing the most precious thing he'd ever had. Spence wanted to ask who Billy was but didn't dare upset anyone more than they already were.

Mum was worrying them, too. Auntie Emily said she'd gone into a world of her own. What if she couldn't look after him anymore? Would he live at 35 or be put in a children's home then never get to grammar school?

Even as this thought stole upon him, he heard the front door being knocked. It couldn't have been his father. He always came to the back. It was Auntie Vron.

Spence crouched near the top of the stairs to hear better. He caught Auntie Vron saying they couldn't just put Mum away.

'The doctor said they could get a court order if necessary,' Miss Arbib said.

'But Joan's no more insane than you or me.'

'Maybe not but I've heard her having a long conversation with your dead father and so has Spence. That's got to be a concern, hasn't it?'

Everything went quiet for a moment. Then Auntie Vron said she'd also heard Mum talking to herself.

'I'm not looking forward to telling her husband,' Miss Arbib said. 'But upsetting though it is, it's got to be done.'

'Yes, he should've been back by now. Anyway, you've done all you can to help but Joan's my sister so I'll deal with John Henry.'

'Forgive me, but has he always been this inconsiderate where Joan's concerned?'

'No, quite the reverse,' Vron said. 'You couldn't have found a more attentive husband at first but couples grow apart... and the war changed the people we thought we were.'

'That's true. A man you thought you knew so well, knew the very heart and soul of him, could come back a complete stranger.'

Spence watched from behind his curtains as Miss Arbib drove off. He climbed back into bed and lay on his front with the pillow over his head. There was nothing more he wanted to hear or to know.

*

Zilla Arbib undressed for the night. Despite her best intentions, she was thickening out where she wished she wasn't. She would yet become her mother. For the moment, tired and pre-occupied, she was simply relieved to have been saved from the unpredictable John Henry. He might've turned awkward and denied the truth of Joan's condition. No man would want the stigma of a mad wife.

By all accounts, his capacity for the logical resolution of problems was limited. He either didn't have - or didn't use - language to express or reveal emotions. Maybe the war played a part in how he'd become yet Zilla felt events in his formative years were a more obvious and likely cause. But even Joan knew little about John Henry's upbringing. He never talked about his father.

His mother's family were rumoured to be wealthy and from somewhere in the south. They cut her adrift after she disobeyed them and married a would-be artist and picture restorer well beneath their social class.

Sadly, love didn't conquer all. She died penniless in the influenza epidemic after the Great War. John Henry - the youngest child - was raised by his sister, Evelyn. It all read like a cheap novelette, a melodramatic parable of refined misfortune with heroes and villains, sacrifice and tragedy.

When John Henry met Joan, he wanted only to have her as his wife, a home of their own and a son to spoil with love he'd never had. But the rent for such security was beyond his limited means. He would only ever be the sum of his contradictions.

Money was found for beer but not family holidays or violin lessons for Spence and his two-string fiddle. He would deny Spence the best education but could shiver with appreciation of operas he didn't understand. Politically, he'd not a progressive bone in his body. All his experience should make him a socialist but he voted Conservative and saw no irony in thinking of himself as middle class.

She switched off her bedside light but an image of John Henry remained in the dark. Vron thought him thoughtless and selfish. Zilla didn't accept this. The blame wasn't his or workers like him. They were just victims of the capitalist system, imprisoned behind bars of ignorance they could not see so could not break.

*

Edgar reached across to Frances's side of their bed and ran his palm over the emptiness of the sheets where once she lay. *You're a good man, Edgar Sydenham.* That's what she'd say. *Good enough for me.* There'd be warmth in her voice in the privacy of the moment. They were never ones for public displays of affection.

He lit a Park Drive with a match which made shadows and rendered the familiar strange and threatening.

The moon could do that at the Front... that and the firework flares illuminating the dead and dying in no-man's land to give the snipers a job to do.

Sometimes, the night air brought the conversations of German soldiers not a hundred and fifty yards away. A joke might be told and there would be laughter or a man could drop something and curse or be cursed.

Even a piano was heard, once. Imagine... a piano in a trench on a battlefield. *Rustle of Spring.* The melody came across in a drift of marsh mist and the putrescent gases from those who could no longer listen.

But then, his own comrades had put looted French furniture in their trenches – a gold chair and settee, ornate and carved, with velvet seats of the deepest burgundy and fit for a sun king. So a piano playing wasn't that out of place, no more than any of the bloody insanity which took hold of them all. Mad things happen in nightmares.

Yet other days of judgement were coming, days Edgar would want over and done with yet which he'd have to endure for the love of Joan and Spence - and in memory of Billy.

Twenty-One

On the morning of Joan's incarceration in a mental institution, Zilla couldn't stomach breakfast. Spence opened the door to her. John Henry sat in the front room in his demob suit; confused by events he was powerless to stop.

Joan stood pale and bone naked in a galvanised tub by the kitchen fire. Kitty was washing her with a flannel and soap. An outfit of clean clothes lay over the back of a chair. Joan had reverted to childhood, obedient to every command. Kitty ladled out the bath water into the sink with a jug then carried the tub outside to hook back onto its nail on the lavatory wall. Zilla helped Joan to towel herself dry and put on underclothes and a summery dress of pale blue flowers which had once been Vron's.

Emily arrived, her face set with self-righteous anger.

'Well, Madam Arbib - I hope you're satisfied with all the trouble you've caused.'

'Please, this is upsetting enough as it is.'

'I told you to keep out of our family's affairs, you and your damned money.'

She pushed a flop of lustreless black hair back from Joan's face. Joan seemed not to understand anything of what was going on around her.

'I've only tried to do what's best,' Zilla said.

'Then let me tell you, lady - we'd be a damn sight happier if you stopped trying.'

Emily's raised voice brought Spence in from the front room. He stood watching his mother picking distractedly through the contents of her cardboard suitcase.

'Mum? What's happening?'

'It's all right, love. Don't you worry about anything. It'll all be all right.'

Zilla checked her watch. They needed to leave soon. John Henry came into the crowded kitchen looking as lost as his son. Joan bent towards Spence and kissed his forehead. She smiled into the circle of Judas faces around her, the victim of their benign conspiracy and concern.

'It's for the best, Joan love,' Kitty said. 'You'll soon be home again.'

'Of course, I will. You'll look after everything while I'm gone, won't you?'

They moved in an awkward procession towards the front door and Miss Arbib's waiting car. Neighbours watched from their windows.

It was all beyond Spence's comprehension. He ran upstairs to his bedroom, almost blind with fear but could see his mother being taken away. He waved and waved but she didn't turn round and he couldn't help it but he pissed his pants where he stood.

*

Within an hour, two nurses had separated Joan from her husband, her family and Miss Arbib. Farewells, such as they might be, were deliberately kept short and without fuss. Outsiders were not to witness the start of the journey through a land of locks and keys which Joan was about to make.

They stripped off her own clothes. Each item was described in a logbook then bagged in a brown paper sack to be stored. Joan was deemed a high suicide risk so given a stitch-quilted moleskin dress which couldn't be ripped and made into a noose.

For her own protection, she was then led to an isolation cell, eight feet square and with slit windows higher than she could reach. Her bedding was canvas so couldn't be torn, either.

The walls were padded with horsehair and nailed over with more thick canvas. At the base of each wall was a cement gully to be used as a toilet.

Over the next three days, shifts of nurses watched her through a spy hole in a stout wooden door. Each was personally responsible for ensuring Joan didn't kill herself.

They gave her paraldehyde, a calming but addictive drug, which also disorientated the patient. It smelled like pear drops and petrol and dried out Joan's mouth, causing her tongue to crack. Thus dosed, she was induced into a state of semi-narcosis. She had to be turned every few hours to combat the risk of thrombosis or pneumonia. When at last she woke, it was with an immobilising hangover. She stumbled into the ward, already displaying signs of a shuffling, institutional gait not improved by the suicide watchers removing her shoelaces.

They observed her even at table where the cutlery cabinet was locked and blunted knives and forks were counted back before anyone was allowed to leave. After each meal, Joan was herded to the toilets with fifty other females. Bodies were required to function to the hospital's convenience, not their own.

Within the week, Joan received her first session of electro-convulsive therapy. An electric current passed through pads attached to her temples and into her scrambled brain. They said it was for her own good. It would shock her out of her depression. She was given muscle-relaxing injections beforehand so she didn't bite off her tongue or grind her teeth too hard.

Joan never complained, never refused to take her medicine. Had she done so, they would have gone ahead anyway. So she lay like the good girl she believed herself to be and when the switch was thrown, her limbs tossed and flailed like those of a shaken doll. But who could say what memories had fallen from her, whose faces she might never recall?

Staff would decide when visitors would be allowed in to see her for the first time. Her family and friends would want to know what progress she was making, when she'd be coming home.

It was important they didn't get to know Susan, the patient who set the table and helped to serve meals. She'd lost a baby like Joan. They found her howling at the moon with grief. But that was long ago when she was seventeen and the Great War still had another year to run. And yet she was still locked up.

*

'Joan? Joan, love?'

'Is that you, Dad? What's going on? Where am I?'

'You're in hospital, my lovely.'

'In hospital? Why am I in hospital?'

'It's about the child.'

'I'm sorry, Dad, but I had to... I hadn't a choice.'

'No, not the baby... not this time.'

'Then what? Why am I here?'

'It's about Billy. You remember him, don't you?'

'Of course I do.'

'Then you'll remember what happened to him, won't you, love?'

120

Twenty-Two

Joan fitted the classic profile of a post-natal depressive, according to the medical books Zilla consulted. Here was a selfless mother and wife trying to please everyone, pretending to cope in the face of overwhelming odds.

But her crisis didn't lack for other triggers. By accident or design, she'd aborted a baby she didn't want. Her father began to appear in visions like some consoling Holy Ghost to hear her confession. The death of her mother-substitute, Frances, brought Joan even lower. Her way back to them would be long and hard, even without the unexplained attentions of the detective, Challis.

The thought of him invaded Zilla's mind as she sat in the synagogue on that Sabbath morning, the bride of days when a woman was allowed to be a priestess and the king and the pauper were equals in their communion with the Almighty.

Zilla closed her eyes, wishing for the cantor's paradisiacal voice to banish thoughts of Challis and lead her instead to that calm, still centre which all of daily life conspired to make unreachable.

Yet even as she bowed her head, a passage from Proverbs reminded her of how spiritually unfitted she was for the quest.

Strength and honour are her clothing...
She openeth her mouth with wisdom...
Her children arise up, and call her blessed;
her husband also, and he praiseth her.

Truth had more than one face - and she must not lie to any of them. What was she really doing in Zion Street?

Whose life was she trying to save? She should talk to the rebbe. He was there to guide the uncertain. But he'd only complicate her perplexities with philosophy though he - and she - would know her meddling was simply a ploy to deny an empty bed and an emptier womb. Why ask questions when the answers were known?

Zilla left the synagogue and walked to her car, parked alongside the croft that was Spence's playground. She saw a blue Wolseley just behind it. Even as she made the connection, detective Challis got out and feigned respect by raising his trilby. Her first thought was how unkind sunlight was to his pocked face. Then, she was just furious.

'How dare you start following me.'

'I don't know what you mean. I'm going about police business.'

'And that just happens to bring you outside my place of worship, does it?'

'It's a free country - at least it is till the likes of your friends take over.'

'You've no right to harass me like this.'

'You don't know the meaning of the word, love. I haven't even started.'

He turned and strode across the croft, through the dust being raised by the skipping ropes of little girls and made for the corner shop on Meadow Street.

Zilla's anger was giving way to fear. Challis could be playing some devious game, getting her to spy on Joan only to blackmail her later into doing the same against the Party. Yet if she confessed this suspicion to the leadership, they'd never trust her again. He was deliberately unsettling her - but why?

Her politics, like her religion, represented a search for order and form, a desire for mankind's future to be better than its past. Something about Challis summoned up her inherited dread of underground cells. The British liked to think they would never have collaborated had the Nazis invaded. Such a view was misguided.

*

For Spence, there was no music in Zion Street any more, no sound of scrubbing or mopping or the sting of coal smoke when the fire was first lit and Mum put a stew in the oven. The heart of the place was still. Dad heated up whatever dishes Miss Arbib left or just bought fish and chips.

Their clothes got washed but never ironed. A neighbour offered to clean but was sent away. Even Robert Heaney's mother with seven children and barely enough money to put shoes on their feet, asked if they wanted anything from the shops.

Dad disappeared into himself, functioning as if from memory - waking, shaving, riding to work on his bike. He was straight home every evening. But without a drink inside him, he hadn't any words, not even for his made-up songs.

He'd been to see Mum the previous night. Spence thought he heard him crying in the early hours. He felt sad for him like he had for Uncle Edgar and wanted to comfort him and say he was upset, too. Yet for all his supposed cleverness, Spence didn't know how to mend what was broken between them.

No one knew how long Mum would be in hospital and he didn't know for how long he could be brave. That was why Miss Arbib told the nurses they had to let him see her. People took notice of Miss Arbib.

*

A shrieking band of boys played a lawless game of cricket with a slat of wood and a tennis ball in the

123

street outside the surgery where Edgar Sydenham waited his turn. He saw in these kids the child he once was but Billy could never be.

Edgar was called through. The doctor, ex-army but not entirely without compassion, read through the results of Edgar's tests.

'Passing blood, not good at all. They say you need an operation.'

'And will that sort me out?'

'We're both old soldiers, Mr Sydenham. War isn't without risks.'

'I'm due to retire soon.'

'Then we can't have you falling at the final hurdle, can we?' the doctor said. 'The hospital will send for you in the next month or so but I'm going to write out a sick note because it's preferable you take it easy till you go in.'

Edgar had never been one to skive off work. But this would give him a chance to put pressing matters in order before he was sent up the line forever. He felt an odd sense of peace spreading through him, a warmth like rum before battle. What he had to do was settled in his mind now. It stood to reason that he'd eventually be hit by the embrasured guns, maybe not today, not next month.

But his time was surely coming and when it did, he'd fall into the denatured earth knowing his duty was done.

A girl of four or five clacked along the pavement beside him in her mother's cast-off high heels, pushing a cheap tin pram to a make-believe shop in readiness for life as it would be. Her innocence touched him but his own salvation would rest in Spence, his confessor, someone to listen and understand and then, please God, to forgive.

Emily and Kitty were sorting through Frances's possessions – what to keep, what to give away, what to throw out. Edgar wanted rid of everything save her wedding ring and a few of her favourite brooches. Joan was the greater concern now.

Her deterioration had shocked them all. It had been coming for months but no one noticed. Joan was Joan, always looking up, never down. They'd taken her smiles for granted. God alone knew when she'd be allowed home.

For the hospital, these were early days. Kitty still worried about Spence.

'We can't allow him to run wild like some little ruffian.'

'Vron couldn't get a word out of him yesterday,' Emily said.

'He's probably not eating properly, either.'

'It's a good job it's the holidays or he wouldn't be getting to school.'

'I think he should come and live with us at 35 till Joan is better.'

'I can't see John Henry going along with that.'

'Then Edgar will need to talk to him man-to-man. It'd be for the lad's own good.'

*

Spence had got his mother presents and wrapped them in paper left over from Christmas. He knew she wouldn't mind. The hospital wasn't far. He'd been made to wear his best blazer and grey pants to look presentable. Miss Arbib would have had the barber cut his hair but there wasn't time.

They turned into a long drive with trees either side that met in the middle and shut out the sky. The hospital was as big as a warehouse and built in the shape of a cross with lawns and flowerbeds on every side. But the windows had metal bars and faces stared out from behind them and this made him nervous. A nurse met them at the main entrance with a bunch of jangling keys at her belt.

She led them down a corridor with walls painted green and brown. Each door they passed through was locked behind them. The cries of women they could not see carried out of wards they could not enter then were lost under the echoes of their footsteps.

Miss Arbib gripped his hand. Mum was waiting for them in a visiting room. She wore more of a gown than a dress and appeared tired, as if she'd just woken up and didn't know where she was or who they were. It looked like her but then, Dad seemed like Dad but wasn't the same person any more.

'Joan, it's lovely to see you,' Miss Arbib said. 'And look who's come with me.'

Spence smiled and held out his parcel, hoping she'd kiss him or say his name. She did neither.

'Where is my Dad?' Joan said. 'Why isn't he with you?'

'Maybe he'll come another day but Spence is here instead.'

She turned towards him but her face didn't light up like it used to. All the affection had gone from it. He put his arms round her neck and hugged her but felt no response.

'We're missing you, Mum. When are you coming home?'

'Home?'

'Yes, to Zion Street. When are you coming back?'

'I don't know. Why am I here?'

'We'll find out, Mum. Miss Arbib will make them tell us when you're coming home.'

'Have I been here long?'

'Too long. We want you back with us.'

'I can't seem to remember what's happened.'

'You'll be well again soon enough, Joan,' Miss Arbib said. 'Why don't you open the present Spence has brought for you?'

Her hands seemed stiff and clumsy so he helped to rip off the paper. All the presents fell off her lap onto the carpet – twenty Woodbines, four bars of Fry's chocolate and a box of Hartley's strawberry jelly.

'I got them for you, Mum.'

*

Keys, locks, the slow dragging of feet and the vacant stares of chemically dulled eyes. It smelt of human waste and felt airless and oppressive, a place of mental torment.

Zilla inwardly rejoiced when the last door was bolted behind them. It was awful leaving Joan. Spence didn't want to but the nurse just led her away. He managed not to cry but she noticed how he'd started screwing up his eyes every few moments. It wasn't blinking, just an unconscious nervous tic.

Things couldn't go on as they were. And those presents – there wasn't a penny in the house so how had he come by those? She dreaded to think.

They drove away in silence. Zilla hadn't any words of comfort. She could only feed him every once in a while and try to maintain some balance and certainty in his life. It was doubtful that his father could provide much of either.

'What shall we get for tea, Spence?'

'I don't care,' he said. 'Robert Heaney says Mum's a loony but she's not, is she?'

'No, she most definitely is not. Robert Heaney is a very stupid boy who doesn't understand what happens to grown-up people.'

'So what's happening to my Mum?

'Spence, listen... you know how we can become poorly in our bodies, don't you?'

'Like getting polio?'

'Yes, like getting polio... well, you can become poorly in your mind, too.'

'But what's made Mum poorly in her mind? What's done it to her?'

She'd been dreading this. Did it really fall to her to tell him? And would a boy, however bright and intuitive, understand the unpredictable imbalance of hormones and chemicals in the post-natal female body when husbands certainly didn't and even doctors weren't sure?

Zilla knew of depression, its blackness and hopeless panics. If Spence understood this, it might provide context for what had overtaken his mother. The alternative was him blaming himself for Joan's pitiful state because he'd not run for help sooner. That was unthinkable. Spence was fragile enough already.

*

John Henry appeared reluctant to let Zilla in when she took Spence home. They stood awkwardly in the front room. Spence went upstairs. John Henry was on edge. Whatever his faults and failings, Zilla felt only compassion for him.

'It's going to be hard for Spence to cope with all this,' she said. 'He's such a sensitive boy anyway. He'll need even more careful handling while Joan is like she is.'

John Henry made no reply. He was motherless, too. Zilla wanted to leave but saw his collection of records

128

leaning against the radiogram - Gigli, Tauber, Jussi Bjorling. Yet it was Callas's aria from *Tosca* that she wanted to hear... *Vissi d'arte, vissi d'amore*.

She slid the record onto the turntable and the dismal little room in that street of slums filled with a voice divine and blessed which came from God.

I gave jewels for the Madonna's mantle,
and I gave my song to the stars, to heaven,
which smiled with more beauty.
In the hour of grief
why, why, o Lord... do you reward me thus?

They listened together and for those few minutes, the disconnect between them and their worlds was immaterial. Only when John Henry abandoned himself to a chair, head in hands, did real life impose itself once more.

Zilla knelt and put an arm around a man she didn't know but had to comfort. And in the silence, Spence appeared beside them, stinking of the hospital he'd so lately left.

Twenty-Three

In a life so often surveilled by death, Edgar Sydenham inclined more to thinking than talking. To have heaved the remains of comrades into a mass grave or felt satisfaction at shooting an enemy through the eye were causes for reflection, not speeches. The grammar of war did not require observations from an irrelevance like him. Besides, he hadn't the language to describe those moments when the coin still spun in the air, yet to come down on the side of existence or oblivion.

No one emerged entirely sane from war. Of that, he was more than aware. But how could a young mother fall down the stairs in her own home, lose the baby she was carrying and end up a mental case? Edgar had no points of reference for this.

He passed beneath the asylum's weeping trees, unable to reconcile the wreck of a woman he'd just kissed in fond farewell with his image of Joan, that laughing, loving girl he and Frances had helped to raise.

She seemed lost to reality like those boys in no-man's land, crying out for comfort from those who would never see them again.

'What is it, Joan love? What's wrong?'

'It's Billy. Billy's going away.'

'You've been dreaming, but I'm here, now. I'm with you.'

'He's going away, Uncle Edgar... going across the sea.'

'Try and go back to sleep, love. You need to rest.'

Joan felt herself falling, falling like an angel into one of the institutional iron beds in which she was confined. Yet within her head, she was back in Zion Street, soon to begin her journey to the green island.

*

It is a warm Friday evening. Each mill and factory has closed its gates for the traditional holiday. Joan and her family assemble at the bus stop near the Friendship Inn for a coach to take them to the ferry.

All talk of Hitler and war is forgotten. It will be another two years before the sky throbs with bombers then goes blood orange red and the uneventful lives of those now making tea in houses nearby or travelling home on trams will be brought to an end by the conspiring Fates.

Joan holds one of Billy's hands, Vron the other. Billy in a white shirt. Billy in blue cord pants. Billy in new sandals and ankle socks. Billy, the apple of all their eyes. It's miles to Liverpool and from there, across the Irish Sea to the Isle of Man.

The weather is set fair and they'll all get browner than berries, especially Billy who's not been well. Auntie Frances wasn't going to bring him till the doctor said he'd only got a cold and a week of sea air would do him a power of good.

Uncle Edgar is here to see them off, just back from Dunlop's and still in his overalls smelling of rubber. He's not one for being far from home. Anyway, he's got jobs to do around the house.

Billy wriggles in his Dad's arms, too excited to be tired. He wants to be off on the great adventure. Edgar smiles and understands. He kisses his son, nothing sloppy, just the merest brush of his lips on the child's soft cheek. Billy squeals with delight, hugs his Dad around the neck then clambers up the steps of the coach. The driver stows everyone's luggage. Billy presses his nose flat against the window and Edgar pretends to twist it off from the other side of the glass. The coach moves away. Billy looks back and waves to his Dad, standing alone on the pavement.

*

Joan hovers wraith-like within her psychotic visions, unable to identify the dark, shifting figures moving without noise or purpose just out of focus. But she sees herself and all the wan-faced factory workers disembarking with the dawn to hurry to their rooms in the sugar-frosted houses that sweep the promenade.

Only the smokestacks of ferries will darken the skies today. The *Tynwald, Mona's Isle, Peel Castle*. What pretty names, such innocent times.

And all the while, the birds of the sea swoop and dive through the laughter of a pierrot show and the smells of a thousand guesthouse kitchens. *The Windsor, The Balmoral, The Harlech*. Each a little castle for a week, respite from storms to come.

The rooms are lovely with views across Douglas Bay and clean, too. Billy didn't want breakfast but Auntie Frances makes him eat some porridge to ease his throat which is sore again. Joan and Vron take him into the town to buy a bucket and spade. His Mum and her sisters sit back in the Sunken Gardens just across from their digs, shoes and stockings off, faces to the sun, which lights the golden gorse on the hills above.

Joan wants to see Greta Garbo in *Camille* at the Picture House and Vron might book into a salon doing permanent waves for ten shillings. Joan says they cost seven and six at home so ten bob's daylight robbery.

Billy's dawdling a bit. He must be dog-tired, poor lad. There wasn't much sleep to be had on the boat. But he'll catch up tonight. After church tomorrow, he can romp on the beach all he wants.

They eat cornets and rest awhile beneath a row of spiky palm trees in a park overlooking the sea. A photographer, all smiles and wiles, is buttering up holidaymakers to have their pictures taken.

Vron says they'll have some done. It'll only cost a few shillings and he'll post the prints to arrive long before they get home to 35. He lines them up on a bench, Billy in the middle. *Click. Click.* The man says they're the prettiest sisters he's seen all season. *Click. Click.* Vron and Joan know he's pulling their legs but they're on holiday and don't mind so they're laughing. *Click. Click.*

But Billy isn't.

'Are you all right, Billy love?'

'No, feel hot.'

'It's a hot day,' Vron says.

'No, hot inside.'

'Is it that horrid throat of yours again, Billy?' Joan says.

He nods. Joan puts her hand to his forehead. He's running a temperature. They better get back. She carries him to their guesthouse on Loch Promenade.

Joan gets bad throats, too. She understands how nasty they are. Billy flops listless onto his bed and they look inside his mouth. The back of his throat isn't pink and clear like it should be. It's coated in a thickish blue-white film going grey at the edges and spreading.

Joan doesn't like the look of it. Billy needs a doctor. Vron hurries off to find Billy's mother. But she and the others aren't where they left them. Vron looks across the mile of yellow beach curving away below the promenade railings.

There's not a single square yard of sand that isn't stiff with families from the four corners of the industrial Kingdom. Auntie Frances could be anywhere.

*

Joan and the others watch Doctor Corkish examining Billy. He dries each of his fingers on a towel. Then he instructs the landlady to boil the towel right away and

133

all the sheets on Billy's bed, too. Auntie Frances, only just back from her walk with Emily and Kitty, looks alarmed.

The doctor asks to use the telephone in the hall. They hear him ring for an ambulance. Auntie Frances's hand goes to her mouth.

When he comes back, the doctor's lined face is grave. He says Billy has a serious infectious disease and must be admitted to an isolation hospital immediately. Yet what he says makes no sense. They're on holiday. It's a beautiful sunny day. Trippers are having fun and the air is filled with the *clop-clop-clop* of horse-drawn trams and seagulls calling through the bright blue sky. What is this man talking about? But Joan doesn't need to be told.

'It's diphtheria, isn't it?'

'I'm not quite a hundred per cent sure but it's what I'm afraid of, yes.'

'Oh, sweet Jesus,' Auntie Frances says.

Just the word *diphtheria* could clear the beach. It's a killer. Auntie Frances collapses but is caught between Vron and Auntie Kitty.

Within an hour, Billy is in White Hoe, a hillside fever hospital behind a screen of trees. They are all swept up in the shock of events.

Auntie Frances is beside herself with fear and reproach and can barely sit still as they wait outside the matron's office. Billy was never well enough to go on holiday. What's Edgar going to say? Should she send him a telegram?

The door opens. Matron, plump and kindly, says Billy's having trouble swallowing and breathing. They should go back to their boarding house and wait. There's nothing more they can do here.

It is a night of fitful sleep. They forgo breakfast so that each of them can take the sacrament at St Mary's Church. All pray to God that Billy's only got croup, which is like diphtheria but not fatal.

The landlady is kindness itself and serves them an early lunch then makes ham sandwiches for the vigil at White Hoe later. The waiting is unbearable. They are allowed to see Billy through a glass partition. He's sucking in his entire rib cage for the tiniest breath.

The sound he makes is like a wheezing old miner's death rattle but from within the body of a child. And as they watch, he turns from blue to grey as his blood is ever more starved of oxygen.

Auntie Frances breaks down. There is no helping her. Joan knows the poison in Billy's body is forming a membrane across his throat. He is being suffocated - and all because he's taken in someone else's germs.

She knows this because she survived a mild attack of diphtheria. The doctors told her what happens. Now she can't stop promising to devote her life to God if only Billy is spared and she isn't the carrier who is to blame.

Sweet Jesus, please let him live.

But it is not to be. At three minutes past eight the following morning, Billy Sydenham dies aged five years, six months. The Matron calls their lodgings. The bell of her telephone doesn't ring, it tolls.

Auntie Frances looks around the breakfast table at the others and they at her. The landlady comes in. She doesn't have to say a word. The tears run down her face. Joan gets up and rushes outside.

*

The second post arrives at 35 just after ten thirty. Edgar Sydenham, up since six o'clock, is stripping off wallpaper in the living room. He wants the re-decorating finished before they all get back.

Emily has chosen a floral pattern he thinks too fussy for a smallish room. But no one listens so he'll just slap it on. He makes a brew and sits amid the mess to read a postcard from Frances showing the harbour at Douglas.

Weather v. hot, digs clean. V. good crossing. Billy and me send love.

Also post-marked from the Isle of Man is a stiff brown envelope. Inside is a photograph of Billy looking tired out between Joan and Vron who pout like a pair of glamour pusses. Edgar smiles. Billy can't do without his eight hours.

The picture goes centre stage on the mantelpiece but he mustn't get paste on it or he'll be for the high jump when Frances comes home. There's still time for a smoke before he goes back up the stepladder.

The house is rarely this quiet. Yet even as he thinks this, the doorbell rings. Behind the squares of coloured glass he makes out a figure in a flat peaked cap.

It is a telegram boy, a messenger from the Post Office with a bit of paper on which a dozen words are written in pencil.

Billy dead. Diphtheria. Funeral must be here tomorrow 10 am. Please come. Frances.

Twelve words. One penny each... a shilling to the earth and the moon and the stars. Edgar steadies himself between the swaying walls of the front lobby.

So it'd happened as he always feared it would. What goes around, comes around. Sins are but debts and must be paid off one day - and with interest, too.

Twenty-Four

Hartford, Cambridgeshire, Sunday 4th January 2015

Sir Patrick Prentice rang as White's narrow boat, *Zion*, was being delivered the short distance down the River Great Ouse from Hartford Marina to the jetty below his garden summerhouse. They'd re-blacked the hull against rust, painted the cabin-top scarlet and leaf green then lined it out in daffodil yellow.

Smoke ruffled from the stovepipe chimney of its wood-burner and had White been at liberty to sail off into the distant spring, he would've done so.

'You'd better watch Channel 4 News tomorrow night,' Sir Patrick said.

'I usually try to but why especially?'

'Because they've heard your inquiry's being announced in the morning. They've led the pack on these deaths in Manchester so they'll be banging their drum.'

'Will you be appearing in any programme?'

'Good God, no.'

'What about Luston?'

'He's reading the gospel according to his minister to anyone not too busy with the election to care but there will be no more publicity till you formally open the inquiry.'

'Still with a press conference beforehand?'

'Absolutely. Everything has to appear open and above board,' Sir Patrick said. 'Goes with the territory I'm afraid, but it'll be nothing you can't deal with.'

White switched off his mobile and stepped aboard *Zion*. He felt the swirling river's push and pull as he made himself coffee in the galley.

A bundle of briefing papers from the Ministry of Justice awaited him and he'd yet to agree final arrangements with the inquiry's secretariat. But he'd an urge to steal a few hours for himself. There was just enough time to sail down to the medieval cutwater bridge in Huntingdon and back. He couldn't be sure when he'd have the freedom to do so again.

*

White approved of Channel 4 News, liked its intelligence and independence if not the gaudy ties of the main presenter, Jon Snow.

That night's bulletin led with a childhood obesity story followed by a piece about sex abuse. Snow then introduced the third item on the running order.

'An inquiry was announced today by the Ministry of Justice into the deaths in police custody of three men in Manchester.

'It was these deaths which provoked serious rioting before Christmas when no criminal or disciplinary charges were laid against any officer, despite an investigation by the Independent Police Complaints Commission.

'Our correspondent, Sophie Bartells, broke this story originally and sends this report from the city.'

It opened with a montage of bloodied faces, stones and bottles smashing into riot shields, officers on horseback wielding batons and protesters hitting back with staves from placards bearing slogans like *Police Killers* and *No Justice*.

Bartells had the figure and poise of a model and appeared doing a walking piece to camera outside the police station where the riot happened.

'What began as a peaceful march over the deaths of three men quickly turned violent and has already become known as the Battle of Bootle Street.

Ironically, the notorious Peterloo Massacre took place barely a hundred yards from here in 1819 when at least eleven people were cut down and killed by the sabres of the cavalrymen who charged through a crowd of workers.'

A sequence of photographs of the three men who died in police custody was shown.

'Michael Clancy, aged twenty, arrested for alleged drug dealing, died during a scuffle as he was being put in a police van.

'Adrian Kelly, twenty five, arrested for alleged shoplifting, died while being restrained in the street and Luke North, eighteen, detained for alleged threatening behaviour and resisting arrest, died later in a police cell.'

A lawyer acting for the Clancy and Kelly families said the Ministry of Justice had no option but to have a public inquiry, not least because officers from the same police station were involved in each death.

'There's been a whiff of a cover-up here,' he said. 'We now need the truth because we've had only years of indifference from the authorities to deaths like these but what's happened in Manchester is simply a scandal too far which cannot be ignored.'

Bartells then voiced-over stock footage of a smiling, power-dressed woman of about forty walking into the House of Commons.

'This is Rose Lingard, working mother and the former high-flying Conservative MP who was Manchester's Police and Crime Commissioner during the period the three men died.

'She's since resigned as Commissioner in order to return to front line politics as a candidate in the forthcoming general election. If David Cameron wins, insiders say she could be heading to the Ministry of

Justice, the very department soon to investigate what happened when she ran the police in Manchester.'

The report then cut to Bartells confronting Lingard as she got out of a car, her mind on other matters and making for her election agent's office.

'Do you think the Battle of Bootle Street will damage your prospects with the voters, Mrs Lingard, maybe prevent you from becoming a minister in a future Conservative government because of a conflict of interest?'

'I'm sorry but I've no comment on this.'

'What do you say to those who've accused you of a cover-up?'

'There will be a full inquiry so how is this a cover-up?'

'So three men died on your watch and you've nothing to say to their families?'

Lingard knew how politically damaging it would look if she carried on appearing to run away from difficult questions. She stopped and gave Bartells a look conveying sincerity and concern.

'The fact is that the Independent Police Complaints Commission found no wrongdoing by any police officer or in any of our procedures. I welcome this public inquiry and will co-operate fully with it and when it reports, the coroner can resume his investigation into these tragic deaths so there's no basis whatsoever for anyone to suggest that any facts are being hidden. Now, I've a meeting I really must attend.'

Twenty-Five

St Cuthbert's Church, Withington, Sunday 22nd August 1955

Edgar Sydenham only went to church for funerals now. Catholicism was beaten into him by priests uttering threats of eternal damnation for sins that weren't.

The God he was obliged to worship wasn't one of love or mercy. And in the Great War, the Almighty might have been an Englishman but He would perish with the rest for all that. Faith was the least of what they lost.

Yet Edgar found himself alone at the back of the church where Frances's coffin had rested only days before. He wasn't sure why he'd come. The morning service was already over and its incense just a hint in the air. But he'd felt some inner compulsion to kneel in the silence of a holy place. Edgar knew he would soon have to walk his own Stations of the Cross.

Billy should have been eighteen with a girl on his arm and a trade. A young man to make any father proud. But they'd had to give him back and Edgar wasn't there when they did. His contagious little body needed to be disposed of quickly.

Such a wind of grief tore through Edgar that day as it never had when death was ever at his side. How cruel, how ironic for a man who'd slipped so many comrades beneath the earth to be denied a last sight of his son. It was a plain pine coffin Frances chose, only small. Edgar could've carried it by himself.

They gave Billy plot number 273 in a graveyard high above the beach where children played. He knew it was beyond reason but he sometimes tried to convince himself that as he'd not been present at the funeral, it might never have happened. Billy would then just be on holiday, playing in the sand at the seaside, forever young.

It was a comfort and a fiction sustained by the memory of his face getting smaller as the coach drove away, that and the photograph of him sitting between Joan and Vron amid the palm trees on the Isle of Man.

Edgar held to these images for he had little else. But tomorrow, he would take Spence to the fun fair at the zoo. It'd be a treat for them both - and he'd news for the boy, too.

*

Soon after breakfast next day, Zilla Arbib opened her front door to Joan's husband, John Henry. He was wearing his demob suit, not overalls.

'Nothing wrong, is there?' Zilla said.

'No, I'm off work this week,' he said. 'I've come to ask a big favour.'

He'd saved enough for a deposit on a second-hand motorbike and sidecar but needed a house-owner to guarantee the monthly repayments.

'I thought about what you said about taking Joan and Spence for trips out and if I get this bike, I'll be able to do that.'

'And you're sure you can afford to pay for it and run it?'

'If I cut back on what I spend on myself then yes, I can.'

Zilla thought this a commendable change of heart and agreed to help. They walked to the garage on the main road for her to sign the papers.

*

'You're wearing me out, young Spence,' Edgar said. 'I'll have to sit down.'

'No, come on. Let's go and see the lions again.'

The creatures paced through their own piss, up and down the iron confines of the cage, which was their unnatural world. Spence had ridden the dodgems and the big dipper, shied for coconuts and eaten popcorn. He'd laughed at elephants being scrubbed down with a yard brush and seen snarling tigers tearing at haunches of meat. They sat together on the bus home, as content and happy as their lives allowed.

'Listen, Spence, we've decided, your aunties and me, that we're going to look after you for a while and when your Mum gets out of hospital, she'll come and stay, too.'

'Both of us at 35, you mean?'

'Yes. Your Dad thinks it's for the best till everything is sorted out.'

Spence went quiet, sure now that his mother was even more poorly than he'd feared. But Edgar said he should cheer up because the two of them were soon going on a special holiday.

'Honest? Where to?'

'Across the English Channel to France.'

'Where you were in the army, in your war?'

'Yes... where the fighting was.'

'Why do you want to go there? You always said it was horrible.'

'It was that all right... but I have to see some of those places again.'

'But why, if that's where your friends were killed?'

'Sometimes Spence, you do things in this life and you don't know why, you don't understand what's driving you but you just have to do them all the same.'

*

143

Zilla Arbib had never ridden pillion on a motorbike before. She hugged John Henry round the middle as he clipped a bend and zipped through a ford, spraying water high in the air. The sense of speed and danger and the intimacy of human contact made her feel young and alive.

They'd test-run his motorbike by visiting Joan. Zilla was glad of a break from next term's preparations. A nurse said Joan was progressing and could be going home very soon. But to the untrained eye, she still seemed in a dream-like state and when she smiled, her teeth showed slightly yellow from the paraldehyde.

On the way back, they stopped at a pub for a lunch of bread, cheese and beer. They ate outside in the sunshine under a cherry tree being raided by thrushes.

John Henry was well into his second pint and loosening up. He talked of making a fresh start, of opening a café somewhere pretty in Cheshire or farming chickens. But these were back-of-envelope plans, full of child-like optimism and a counter-intuitive belief that all would be well. Below the waves, it wasn't hard to imagine the wreckage of other such schemes.

'It's good that you're thinking about the future,' Zilla said. 'But please don't forget how ill Joan's been or how long it's going to take before she's back on her feet.'

'I know but I've got to put things right, not just for Joan but for Spence, too.'

'You certainly have. He's about to go to one of the country's best schools so if he's to make the most of his talents, he'll need a stable home life more than ever.'

Zilla had always been intrigued by Joan's story about her husband's mother, Harriet, being disowned by her wealthy parents. With a paper on social attitudes in mind, she bought John Henry another beer and asked if it was true.

'Yes, cut her adrift without a penny or a stick of furniture.'

'What do you know about her family background?'

'Not much but I think they were from Gloucestershire but whatever happened back then, it was obviously a very painful episode and never mentioned openly in our house, certainly not by my Dad.'

'But they didn't approve of him?'

'Can't have done, can they? He barely scratched a living as a picture restorer so in their eyes, he was never going to be the sort of middle class, professional husband to keep their daughter in the manner they would've wished.'

'Yet she must have been very much in love with him to defy her parents.'

John Henry lit a cigarette and Zilla could see him thinking about how best to respond.

'I never knew my mother,' he said. 'But I'm pretty sure she must have been pregnant with my sister before any wedding took place.'

'Conceiving a child out of wedlock? That would've been a dreadful scandal then.'

'And my God, how she ended up paying for it.'

'In what way?'

'Condemned to a life in the back streets, no money, five kids to bring up then suffering an early death. Not what Daddy would've wanted for her, was it?'

Zilla considered this for a moment then asked if they could ride back by the house where John Henry lived as a child.

'Why ever would you want to do that?'

'Because places and what happens in them help to make us the people we become.'

*

The fierce afternoon sun shadowed one half of the street of industrial cottages where John Henry was born and bleached all colour out of the other side. Curtains hung limp at open windows and in the distance, the silhouettes of children moved in the smoky light.

His house in Levenshulme, not far from Zion Street, was like the rest - two rooms upstairs, two down, shared toilet outside. Harriet gave birth to her daughter, Evelyn, and four sons, in the back bedroom.

She died in 1920 when her youngest, John Henry, was just three. Evelyn raised him and made sure they all attended classes in the corrugated iron *Tin School* in Chapel Street where some of their classmates didn't have shoes.

'Were you fond of your father?'

'If I'm to tell the truth, there wasn't that much to be fond of.'

'I see,' Zilla said. 'I gather from Joan that he was killed in the Blitz.'

'Yes, in 1941. He was an air raid warden.'

Zilla remembered those nights - that pulse of alien bombers and searchlights sweeping the black skies to trap them. Hundreds of people killed, thousands injured, homes wrecked, factories burnt down. Ash and smoke from the ruins blew into the dirtied faces of demolition gangs, standing to attention when the King and Queen inspected the damage.

'How terrible those times were.'

'By rights, he shouldn't even have been on duty.'

'So why was he?'

'He'd worked all through the raids the previous Christmas but he came down with a bad chest and Joan was nursing him but he insisted on going back on duty before he was better and that was when he copped it.'

John Henry took an old photograph from his wallet. It showed Freddie coming from a pub clutching the left paw of a terrier walking on its hind legs like a circus animal.

'That's him and his dog doing their party trick.'

Freddie would have been about fifty when the picture was taken, dark suit, trousers baggy at the knees, waistcoat, white shirt, striped tie, thin-soled black shoes. He'd silvery, centre-parted hair, an angular face without warmth about the eyes and a cruel, slash of a mouth.

Zilla was sorry Freddie had been killed. But it was the dog which had her sympathy.

*

The front door of Zion Street was knocked loudly as Edgar was making a cup of tea in the kitchen and Spence packed clothes from his bedroom for his stay at 35.

Two men in suits stood on the pavement. The older one had a blotchy face, pitted by the scars of boils, and had the stance and manner of a boxer.

'We're looking for John Henry White,' he said.

'He's not here. Who are you?'

'Police officers. When will he be back?'

'No idea. He's on holiday from work. Why do you want him?'

'That's our business. So who are you, what's your name?'

'Edgar Sydenham, his wife's uncle.'

'Is she here?'

'No, she's ill in hospital.'

'Get on all right with John Henry, do you, Edgar?'

'I don't know why you're after him so that's my business.'

'Well, we think he's a bit of a bad lot... a bit light-fingered.'

'I wouldn't have him down as a thief. He hasn't the bottle for it.'

'What about murder, Edgar? Hasn't he the bottle for murder, either?'

'Murder? You're after John Henry for murder?'

'A lot of deaths during the Blitz, weren't there, Edgar? What was one more corpse back then?'

'You're talking out of your backside, you really are.'

'But with the benefit of a long memory, old man.'

'John Henry's a shiftless bugger but he's no killer.'

'A word to the wise, Edgar... if you're withholding information from my inquiry, I'll have you in the dock with John Henry White as an accessory. Got that, have we?'

Twenty-Six

Malcolm Feingold would have married Zilla but she had refused him twice so he'd not ask again, whatever his mother urged. They still went to the Opera House or the Free Trade Hall when the Hallé Orchestra played but only like brother and sister.

It was difficult for Feingold to reconcile Zilla's communistic leanings with her religious beliefs. But who - or what - was God to the Jews? They clothed Him in many robes.

The victims of the Shoah were not saved yet even when faced with this almighty impotence, Zilla held that to despair of God was to hand Hitler a posthumous victory. So here was the basis of her spirituality - that and the ethical *quiet deeds* she performed for those around her.

They were having supper in the Midland Hotel where sables and diamonds were de rigueur. Zilla, who could afford both, kept to an unadorned austerity jacket and skirt with her hair curled and pinned up as if the forties weren't over. Their talk inevitably turned to the woes of her cleaner, Joan. As Zilla's friend and lawyer, Feingold again advised her not to get involved.

'But why did that awful detective make sure I saw him outside the shul?'

'I keep telling you, no good will come of this business. Just stay out of it.'

'Yes, but if he investigates murders like you said, what's he doing asking questions about Joan? She's not a criminal.'

'Zilla, that's what I say about my clients – but I'm paid to.'

*

149

Edgar found John Henry on his own in the public bar of the Friendship Inn, drinking a pint of Hydes stout. It wasn't his first.

'Edgar, old man - what'll you have?'

'Nothing, my guts are playing up again. But I'm not here to drink.'

'What are you doing in a pub, then?'

'First off, I've come to take you back to 35 to say goodnight to your lad.'

'I was just about to do that very thing.'

'Good,' Edgar said. 'Then once you've done that, I've got something to tell you that'll sober you up.'

*

Spence chattered non-stop to Kitty and Emily about the fun he'd had at the zoo and of going to France with Edgar. It reassured both aunts to see him excited and happy. The boy within wasn't entirely lost, despite all he'd seen and heard.

They made him toast and a boiled egg then he'd fallen asleep in a chair. John Henry came back soon after. He kissed his son's forehead and gathered him up in a rare display of tenderness. Spence woke and put his arms around his father's neck and was carried to bed.

Emily settled to a game of patience. Kitty was clearing their supper plates into the scullery as John Henry came back downstairs. He rolled back his shirtsleeves to help her with the washing up - anything to delay being carpeted by Edgar.

'Spence will be so pleased when his Mum gets home,' Kitty said.

'Won't we all? And just wait till they see the motorbike I've gone and bought so we can have days out in the country.'

'That'll be grand but you've got to take greater care of Joan in future, haven't you?'

'I know, you don't have to remind me.'

'Believe me, John Henry, you never miss the water till the well runs dry.'

'It's just that whatever I do, nothing ever turns out how I want it to.'

'You're not on your own there, love.'

'Anyway, the main thing now is that Joan's on the mend.'

'Yes, let's thank God for that and pray she's turned the corner.'

*

Edgar sat in his own room, waiting for the right moment to confront John Henry. He looked again at the travel agent's itinerary for his pilgrimage to France with Spence. They would go by train to London, stay overnight at the Baron Hotel on Buckingham Palace Road then take the *Golden Arrow* from Victoria Station to the port of Dover. Once there, they'd board the steamer *Invicta,* cross the English Channel to Calais then catch a train south to Amiens and their final destination - the valley of the Somme River.

Edgar wanted to look once more on a landscape he carried like the memory of a medieval painting... of cornfields going gold, chalk hills no more than bumps in a bedspread, ancient woods and soft green meadows yet to be harrowed by ordnance.

Away in the distance were stone cottages and courtyard farms under opalescent skies, gilded crosses on church spires and half-timbered towns where all the fruits of the earth were to be had.

But turn that mortmain soil now, work the plough into the clay and flints beyond the banks of the slow-moving Somme and prepare the altars for a different harvest.

Here will lie the offended bones of Edgar's missing pals... footballers without legs, artists without eyes, lovers without arms. And their skulls like the shells of blown eggs, discarded in the dirt.

So dig deep but dig with care for the artefacts, which remain... the wedding rings and cap badges, buttons tarnished green, spoons, knives and forks and all the dull brass bullet casings, which marked the end for so many.

Edgar had to walk those fields again, more so now his health was failing. But this time, he would be holding the hand of the sleeping child upstairs and praying for forgiveness from one who would never wake again.

*

The young doctor attending Joan had not yet been calloused by the grief and despair of those whose broken lives he was there to mend. They sat together in the patients' lounge. He smiled and said he had good news.

'I think you're ready to leave us, Joan.'

'Am I... really, am I?'

'Yes. I've spoken to your aunts and they're going to take responsibility for looking after you at their house.'

'I lived with them as a girl, you know... lovely people, all of them.'

'I'm sure they are,' the doctor said. 'I've also telephoned your friend, Miss Arbib, and she'll be here in the morning to collect you.'

'She's very clever, is Miss Arbib... teaches at the university, says my son's got the head of a professor.'

'No doubt he'll make you very proud one day, Joan. Now, I must get back to my other patients but I'll see you before you go tomorrow.'

He hurried through the dormitory, his white coat flapping behind him. Joan felt euphoric at the prospect of going home. Yet the world beyond the hospital's locked doors held threats Joan couldn't explain but somehow knew were there.

*

John Henry would have sloped away had Edgar not been waiting by his new motorbike and sidecar.

'Cigarette?' Edgar said.

'For the condemned man?'

'You need to get yourself straightened out, son. You're in the shit.'

'More than usual, you mean?'

'This is no joke. Some detectives are looking for you.'

'Detectives? Why, what am I supposed to have done?'

'They were round at Zion Street today and said they're investigating a murder - '

' - a what?'

'A murder during the war, someone was murdered during the war and they want to question you about it.'

'Dear Christ, Edgar.'

'Why do they want to talk to you about such a thing?'

They were standing under the street lamp outside 35. Its yellow light half-shadowed John Henry's face. He stared at Edgar and his hands began to shake.

'You best tell me what this is all about,' Edgar said. 'This doesn't just affect you, there's Joan to think about and young Spence.'

'Listen, please, you've got to cover for me. I've got to get away. I need to think.'

'What the hell are you hiding, son?'

'Edgar, honest to God I'm sorry. Please tell Joan I'm sorry, really, really I am.'

He then kick-started his motorbike and drove into the night without another word.

Twenty-Seven

Joan was still not sure which side of the dream she was on, if she had really woken up or not. It had felt for so long as if some music hall magician had called her out of the audience and she'd been conjured into a place of disembodied voices where time meant nothing and night could fall without warning. For now, she wanted only to return to her own reality in Zion Street. She left Miss Arbib waiting in the car and stood in the kitchen to re-acquaint herself with the familiar and the mundane.

Here was John Henry's blue and white shaving mug on the windowsill, the cast iron range, cold and unlit, their old Bakelite wireless and above the mantelpiece, the black wooden crucifix on which Christ died every day.

Joan ran a forefinger over the cold pewter bones of His body. There was still so much to confess. But someone had mopped the lino at the bottom of the stairs and scrubbed the draining board clean of its secret.

How she wished Spence was there to hold and hug and to say that all would come right in the end. But he'd be waiting at 35 once she'd collected all that was needed for her stay in Grenville Road.

First, she'd her suitcase to empty of the clothes that reeked of confinement. Miss Arbib had washed others - dresses, slips, cardigans, underwear - and laid them on the bed.

Joan could have rested beside them. She still felt wrung-out. But the doctor said she would until she adjusted to life on the outside. That night, she would lie in innocence with Vron as they had long ago. She wouldn't sleep with John Henry anymore… not in that way. Never again could she go through what she'd just experienced. If only she could talk to her Dad. But for some reason, he'd stopped coming to see her.

*

Zilla carried Joan's case into 35 but excused herself from the welcome-home party that had been laid on. For Joan, it was an ordeal by love and affection.

Edgar gave her a spray of yellow irises and ferns and Kitty said she'd done well on the horses that week so she'd take her to buy a new autumn outfit. Emily paid for meat pies and cakes and set the table with the blue willow pattern plates they kept for best. Spence didn't say much but hardly took his eyes off his mother.

The living room became warmer and noisier. Joan couldn't breathe with all the cigarette smoke and went to sit in the canvas deck chair by the French windows.

Butterflies and wasps flitted amongst the rotting apples from next-door's overhanging tree, taking sweetness wherever it could be found. The fragrance of the Damask roses held best here, too. But the blush of their petals was beginning to fade and soon they would fall to earth. This had been Auntie Frances's favourite spot where, with the sun on her face and her eyes closed, she could hear the laughter of the boy who had been stolen from her.

But Edgar would never talk of Billy - or the Great War. He'd locked the past away and saw no reason to re-live whatever had caused him pain.

John Henry was another who kept his feelings private, even from Joan. She wondered why he couldn't be at 35 when she arrived. Edgar didn't seem to know where he was when she'd asked him.

She hoped he'd been paying the bills in Zion Street. What if he'd fallen behind with the rent? It didn't matter that John Henry was the landlady's brother. Evelyn's agent could still give them notice to quit.

But Joan knew she hadn't to get worked up about anything. That's what they told her at the hospital. She must simply enjoy being fussed and cosseted till she could cope on her own again.

Spence appeared at her side, smiling but in a nervous sort of way.

'Hello, love,' Joan said. 'It's grand to be with you all again.'

He nodded, unsure of what to say or how much to admit. She took his hand and squeezed it and said he should run off and play.

'But will you be all right?'

'Yes, love... I just want to doze here for a bit.'

He walked down the garden's cinder path and looked back at her before climbing over the wall to the tennis courts. Joan felt herself drifting away. Somewhere, she could hear a kettle being filled at a sink, cups and saucers put on a tin tray and children calling one to another. For now, Joan was at peace at last in the rose-scented air and nothing mattered any more.

*

Vron arrived home from her office and asked where Joan's husband was.

'That's what we'd like to know,' Emily said. 'He's sent her some flowers by Interflora with a card saying he was sorry but that's John Henry for you, selfish so-and-so.'

Edgar didn't dare tell them the police wanted to question him about a murder. That would floor them all - as it had Edgar.

He left his sisters-in-law in the living room and retreated to his own quarters. John Henry's disappearance had put the kibosh on the trip to France

156

with Spence. The lad and his mother would need everyone's support when the police caught up with him - as they surely would.

But another cloud was massing on Edgar's horizon. The hospital had written to say they'd booked him in for an operation in six weeks. He'd survived stiffer odds in his day but this was different. What he now faced was an enemy within.

*

Shortly after breakfast next morning, an unmarked blue Wolseley drew up in Zion Street. Two detectives stood with Inspector Challis as he knocked again at the front door of number 3. There was no reply. They went to the rear of the property, climbed over the yard wall and forced the back door with a crowbar. The house was empty but Challis found the two items he wanted hanging in the front room. He tucked them under his arm and led his men back to the car and headed for Grenville Road.

*

Joan sat on the stool by Kitty's sewing machine and lit another cigarette. The kitchen window was open to get rid of the smoke from the toast Emily had let burn under the grill. Joan looked fretful, worried that John Henry still wasn't back and could've been injured on his motorbike.

'We should telephone the police,' she said. 'They'll know if there's been an accident.'

Edgar was on his knees, sweeping out ashes from last night's fire. He played for time and said if John Henry hadn't returned by late afternoon, he'd call them.

Spence, dressed but not washed, stirred three spoons of brown sugar into his Quaker Oats. Everyone was on edge and he sensed it. He didn't know if he should be angry with his Dad for not being there or fearful in case he'd been killed.

Either way, his mother was becoming more agitated by the minute. A sudden hammering shook the front door. Everyone stopped what they were doing. Was it John Henry - or bad news about him? Kitty hurried down the hall. She opened the door to be confronted by three men.

The one with a pockmarked face said his name was Challis and he was a detective with a warrant to arrest John Henry White and Joan White.

'You've a what?' Kitty said.

'Don't muck me about, love. They're here, aren't they?'

'Yes, but - '

Challis hustled past her followed by the other officers. Vron was drying her hair in the bathroom and ran downstairs when she heard raised voices.

'What's going on? What's happening?'

Joan looked bewildered. Spence stood between her and Challis and stared up at the threatening stranger.

'Are you Joan White?'

'Yes, why?'

'Where is your husband?'

'I don't know. He should be here.'

Challis ordered the two other detectives to search the house.

'Joan White, I am arresting you for being in possession of stolen property, namely two pictures belonging to the late Miss Maud Elizabeth Tester of Hulme.'

'I don't know anyone called Miss Tester.'

'So how come you've got her pictures in your house?'

'I haven't stolen anything.'

'No? So you don't know anything about her being murdered during the Blitz, then?'

Joan feared she'd slipped back into the nightmare from which she'd only just woken.

'Poor old Miss Tester,' Challis said. 'Battered to death with a brick in an air raid.'

Edgar laid his hand on the policeman's arm and said Joan had only come out of hospital the day before and was in no state to be questioned.

'I'll decide that,' Challis said. 'Now, one last time, Joan - where is your husband?'

'No-one knows where he is,' Edgar said. 'Get that into your bloody head, will you?'

'Right, Joan, you're coming with me to the police station.'

She was led out into the street, trembling and confused, then shut in the police car. Challis turned to her relatives, all stunned by the speed and enormity of what had just happened in their home.

'If John Henry White turns up, you'd better let me know or I'll be back here to charge the lot of you with obstructing my investigation.'

Spence's whole body shook. The policeman was saying his Mum was mixed up in a murder and they hanged murderers with a rope and it was reported on the wireless and he'd never see her again.

Challis's car started to pull away. Spence ran after it, screaming for his mother all down Grenville Road and even as it disappeared into the main road traffic. But she never looked back. Not even once.

Twenty-Eight

Passengers on the top decks of buses driving down Peter Street stared into Malcolm Feingold's first floor office, each a fleeting witness to the drama unfolding within.

'You cannot put the words *Joan* and *murder* in the same sentence,' Zilla said. 'It's madness, I don't know what the police are talking about.'

Feingold made notes at a desk the size of a dining table in a musty, dusty room lined with box files and law books. Vron, who'd run to Zilla's house as the police took Joan away, asked how serious the situation was.

'I'm puzzled by aspects of what you've told me so far,' he said. 'We need to establish exactly how Joan came by the pictures which the police say are stolen.'

'I'm sure she got them as a present from someone during the war.'

'Which is when the police appear to believe their original owner was murdered.'

'But after all these years, how can they prove that?' Vron said.

'I won't know until we discover how a murder charge can be contemplated without, it would appear, the body of a victim who may also have been injured in an air raid.'

'Yet the police must feel they've the basis for a case,' Zilla said.

'To be pedantic, we only know that Challis thinks he has one,' Feingold said. 'He's an obsessive so maybe he's the driving force here.'

'Being obsessive doesn't equate to being right,' Vron said.

Feingold looked at her over his glasses. He'd already formed the view that the quick-minded Vron was as shrewd as Joan must be naive.

'What's behind your point?' he said.

'Just that I can't believe that it's Joan he's really after,' Vron said. 'I think it far more likely that my brother-in-law is the one with the explaining to do.'

'Why do you suspect that?'

'Because my timid little sister is incapable of either theft or violence but hand on heart, I couldn't swear the same about John Henry.'

'Is there anything else I should know about him?'

'He's impulsive, he drinks and he doesn't consider the consequences of his actions.'

'I see,' Feingold said. 'Do either of you know where he is?'

'No, he's been missing for two days,' Zilla said.

'And what about the son? You say he ran away after the police arrested his mother?'

'He was distraught, poor kid. His uncle is out looking for him, now.'

Vron had to leave for a meeting with overseas clients at her office. When she'd gone, Feingold shook his head at Zilla.

'I'll only say this once, but I did warn you.'

'I know, I know, but you must see that something's not right here.'

'Yes, but a possible murder, Zilla. You're getting dragged into something completely outside your experience and expertise.'

'Look, John Henry might be an inconsiderate husband and not the father his clever son deserves but he's no murderer any more than you or me.'

'Zilla, just because you want something to be true, doesn't mean it is,' he said. 'This man has vanished when his wife needs him most. There must be a reason for that.'

*

Joan was confined in a cell two floors below the secure office in which Bootle Street Police Station's criminal records were stored - fifty thousand card indexes and photographs of offenders in sixteen grey metal cabinets set between walls of shelves bending under even more files. Challis sat at a desk reading one as he waited for Inspector Gormley of Special Branch.

Gormley was a monk of a man who tapped the phones of communists and other subversives threatening Queen and country. They had joined the city force together as cadets then been detectives during the war. He and Challis were members of a very private ways and means committee, close enough to do each other discreet favours.

Gormley appeared noiselessly in front of Challis - oiled black hair, dark double-breasted suit and a bluish chin needing shaving twice a day.

'I've only got a minute,' he said. 'But your suspect's got a solicitor already.'

'Has she, now? Who?'

'Feingold, one of the partners at Feingold & Abel in Peter Street.'

'I don't need to ask who fixed that up.'

'No. She rang Feingold almost before you got the cleaner back here.'

'OK, thanks. If you hear anything else of interest, you'll let me know, yes?'

Challis returned to his office. The pictures recovered from Joan's house were leant against his chair.

He looked again at their descriptions in the witness statement of a Mrs Turner, the owner's next-door-neighbour in Hulme.

The first one shows the quay of a fishing village, which looks Scottish. A fisherman in braces is kneeling down on the beach to show his catch to a woman standing nearby with a basket and there are several small boats in the sea behind them.

The second shows two men in a rowing boat on a lake with some cottages in the background and a windmill by a house with a curved gable end which Miss Tester said was the Dutch style of building.

They were clearly prints but with the name *Alex Lawson* forged in the left hand corner of each. This was why Challis's snout knew Joan was trying to pass off duds without value. But the key to re-opening the case so long after the event turned on Challis remembering the artist's name. Alex Lawson had exhibited at the Royal Academy in London and painted the third picture stolen from Miss Tester - a genuine watercolour of Caernarfon Castle in a plain gold frame.

Mrs Turner's statement mentioned the missing stamp and coin collections, the canteen of silver cutlery and the handbag of cash, and went on:

Miss Tester spoke very properly and seemed from a different class than the other residents of our street. I never saw any visitors to her house and she did not mention to me that she had any living relatives. I got the impression that she came from the south of England but Miss Tester was not the sort of lady you could question. I just cleaned her possessions each week and they struck me as being valuable.

Challis believed then - as he did now - that whoever robbed and killed Miss Tester knew what they were after.

He looked again at Mrs Turner's photograph of her, taken around the time of the Great War. It showed

Miss Tester in period clothes - long skirt, side-buttoned boots with a shirt-like top and satin choker. Her hair was wispy and dark, pushed up beneath a straw hat with a floral ribbon around it.

She would not win any beauty contest but her smile displayed an intelligence and a reserve which gave nothing away.

Challis headed downstairs to question Joan. In his hand was a teleprinter message from the army confirming that Private 4130410 John Henry White was on an authorised three-day leave of absence at the time of Miss Tester's death.

The value of her stolen property gave White the motive. Challis now had proof that he also had the opportunity.

*

Maybe it was guilt or a fear of the unknown or simply the thrill of the questionable legality of what she intended doing. Whatever it was, Zilla had rarely been more alert. Colours seemed brighter, images sharper and the sounds of the city never more distinct. Trains coming, trains going, steel-rimmed cartwheels on granite setts, trolleys, lorries and the shouts of market traders, all this filled her ears.

University commitments could wait. She had to help Joan despite Malcolm's warning that she'd only muddy the waters of due process by meddling in matters she didn't understand. She'd left him arranging to interview Joan and get her formal instructions to act for her.

Zilla arrived at The Old Wellington Inn, an oak-framed pub built when the city was a village. A dray drew up to deliver barrels of beer. The horse pulling it gleamed with sweat in the autumn sun, stamping its iron shoes and jingling its brasses.

It took a moment for Zilla to adjust to the bar's tobacco-stained dimness. The *click, click, click* of ivory dominoes came through the laughter of men with pint pots in their hands. She ordered a tonic water and sat alone at a table in the best room. Standing around her were lawyers, newspapermen, detectives, a favoured circle of initiates who knew what others didn't and whose currency was information.

The man she might once have married came here, too. Elliot would surely have answers to her many questions. But would he have the courage to risk helping her?

Zilla lit another cigarette to calm herself, aware of being adrift on a tide she couldn't control and which might drag her under. She went to the bar for another drink.

Behind her, a man ordered a pint of bitter. Even in all that noise, she didn't need to see his face or look into his sad, lambent eyes to recognise who had just spoken from the past. She turned and each smiled at the other in that knowing, wordless way only old lovers have.

*

Joan wanted to scream but no sound would come. They'd locked her up once and now they'd done it again. And both times, she'd seen into the despairing eyes of those who loved her and they'd been powerless to keep her with them.

Where was Spence? Where was John Henry? Why was a pig of a man shouting in her face?

'Joan, I want you to look at these pictures.'

'They're my pictures.'

'No, Joan, they're not yours. Where did you get them from?'

'From Freddie.'

'Freddie? Who's Freddie?'

'I want to go home.'

'You'll not be going home till you've answered my questions. Who is Freddie?'

'They're mine, the pictures are mine.'

'A woman was murdered for these... had her head bashed in.'

'I want my boy, I want Spence.'

'Joan... you're in big trouble. You need to think about that and start telling me the truth if you want to see your lad again. Your husband stole these pictures, didn't he?'

'They were a present, they're mine.'

'Where is that husband of yours, Joan? Where is John Henry?'

'He'll be home soon... he'll be wanting his tea.'

Joan was led back through a narrow corridor with iron barred windows on one side and eight metal doors on the other. It was like before, just as she knew it would be. The tumblers of the lock fell into place, leaving her trapped in a cell not three paces by five. The walls loomed over her. She crouched in a corner and folded her arms around her knees to make herself small and began to rock to and fro, to and fro. The bricks were hard to her back. She rocked a little quicker and hit her head again and again. Her blood, like her spirit, began to ebb out through her pain, through her hair and down her face and onto the cheap print frock she wore.

*

It was past eight and Spence was still missing. Edgar had tramped the streets all day, searching every garden, allotment and shed where a boy might hide but he'd gone to earth like a hunted cub.

The gates of Platt Fields were shut but a few railings had been forced apart by kids, so Edgar could get in. He found a bench to rest and have a smoke. The moon sculled across the boating lake and silvered the wooded island in the middle.

He called Spence's name into the evening air.

'Come on, son! It's late. Let's go home.'

No one answered and he felt again that dread of the night and what it might bring. In such hours as these had he once prayed.

I confess I have sinned exceedingly, through my fault, through my fault, through my most grievous fault. I beseech all the saints to pray for me.

His guilt weighed heavier as the end came nearer. He could still see those Germans, flushed from their funk holes, arms raised, no longer demonic savages but the most ordinary of men, begging for mercy with their eyes. But Private Sydenham was off the leash, brim full of hate like the others whose own deaths had only been postponed. No prisoners. That was the nod they got.

So they closed in with bayonets, stabbing at enemies with no more than a prayer in their hands. Lunge, twist, pull. Down they went, bellies bursting, sticky and warm, their dirty grey uniforms turning brown. Stab, stab and fucking stab. That was for my brother. That was for my mate. That was for winter in the trenches. And blood bubbled from mouths with nothing more to say.

War crimes hadn't been invented so couldn't be committed. Yet Edgar still looked down on his younger self all these remorseful years later, this instrument of death, cruel and unthinking.

In the silence by the lake where he sat, he still did not know from where he might get absolution for such sins. And that wasn't the worst of it.

'Spence! Spence! Answer me, please!'

167

Something small and pale seemed to pass through the trees. Edgar went to the water's edge and shouted again.

'Spence! Is that you, son?'

Whatever it was disappeared in the undergrowth. It could only have been a trick of the light, a moving shadow that his heightened awareness misread. The half hour chimed from the clock of Holy Trinity Church. Edgar, exhausted and unwell, couldn't carry on. The spasms gripping his guts weren't just from hunger.

He began to walk the hard mile home. As he turned a corner between the rhododendron bushes, a boy appeared from nowhere, backlit by the moon on the path ahead.

In that dreamlike moment, Edgar Sydenham thought the figure could only be an apparition of innocence lost, a vision summoned by the gods as a final warning for him to repent the evils of his life.

But then the child opened his arms and ran to his uncle. Each had more need of the other than either could put into words.

Twenty-Nine

Spence had managed to run behind the hangman's car until the Friendship Inn when his mother finally disappeared from view. He'd dropped to the pavement, out of breath but not of tears and rage.

Where was his Dad when a raised hand might've done some good? Why didn't anyone at 35 stop Mum being taken away? He'd thought about going to Miss Arbib's house but why should he trust another grown-up ever again?

He made for Platt Fields instead, a boy in a park, hiding in plain sight. Often in the past, he'd wanted to run away from where he should've always felt safe yet didn't. But this would've needed more courage than he had so he drew comfort from another of Auntie Kitty's pet sayings - that the devil you knew was better than one you didn't.

Spence didn't see any boys from around Zion Street in Platt Fields. But he'd not wanted to play any games that day.

He climbed the chestnut trees beyond the boating lake to be on his own. As each hour passed, he became hungrier. But the man at the ice cream kiosk paid threepence for empty pop bottles. Spence searched beneath the bushes and found two - enough for a bar of chocolate.

The sun moved across the sky. People drifted home, the skiffs were chained up and the park-keepers locked the gates. It became darker.

Whatever rebellious spirit he'd had earlier gave way to anxiety. What if Auntie Kitty had called the police and they were looking for him? Might this make things worse for his Mum?

He sought shelter under the rhododendrons by the lake. It was then he'd heard his name being called across the cold black water and he was no longer lost.

*

'Why's my Mum been taken away, Uncle Edgar?'

'I wish I knew, son. It's all a muddle and no mistake.'

'But she'll be coming home again, won't she?'

''Course she will. I'd stake my life on it so don't you worry about that.'

'We're not still going to France, are we?'

'No, your Mum needs our help so we best stay here.'

They'd left the bus and were walking to the Salutation, the pub near the factory where Edgar worked. He knew the landlady well and explained what'd happened. She made them beans on toast in her parlour and said Edgar could use her phone. He rang his neighbours at number 15 to say Spence was safe and could they tell everyone at 35.

The landlady smiled at Edgar with fond concern as they left and urged him to take greater care of himself.

He and Spence walked through a street of derelict terraces awaiting demolition. Curtains still hung at some windows and stars were visible through missing slates and the bare ribs of the roof timbers.

Edgar paused outside one of the houses. Spence felt his uncle's hand tighten around his own. They went to the back and Edgar forced open the kitchen door. Inside, the floor was crunchy with broken glass and rubble amid paper that'd peeled away from walls made damp by rain.

All about were traces of life as it had been for those who had gone - a mirror on a shelf, a cup without a handle, a saucer, a chair with a once-red velveteen seat now thick with muck.

'What are we doing in here, Uncle Edgar? Won't we get in trouble?'

'No, son... we're just looking, that's all.'

'Did you know the people who lived here, then?'

'Yes... I knew them.'

Edgar gazed at the broken heart of what had been a home - at the brown earthenware sink, silted up with dirt where a woman would have stood to wash clothes, the rusting grate she'd have black-leaded once a month and the table where her family had fed, collapsing now under the weight of fallen bricks and plaster. He had seen enough and turned to leave.

'Come on, young Spence, we should be getting you home to bed.'

For Spence, it'd been a day when his senses had been heightened by anger and fear but one which also felt unreal, as if he'd been appearing in someone else's dream. To go back to 35 now and find that his mother really had been taken away would be to wake up and be required to confront what he dreaded most.

'Can't we stay here a bit longer, Uncle Edgar?'

'Why would you want to do that? This building isn't very safe.'

'No, but I'm not tired and we could make a fire and you could tell me some stories from your war. You're always promising you will.'

The man considered the boy. Here, in what remained of the place from where Edgar had set out on his own long march, was as good a confessional as any field in Flanders would have been. It didn't seem to matter that the moment had presented itself in this way, unplanned and unrehearsed.

He screwed a few balls of paper into the grate, laid a criss-cross of laths on top and put a match to it. The flames and the slants of moonlight threw strange shadows around them. Edgar wasn't normally given to speeches. He thought people who talked a lot heard only what they already knew. Those who listened, learned. But this night had to be different.

*

'It's the colours that stick in your mind, Spence... like the lilac flower of vervain, just a weed somehow still growing in all that mud or put in some bloke's letter to his girl then we'd find it in his pocket before we put him in the ground and he's just a shape on the canvas of the stretcher till the next one... just bloody Shrouds of Turin, all of them, all of us.'

He was sitting on the floor leaning against the staircase, knees drawn up and his face lined like a woodcut, staring into somewhere far away and long ago.

'But you still wanted to go back there,' Spence said. 'You must have had a reason.'

'I'd a reason all right... make no mistake, I had a reason.'

Edgar lit another Park Drive. The fire which had flared out sparks like little tracers was dying down. The uninterrupted rumble of the city's heavy industries and the crump of a drop forge came on the evening air as if from a distant battle.

'It's about Billy, Spence... all about our Billy. They said it was a disease that took him down, that's what the doctors said but it wasn't... not if I'm to tell the truth.'

'What was it, then?'

'It was me... I as good as killed our Billy in France even before he was born.'

Edgar took a strip of lath and forced it between his big, bony hands until it splintered in two with a crack and a puff of dust.

'This is how men are, Spence.... strong enough to bear many a load but there's a point when we can't take any more and we can't ever be mended.'

Edgar Sydenham finally broke, not when a whistle went and he clambered out of his trench to go up and over the bags and into the leaden wind once more, but on a quieter mission when death was busy further up the line.

'We're quartered in this village, all bombed out and ruined like where we are now and there's a lull but we know it won't last. I've had three years and more of this, being a corpse waiting my turn and me and another bloke have been ordered to scout the lie of the land then something moves in the undergrowth to the side of us and I don't care what it is, my finger's on the trigger and I'm going to kill it before it kills me.'

They heard a cry but fire wasn't returned. Edgar crawled on his belly to finish off the enemy. What he found in the dark of that night was a child, a scavenging, malnourished boy who'd no business not being in bed.

Edgar carried him back to their billet. Men desensitised by killing to live gathered in a circle and looked on in silence. An oil lamp was held aloft. The bullet had torn a path across the boy's throat. The last of his blood boiled up from a wound no field dressing could staunch. Someone thought they'd seen him earlier in the day. There was a cottage a mile or more back. A family holding on to their land for there was nothing else.

They were fetched. Edgar was beyond comfort. The mother came and shrieked against the pitiless war. If only kisses could raise the dead. Her husband gathered their son in his arms and held out his lifeless little body as if it were a sacrificial offering.

Then he spat in Edgar's face and damned him.

'*Puisses-tu avoir un fils et fasse le Ciel que tu souffres comme nous maintenant.*'

All those years later and the words wouldn't leave his head nor the pain his soul.

'What was he saying, Uncle Edgar?'

'That he hoped I would have a son and if I did, that before Heaven I would come to suffer like he was suffering then.'

'But it was an accident. You didn't mean to shoot him.'

Edgar shook his head. That was what his comrades had said. But they hadn't seen into the father's eyes or taken his curse into their own. All sins had a price and had to be paid in full, however long it took. That was a law of nature.

'How old was the boy, Uncle Edgar?'

'Five... five years, that's all.'

'Same as Billy?'

'Yes... same as our Billy.'

There was nothing more to tell, nothing more to say. Spence understood.

Thirty

Grenville Road, Fallowfield, Saturday 17th January 2015

The advice is well-founded - never go back, never return to places where memories were formed and try to nail one's pictures of the past on the walls of the present. They will not line up.

So it was with His Honour, Judge Spencer White, treading streets he had known as a boy but which time had rendered as unrecognisable as him.

He stood on the pavement across from 35 Grenville Road, hoping to glimpse the spirits that must still dwell within. Somewhere behind those blank windows, *Mrs Dale's Diary* would surely be on Uncle Edgar's wireless and the line calls of tennis players just about audible from the courts beyond the perfumed roses of the garden.

In that moment, White was less a learned judge governed by evidence and logic and more a man conflicted by the journey he'd made thus far.

He was also aware that the curtain had yet to fall on the drama of his formative years. If only he could walk up that tiled path once more, peer through the squares of coloured glass in the front door and see the approaching shadows of those who had held him dear.

They would take him into their hearts again as he had never been since and he'd be at peace with himself - and maybe even with all that made him so apprehensive about what he was soon to undertake.

But these were fanciful musings, laid waste by other images which would not fade either... his mother being driven from there to be locked up, Edgar falling to his knees in drunken grief and where, every once in a while, a hearse had pulled up until at last, all the characters in his story were gone and he was alone on the stage.

Time had passed without seeming to have done so. The impermanence of people and places was all around. White turned and made for the main road.

What were once family homes were now divided into flats for students, gardens which had been carefully tended, had become dumps for mattresses, broken furniture and dustbins spilling waste into the weeds around them. Of Zion Street and its cobbled maze of sooty brick terraces, nothing remained. In its place was an estate of boxy little houses with bathrooms and inside toilets and chimneys from which coal smoke did not rise, just the hazy fumes of central heating systems.

White knew now why he'd stayed away for so many years. He cursed himself for not having the wit to resist Dan Luston's flattery and the shrewd manoeuvrings of Sir Patrick Prentice to set him up as the public face of a political embarrassment in this prelude to a general election.

It began to rain. He put up his black umbrella and bent into an icy wind. The cold bit into his bones. His polio arm always ached more acutely in damp weather.

But the Lady Barn Hotel where he'd arrived the previous night was not far. It was sited where White remembered greenhouses and a market garden from Fallowfield's long-lost agrarian past.

He'd have an early supper and prepare for his conference call with Luston next morning. Luston wanted to role-play the press conference which White would chair on Monday week to launch the public inquiry.

'My minister is very keen that we're all on the same page,' Luston had said. 'The media won't necessarily

176

be onside so we've got to agree the most appropriate responses to any hostile questioning.'

A room service waiter brought White three grilled lamb chops which he ate well salted and with a glass of house red. He'd not much of an appetite. Graffiti sprayed on the metal grills of shop fronts near the Friendship Inn - now an upmarket café-bar - demanded *Justice For The Bootle Street Three*. Alone, and a stranger in a place he had once known well, White was starting to feel unequal to the task of providing it. Nerves were to be expected before any big case but what he was sensing had more to do with confidence - or the sudden lack of it.

*

It had snowed on and off for most of the day in Hartford. Elspeth White arrived home from Cambridge, garaged her Mini Cooper and unlocked the connecting door into the kitchen. She was tired. That was the way of it these days. A single malt would help. Elspeth poured a measure into a cut glass tumbler and went into the sitting room.

She called Archie, the cat, who didn't come. He was probably on their bed, which wasn't allowed, but she couldn't be fussed to check. The red light on the phone was flashing with a message.

'Yes, hello, it's me. I'm in Manchester, in the hotel. Not much to report so no need to ring back. Launch day looms so fingers crossed. Luston says we might get on television if it's a thin news day. Can't say I share his enthusiasm for publicity. Anyway, I think I'll turn in. I might call you tomorrow if I get a chance. Bye.'

How like Spencer not to seize the moment. She thought about refilling her glass then the security lights came on beyond the French windows. The curtains

177

hadn't been drawn and she saw the fox which had crossed the beam. It stared back at her, russet brown against the blinding whiteness of the snow, defiant and on its way to a kill. Elspeth stood up and it padded away into the darkness.

This would-be intruder triggered a belated thought - why wasn't the burglar alarm beeping when she came in? She hadn't needed to de-activate it. Elspeth checked the front door. It was unlocked. But she felt certain she *had* locked it before leaving for her daughter's - and that she'd entered their security code into the alarm, too. It frightened her how mixed up she was becoming. God forbid it was Alzheimer's.

There was still no sign of Archie who was old and never strayed outside. His dirt tray looked wet so he must be in the house somewhere. But she couldn't find him, not downstairs or in any of the bedrooms.

Elspeth put on her coat and went into the garden with a torch, puzzled and not expecting to find him. Every door and window was closed, even if unlocked. She shone a light across the lawn and into the bushes where he might be hiding but he didn't come when she called.

Only as she returned to the house did she notice a ball of black fur curled up on the path beneath the utility room window. It was Archie and he wasn't moving. But how had he got out? He'd been in his basket when she left home. She was sure of it.

Elspeth knelt and gently picked him up. He was frozen stiff, poor creature. It was then she noticed indistinct footprints in the snow. They had to be hers... hadn't they? But the thought gripped her that a burglar could've gained entry to the house through this window, somehow disabled the alarm and robbed them.

She hurried indoors still carrying the cat's body. Her jewellery remained on the dressing table, their paintings where they hung and no antique silverware was missing from the dresser. Everything was as she'd left it eight hours before.

There was, however, a small puddle of water on the utility room work surface just below the window. But that was where she'd left Archie so it was probably melting snow.

Only Spencer's study remained unchecked. She rarely went in there. It was on the dark side of the house, a man's room heavy with books and dominated by the button-backed chesterfield where Spencer sometimes slept. Each of his six desk drawers was locked and nothing seemed out of place.

Elspeth realised she'd need to be far more security-conscious in future. It was better not to mention this lapse to Spencer, not to distract him as he embarked on the last assignment of his career - and one with such an exciting honour at the end of it. She closed his study door and prepared for bed, upset about the cat which she would bury in the morning but mightily relieved that they'd not been burgled.

Had Elspeth looked in Spencer's en suite dressing room, she might have noticed a silver hairbrush was missing. And had she known about the contents of a black metal box no bigger than a biscuit tin and kept in his bureau, she would have seen that a dangerous and unregistered Great War memento brought back by his late uncle, Edgar Sydenham, was no longer there, either.

Thirty-One

Manchester City Magistrates' Court, Wednesday 26th August 1955

Joan was led into the dock from the cells below. She looked disorientated and seemingly unable to acknowledge Vron, Edgar and Miss Arbib in the public seats. The clerk outlined details of the charge under the Larceny Act 1916. Detective Inspector Challis got to his feet for the prosecution.

'Your worships, this case arises after two stolen pictures were found at the home of the defendant but as of now, my inquiries are far from complete and I would ask for a remand in custody for a further seven days.'

Malcolm Feingold immediately objected and applied for bail.

'Mrs White is a respectable wife and mother with an excellent character who has no intention of absconding. I can produce medical evidence about her recent stay in hospital and it is her doctor's opinion that her well-being would be imperilled were she not allowed to continue living with her aunts. I should also say that her employer is willing to stand surety in whatever sum you might set.'

Challis stood up again, his neck muscles clenched like fists, reddening above the collar of his white shirt.

'I am constrained by what I can say at this stage in my investigation but there is a separate and far more serious offence to be considered here which, with respect, makes a remand in custody a more suitable course of action.'

The magistrates' chairman leaned forward and asked what he meant.

'Sir, I have a warrant for the arrest of the defendant's husband who has disappeared. In due course, I expect to bring a charge in relation to a suspicious death during the Christmas Blitz in Manchester in 1940, which is linked to the pictures referred to in the matter before you today. These offences could involve murder.'

Reporters on the press bench began scribbling hard. Here was a whiff of red meat. They looked across at the agitated woman in the dock. She was more than just a paragraph on an inside page now.

The magistrates refused bail. Challis bowed to the bench. Joan was taken down the steps to be replaced in the dock by a prostitute.

*

Vron vented her sisterly anger outside court and said Joan was obviously being used as the bait to hook John Henry.

'How can that appalling and vindictive policeman be so cruel, Mr Feingold?'

'It isn't personal. It's a sort of game to him but one he intends to win.'

'It shows the wickedness of the man,' Zilla said.

'And the selfishness of John Henry,' Vron said. 'He ought to have the backbone to come home and not leave Joan to face the music for whatever he's done.'

'But how did he know the police were going to arrest him?'

Edgar, who looked drawn and jaundiced, now appeared shame-faced.

'It was me,' he said. 'I told him.'

'You, Uncle Edgar? But how did you know?'

'That copper, Challis, came to Zion Street while I was there with Spence. I never thought John Henry would do a runner.'

181

'You're best keeping all that to yourself, Mr Sydenham,' Feingold said. 'This situation is problematic enough as it is.'

Vron had to return to her office and Edgar to Grenville Road to make sure Spence wasn't left on his own for too long. Feingold invited Zilla for morning coffee.

'Sorry, Malcolm. I've someone to see.'

'Someone to see about Joan?'

'I can't tell you.'

'Which suggests it is and you refuse to tell me even though I'm Joan's lawyer?'

'I have my reasons, honestly.'

'Zilla, for the last time, you could be making a dangerous situation even worse.'

'That's unfair, Malcolm. I'm doing my best as Joan's friend.'

'But you heard Challis. He means to make a charge of murder stick here. It's a hanging offence, someone's life may well be at stake.'

'That's the point, don't you see? I can get information that'll help her.'

'You're a sociologist, not a criminologist. You should keep to what you know.'

She left him on the pavement and went to her car. Elliot had agreed to meet her on a particular bench by the Irwell near Salford Crescent. He was taking a great risk. But how wonderful it'd been when they'd met at The Wellington. It was as if they'd never broken apart all those years ago. They'd fitted back together again so easily.

Zilla was early. The oily black Irwell poured itself between the backs of factories and over a weir to form the chemically polluted suds floating downstream like mounds of dirty cotton wool.

Malcolm's dismissive words offended her. But he wasn't to know her motives, still less understand them. It had begun with Spence, newborn and fragile. His mouth would seek her breast, his infant heart against hers. Joan might be scrubbing on her hands and knees so Zilla would bottle feed him or change his nappies. She did not covet the child, not then. She still had Elliot.

But in war, men become killers or corpses or lose themselves on the long journey home. So it was with him. Elliot returned from soldiering remote and changed, the sum of his fears and experiences.

Yet she was different, too. Hitler had seen to that... his factories of extermination and the encaustic stares of those who waited behind the wire as she might have done but for an accident of history.

Then came the stemming of her blood and for this or some other reason she couldn't know, Elliot slipped from her life till she went looking for him once more.

He was also a lawyer in Manchester. She'd sometimes ask Malcolm how he was faring. He would tell her but wish she didn't want to know.

When they finally met again, she felt no aftertaste of bitterness, no sense of recrimination, not even at the ring on his wedding finger. All hurt decayed with time.

An Evening News van dropped off a bundle of first editions at the shop across the street from where she sat. The newsagent pinned up a billboard outside - MURDER MYSTERY IN ART THEFT CASE.

Zilla, full of dread, bought a copy. Joan's case was on the front page.

Two stolen pictures could be linked to an unsolved murder during Manchester's Christmas Blitz in 1940, the city's magistrates heard today.

Housewife Joan White, 38, of 3 Zion Street, Fallowfield, was accused of being in possession of the pictures and remanded in custody for five days.

Detective Inspector Vincent Challis said a charge of murder could yet be laid in connection with this matter.

Police have a warrant out for the arrest of the defendant's husband, John Henry White, also 38, a van driver and former Cheshire Regiment private who has been missing for several days.

He is described as 5ft 8ins, stocky and dark-haired with a tattoo of a woman's face on his right forearm and the name 'Joan' underneath.

The damage Challis intended had been done - in public and with a vengeance. What did he care if he destroyed a mother and wrecked her son's future? He was ahead of the game. But the contest had a way to go yet.

'Zilla?'

Elliot stood behind her, smiling, his face more lined in the harsh daylight, his hair thinner, greyer and those laughing green eyes she'd adored, showing something of life's disappointments and regrets.

'I'm so grateful for you meeting me,' Zilla said. 'I really need your help.'

'Yes, but you're asking me to break professional confidences.'

'Better than breaking hearts, Elliot. But let's go for a walk. It's hardly the banks of the sweet Afton but we won't be seen.'

Elliot's own legal firm hadn't prospered so he'd joined the prosecution department of the city police. All Challis's paperwork about Joan's case passed across his desk. He told Zilla that the police could show John

Henry had motive and opportunity to kill the original owner of Joan's pictures - a Miss Tester.

'But Challis will need more than this to prove murder, won't he?' Zilla said.

'Yes, not least because we've obviously no actual body, the post-mortem photographs cannot be said to demonstrate a deliberate killing and the police doctor who attended is dead.'

'So why is Challis so sure of his ground?'

'That's what you have to understand about him as your enemy.'

'What do you mean?'

'Well, it's fifteen years after the event and he still has an almost pathological need to be right. The old sweats in Bootle Street say he's always been like this, refuses to believe he's ever wrong.'

'Do you think it was murder?'

'I can't say if it was or it wasn't.'

'Then neither can Challis.'

'You're forgetting he was actually there at the scene, Zilla. He examined the lady's body and he's a shrewd and wily interrogator who gets confessions and add to that, he's a persuasive witness in the box as many a man on the scaffold could've told you.'

'So it looks bleak for Joan's husband?'

'Ask yourself why an innocent man would run away.'

But he offered Zilla one hopeful inside track.

'Miss Tester had a cleaner, lived near her in Scott Street. Reading between the lines, she obviously didn't warm to our friend, Challis, but she's not alone there. I'm sure she held things back from him.'

'What's her name?'

'Mrs Turner, first name Joyce, a widow, getting on in years, moved house not long since so ask around her old neighbours and someone's bound to know where.'

'Anything else?'

'Only this... I did a little bit of digging into Miss Tester, not for Challis, but just to keep my hand in and you need to remember that almost without exception, a murder victim either knows their killer or is related to them.'

'So are you saying there's a connection between her and John Henry?'

'No, I'm saying that you should cosy-up to Mrs Turner and see where she leads you.'

'And that's it? You can't tell me anything else?'

'Come on, Zilla, I just can't take the risk.'

'Because you've got a wife and family, now. It's all right, I know.'

Then Elliot squeezed Zilla's hand in farewell, his guilt assuaged, his debt more or less paid, and left her life for a second time.

Thirty-Two

The station buffet was as smart as many a restaurant in town - laundered white tablecloths and linen napkins, waiters with slicked-back hair and dickie bows.

Spence stared out of the window to the platforms beyond. The figures of strangers crossed from left and right, lit for a moment as they passed through the dusty beams of sunshine coming down from gaps in the canopy above.

He would soon follow them. But for now, everyone was being extra kind to him. Auntie Emily helped him to a second serving of ice cream and Kitty gave him a ten-shilling note.

'I've been lucky on the gee-gees, love, so buy yourself a treat when you arrive over there,' she said.

Uncle Edgar winked. Both knew he was being buttered up, though for what purpose, Spence couldn't be sure. He was aware only that they wanted him out of the way, however much he protested. But it had been agreed. He was to stay with his Dad's sister, Evelyn, and her husband on the other side of the country.

Uncle Edgar had phoned her from Miss Arbib's house and said he'd bring Spence across on the train.

'I know you're upset about this, son,' he said. 'But your Mum would want you to be brave while Miss Arbib and the rest of us try to sort everything out.'

'But I could help and so will Dad when he gets home.'

'I'm sure he will, Spence, but till then, it's up to all of us to do everything we can to get your Mum home. That's what you want, isn't it?'

The station announcer called the imminent arrival of the Liverpool to Harwich train. Spence picked up his small leather suitcase. Then he walked alongside his uncle, through an oily drift of steam from an engine

187

which, before nightfall, would set him down in a place he did not know amid relatives he had never met.

Kitty and Emily watched and waved until the last carriage was out of sight.

'Poor lad,' Kitty said. 'Still, he didn't get to read the Evening News and he'll not have other kids calling his Mum and Dad murderers.'

'No, but he's seen enough already to know something dreadful is happening.'

'Miss Arbib doesn't think he'll be able to start at that grammar school, not yet, not with all this hanging over him.'

'That woman has too much influence in this family,' Emily said.

'Maybe you're right but Edgar says she knows people, people who are important and who could help our Joan.'

'Does she, now? Come on or we'll miss our bus.'

*

Zilla found a past voters' register for Hulme at the Central Library and checked the numbers of the houses where Miss Tester and Mrs Turner had lived.

Scott Street was as dismal as a thousand others - a corner pub, a corner shop, gritty, unclean air that left shadows on lungs and washing alike. Of Miss Tester's bombed-out home, only mounds of rubble remained, colonised now by dandelions and buddleia.

The house of her former cleaner, Mrs Turner, was boarded up and awaiting demolition. Several families were new to the area and didn't know either woman. Finally, an elderly couple thought Mrs Turner had moved to a terrace by the yard used by Finglands, the coach firm in Rusholme.

Zilla waited an hour for her to arrive home. She'd not see seventy again and wore what could've been an

Edwardian shift, buttoned up to a lace collar at the neck.

Mrs Turner listened respectfully to Zilla's preamble about Miss Tester then invited her in. The kitchen was predictably clean and neat with a polished brass artillery shell containing a poker, standing in the tiled hearth. On the mantelpiece was a silver-framed photograph of a young soldier in uniform.

'My husband,' Mrs Turner said.

'What a handsome man.'

'In the 19th Manchesters... didn't come back, though.'

'That must have been unbearable for you.'

'On the Somme... never found him. His name's on that big monument over there.'

There were no other photographs around, not of children, not of grandchildren.

'Were you married long?'

'Didn't quite make our first anniversary.'

She turned the ring on her wedding hand with fingers red and rough from housework. Nothing more could be said on the subject.

Zilla began to explain about Joan and her disputed pictures but made no mention of Miss Tester allegedly being murdered for them.

'I'm afraid Joan has really been quite ill, a mental breakdown, and she either can't or won't say how she came by the paintings.'

'I've told the police all I know,' Mrs Turner said. 'And it's not much.'

'Yes, I understand that but this poor woman needs help, not locking up.'

'All I can tell you is that lots of things got taken from houses after the bombings.'

'Stolen, you mean? But who would do such a thing?'

'Folk who should've known better.'

Mrs Turner wouldn't be drawn, didn't want to get in trouble by speaking out of turn. But she confirmed what was missing from Miss Tester's - a handbag containing a few pounds, silver cutlery, a stamp and coin collection and three pictures in gilt frames.

'Was she in reasonably good health for someone of her age?' Zilla said.

'Well, if I'm honest, she'd started to go a bit odd, I'd say.'

'How do you mean, exactly?'

'A bit senile, I suppose.'

'A little absent-minded, that sort of thing?'

'That and worse,' Mrs Turner said. 'She wasn't keeping herself clean and she'd always been a tidy sort of soul of good breeding but she began to forget personal matters but the war didn't help, terrified of the air raid sirens, she was... cowered in the corner like a child when they went off but then, we were all scared, weren't we?'

'With good reason,' Zilla said. 'But before this, did she ever say what brought her to live round here?'

'Not to me, she didn't.'

'Did she have any relatives or friends who visited her?'

'If she did, I never knew about them.'

A cup of tea wasn't offered as Zilla had hoped. But she needed to keep Mrs Turner talking.

'She came to a terribly sad end that Christmas, didn't she?'

'As far as I know, part of a wall fell on her but they never tell you the truth, not in wartime they don't.'

'You think there's more to her death then, do you?'

'There's no smoke without fire so there must be some reason the police are raking it all up again.'

Zilla asked if Mrs Turner had any of Miss Tester's personal belongings - letters from people she knew, a diary or an address book.

'I've got some bits and pieces,' Mrs Turner said. 'After the bombing, there were a few papers and things lying about in all the mess so I picked those up because they were no-one else's business but hers, private things.'

'Did you show them to the detectives who came to see you?'

'They never asked.'

Mrs Turner opened a drawer in the dresser where her best blue and white dinner plates were arranged and pulled out Miss Tester's rent book. It contained a few household receipts but nothing of any interest.

But there was also a catalogue from an auction held by Provis & Barter in the town of Coleford in the Forest of Dean, Gloucestershire.

This gave details of household furnishings and effects from *homes of repute and substance in the locality* to be held at the Angel Hotel, Coleford on Monday the 29th of October 1928. Among the items offered for sale, Lot 32 was actually shown - a watercolour of Caernarfon Castle.

It was described as *...a painting by the noted Victorian landscape artist, Alexander Lawson, who exhibited 17 times at the Royal Academy.*

'That was one of those that disappeared,' Mrs Turner said. 'She always said the other two weren't up to much but the castle picture had pride of place in her front room. Loved it, she did, would often sit there of an evening and gaze at it.'

Mrs Turner had rescued her employer's bankbook, too. Zilla tried to hide her shock as she read the final entry. On Tuesday the 24th of December 1940, five days before she died, Miss Tester went to Martins Bank in

Cheetham Hill Road and closed her account. She withdrew every penny of what was then a huge fortune - £5,573 in cash.

Zilla couldn't decide if this was a sign of irrational behaviour or, more conspiratorially, the result of someone exploiting her fear of air raids and suggesting her savings would be safer at home.

But if that someone was John Henry, on what could he have possibly spent so vast a sum? His wife wore her sister's cast-offs, they rented a house in a street of slums, their furniture was second-hand and he'd needed Zilla to stand guarantor when he bought a motorbike on hire purchase. Based on this, he'd either salted away Miss Tester's money for fifteen years and chosen to live in comparative poverty - or he wasn't the killer. Whichever it was, Malcolm Feingold had to be told.

This didn't explain how Joan came by the two other pictures and neither did it answer the pointed question of why, if innocent, John Henry had run away.

As Zilla learned more about Miss Tester, what had been too personal to be just a puzzle became a mystery.

For some unknown reason, this wealthy woman had moved to the dirty back streets of Hulme. And through the auction catalogue, she had a connection with Gloucestershire, the county where John Henry's disinherited mother came from. Was this a coincidence or what Elliot was hinting at?

Of Coleford and the Forest of Dean, Zilla knew little save for it having ancient mine workings and quarries and the oaks from which Britain's great Elizabethan fleet was built.

She hadn't much to go on. But first principles dictated this was where Zilla should start looking for the enigmatic Miss Tester - and maybe even John Henry White himself

*

'Uncle Edgar, you've got to tell me where my Dad's really gone.'

'He's gone on some business somewhere but he's not told us where it is.'

'But he'll be coming back to help Mum, won't he?'

'That's what we all want, son.'

Their train rattled east across England, by factories and fields and taking Spence further away from Zion Street than he'd ever been before. His nervous habit of rapid blinking was becoming more pronounced.

So, too, was Edgar's anger towards John Henry. But that account could only be settled on another day.

'Why must I go to Auntie Evelyn's?'

'Like we've told you, we're all going to be busy. There's no-one to look after you.'

'Not even Miss Arbib?'

'Least of all her. She's even gone sick from work to help your Mum and her solicitor.'

Spence went quiet, disappeared into himself, his eyes full of reproach and hurt. His Dad would've called it dumb insolence but Spence's regard for his opinions diminished a little more each day.

How could he be proud of a father who might come home singing drunk, even hitting drunk, but wasn't there to protect them when it mattered? Even so, somewhere within the bones of the boy was a sense of love for this hopeless, helpless runt of a litter which had only a dubious pedigree anyway. But was what he felt familial love or simply compassion and pity at the sadness of what he saw and understood?

Mature for his years he might have been yet in such a confused state, how would Spence know the difference?

Thirty-Three

Malcolm Feingold read the Evening News report of Joan's second court appearance with professional - and personal - satisfaction.

A solicitor today accused police of using a mentally ill woman like 'cheese in a trap' to trace her husband who is wanted in connection with an alleged suspicious death during Manchester's Christmas Blitz in 1940.

Malcolm Feingold told the city's magistrates that keeping housewife Joan White in custody on a minor charge to allegedly lure him back was 'cruel and unnecessary'.

Mrs White, 38, of Zion Street, Fallowfield, is accused of being in possession of two pictures said to have been stolen during a German bombing raid which killed hundreds of people.

Detective Inspector Vincent Challis told an earlier hearing that he had a warrant for the arrest of Mrs White's husband, John Henry, a van driver and former soldier, who disappeared before he could be questioned.

Detective Inspector Challis objected to bail today, saying his inquiries into the death were still incomplete and that a charge of murder remained likely.

But Mr Feingold said: 'I have not been shown or heard of any evidence to suggest that a charge of murder is sustainable in this matter.

'To use my client like cheese in a trap is both an abuse of process and of power, not least when I am told that she will have an entirely innocent explanation for her possession of the pictures.'

He had a written opinion from Mrs White's psychiatrist saying her mental health had deteriorated so badly in custody that she could barely communicate coherently.

'This makes taking her instructions singularly difficult but meanwhile, I have sworn statements from her closest relations saying they do not know where her husband is and to the best of their knowledge, neither does my client.'

Magistrates granted bail on condition Mrs White lived with her aunts and received urgent medical attention.

Having now observed Challis in action, Feingold saw in him a man often in error but never in doubt, a self-aggrandising *chutzpanik* who'd not hesitate to bend the facts to fit his theories - as he must surely have done in other cases. Challis was a dangerous and potentially vindictive opponent.

Getting bail for Joan was to win a battle, not a war, as Feingold would have told Zilla had he any idea where she might be.

*

Zilla checked in to The Angel Hotel, an old coaching inn on the market place in Coleford and freshened up after her long drive south.

She found the Dean Forest Guardian office in Newland Street, next to Fowler's ironmongery, hung with galvanised buckets, chicken feeders and watering cans. The fumes of paraffin and creosote came on the warm afternoon air

All newspapers had a dingy, out-of-the-way little room called a *morgue* where bound copies from years ago were stored. Here, all that was once fresh and important slowly mouldered into yellowing flakes of newsprint and then to dust.

One of the Guardian's receptionists was arranging that week's window display of published photographs. Zilla told her she was researching family history - which was true - and asked to check some information in the paper during 1928.

The morgue was in an attic in what had been a three-storey town house. It was lit by a bare bulb and the 52 editions from each year since the 1870s were bound in green book cloth and stacked along wooden shelves, bending under their weight.

Zilla knelt on a square of carpet and turned the pages of the 1928 file until she found Friday the 2nd of November. With winter coming, adverts appeared beneath the Guardian's Gothic masthead for rain-proof gabardine coats at twenty five shillings and Beechams Powders to *fight the 'flu*. What Zilla sought was on an inside page - a report of the Provis & Barter auction earlier that week.

She checked the list of who'd bought what but was puzzled to read that the Caernarfon Castle painting hadn't been knocked down to Miss Tester but to a Mrs M.E. Bethel - same initials, different surname.

Her address was shown as Gorsty House, Coleford. The receptionist said it had been a grand place in its day but was converted into a nursing home before the war.

'So were the Bethels important people around here?'

'Not that I remember,' the receptionist said. 'I could check our cuttings library to see if we ever carried a story about them.'

She returned a few minutes later with a brown envelope containing a single item from August 1917.

It is with the greatest regret that the death has been reported of Captain Huw Owen Bethel of the 13th

Glosters during action on the Ypres Salient at Passchendaele.

He originally came from North Wales where he studied mine engineering and moved to the Forest of Dean as a manager with Dean Mines & Quarries Ltd.

Captain Bethel was commissioned in May 1915 and fought with bravery and distinction on the Somme the following year where he survived numerous enemy attacks during trenching and other dangerous operations.

His death is all the more poignant coming as it does just four weeks after his marriage to Miss Maud Elizabeth Tester at Coleford Baptist Church.

Mrs Bethel is the elder daughter of the late Mrs Honoria Tester and Mr M.R.W. Tester, JP, of Gorsty House, Coleford, chairman of Dean Mines & Quarries Ltd.

So Miss Tester *had* bought the picture. And like her cleaner, the Great War had widowed her. She can't have mentioned this or Mrs Turner would surely have said.

These few sad lines explained Miss Tester's wealth if not her decision to revert to her maiden name and leave such gentle, wooded countryside for the back streets of Manchester - and there to die violently in a terrible war, just as her husband had.

But how - if at all - did this fit with John Henry's family secret about his disgraced and disinherited mother?

*

Spence didn't like the look of Auntie Evelyn and sensed she had doubts about him. Her stick-out backside balanced her stick-out chest. One without the other would cause her to topple over.

198

Each of her seemingly boneless bare arms ended in a roll of flesh, not a wrist. Her hair was yellow, straight and fine, her eyes faded blue and set in a face of pinkish dough.

Spence remembered seeing such a face before - in a butcher's shop window with an apple in its mouth.

He and Uncle Edgar were met off the train by Evelyn's husband and driven to their house in his new Jowett Bradford van. It had his name and address painted on the sides - *James McKillop, Furniture Restorer, Lutton Hall, Fenbeach, Lincs.*

'So you're the young brain box we've been hearing all about?' he said. 'It's a good job you've come because I've been needing an apprentice for weeks.'

Spence saw he'd kindly eyes behind his spectacles. His bib and brace overalls smelled of linseed oil and beeswax and he'd a fleck or two of sawdust in his hair, combed straight back and going grey. He sounded northern but Auntie Evelyn spoke like the ladies on the wireless.

Lutton Hall was a mansion with a garden of butterflies, bright flowers and an orchard of apple and pear trees. Spence and Uncle Edgar were led in through a door from the yard where a soft-top MG Midget was parked in a stable by his workshop.

'Like sports cars, do you, Spence?'

'I've never been in one.'

'Then we'll have to put that right, won't we?'

They passed through a small room, cool like a dairy, with a pump by the Belfast sink to draw water from a well beneath the stone-flagged floor. Jars of Evelyn's homemade marmalade, jams and chutneys were arranged on shelves and a set of copper pans hung from hooks in a beam.

Three steps led up to a tiled passageway to the kitchen. Evelyn had laid a table with floral teacups, plates of sandwiches and a cake stand of iced dainties. When they'd eaten, Edgar went to light a Park Drive. Evelyn said if he had to smoke, he must do so outside.

He knew enough about Evelyn's early days to recognise the sleights of hand and conversation she must have deployed locally to obscure her true origins. This meant he couldn't even hint that her brother was wanted by the police, still less for possible murder. Any suggestion of scandal and Evelyn would put Spence on the next train back to Manchester.

It was getting late. Spence was travel tired and Uncle Edgar ruffled his hair in lieu of a goodnight hug and kiss. Uncle Jimmy took him to the attic where two single beds had been made up under the sloping ceiling.

A dormer window was open but the heat of the day remained trapped within. The floorboards sighed one against another and Uncle Jimmy's grandfather clocks chimed and clanged in different parts of the house to mark the passing of another hour.

Spence, barefoot and in pyjamas, went one floor down to brush his teeth in the bathroom above the kitchen. He could hear the grown-ups talking.

'So what's really happening with Joan?'

'Having it rough she is, and that's a fact,' Uncle Edgar said. 'Had a nervous breakdown a while back and went into hospital and now she can barely look after herself, let alone anyone else.'

'So that's why the rent hasn't been paid,' Auntie Evelyn said. 'I always thought Joan was off her head to marry my no-good brother. But why can't he take care of her and the boy?'

'That's the trouble, you see... we don't know where he is.'

'I don't follow.'

'I mean he's scarpered, disappeared. No-one knows where.'

'But why would he clear off when his family needs him?' Uncle Jimmy said.

'Because my brother's never shouldered his responsibilities.'

'Always seemed like a decent bloke to me.'

'That's because you're too softhearted, Jimmy. John Henry is a waster, always was and always will be.'

'I'd look after the lad but I'm going into hospital myself,' Uncle Edgar said. 'Our Kitty and Emily aren't as young as they were and Joan's sister works full time so it'll really help us by you having him for a bit.'

'We'll be glad to,' Uncle Jimmy said. 'It'll be good having a youngster around.'

'John Henry is the only one in my family who's turned out a failure,' Auntie Evelyn said. 'The only one who's not made something of his life like the rest of us.'

Spence pulled the lavatory chain. He knew all she said was true but didn't want to hear any more. For all his faults, his Dad was his Dad. And his Mum wasn't off her head. Miss Arbib said so. Anyway, it was wrong to listen to other people's conversations. You only ever heard them say bad things.

*

Zilla drove to Gorsty House where Miss Tester might have expected to live a long and happy life with her husband, raise children and be proud of all they would become and all they might achieve.

But the madness of men had different plans.

The house could once have been a large Victorian rectory, painted creamy white with tall windows and a glass veranda along one side where invalid residents in bath chairs and blankets took naps in the sunshine.

A sentient few looked up as Zilla pulled into the drive, each hoping it was a visitor for them. She got out of her car and gazed at the landscaped lawns and specimen cedars. The contrast to Miss Tester's final surroundings couldn't have been starker.

Zilla was spotted by the matron who came across.

'Hello, giving us the once over?'

'I beg your pardon?'

'People often look around if they're considering placing a loved one with us.'

'And I'm sure they're impressed by all they see but that's not why I've come.'

'Is it about a resident, then?'

'No, a former resident I suppose, a lady who lived here before it was a nursing home.'

'Really? Who was that?'

'She was a Mrs Bethel but her maiden name was Tester, Maud Elizabeth Tester.'

'Are you a relation of hers?'

'No, but I'm researching Miss Tester's family history for a good friend of mine.'

'Then you've come to the right place,' the matron said. 'Our Miss Pont is the very person you should be talking to.'

'Why's that?'

'Because Miss Pont was in service at Gorsty House until the original owners sold up.'

'So she could've known Maud Elizabeth?'

'Almost certain to and now she's back here but not as a servant. It's funny how our lives can turn out, isn't it?'

Thirty-Four

It was the oddest sensation Spence could ever remember experiencing - setting foot in a place where he had never been but which somehow seemed familiar. He couldn't explain his primitive sense of return as he walked onto the desolate wallow of marsh. The first instinct of the child within was to run into the waving reeds, arms outstretched like wings, to fly across the creeks and the shining mud flats and to the very sea itself.

But some impulse stopped him; a feeling that he was meant to be there that morning for a reason yet to be revealed.

Uncle Jimmy had fettled up a second-hand bike for him and put a chocolate bar and a bottle of Vimto in the saddlebag.

'You enjoy yourself, kiddo,' he said. 'See you when you get back.'

Spence rode away between swaying expanses of corn and barley and the stubble of that already harvested waiting to be burned off. He did not know where he was going until he arrived.

And then he lay on his back beneath luffing clouds crossing the infinite blue of the heavens. All was quiet save for the calling, falling curlews, blown by winds from lands far away.

He imagined them looking down on the solitary figure that was Spencer William White, a boy at the edge of his known world.

He wished the pictures in his head would leave him - his mother, collapsed in her own blood, the hangman taking her away, Uncle Edgar confessing he'd caused the death of his son by killing another man's child.

Nothing taught by school or church had prepared him for his parts in these dramas, those of adults whose words and strengths he'd never doubted until they took him behind the scenery and he saw the illusion for what it was. Now, they'd exiled him to this wild and remote place.

Under this sun and these skies, where was his mother, where was his father? He could not be sure of anything except that the certainties of Zion Street were no more. Was that the moment he knew that if he were to gain the prizes Miss Arbib foretold, he had to put away childish things and by so doing, accept that in life, grief comes to all and evil to some?

*

Hilda Pont had tidied away any unpleasantness from her time of servitude at Gorsty House and now commanded the very drawing room where she had waited on the ghosts still flitting across her memory.

New residents were required to hear her stories of how the Tester household ran during the grand pre-war years - the elegant supper parties, the county's social elite discussing great political issues of the day, *Madam* as the beautiful hostess, *Sir* in his pomp and the epitome of a beneficent Christian employer to those who toiled above and below ground to create his fortune.

Zilla listened as others had, imagining goblets of brandy, drifting cigar smoke and the chauffeured Lagondas and Daimlers, bonnets polished, engines bubbling, waiting in the moonlit drive to take guests home.

'Such times they were,' Miss Pont said. 'It was so lovely to be part of it.'

Miss Pont smiled and swept imaginary specks from her plain blue skirt with hands afflicted by arthritis.

She spoke with an engaging Gloucestershire burr and had the features of a pot doll, shiny and rouged but with hair so thinned by age that her scalp showed through, pink and clean.

She'd been buoyed up with pride to be consulted by a visiting academic and expressed genuine sorrow when told of Maud Elizabeth's death in an air raid.

'A brilliantly clever person,' she said. 'But the whole family were highly intelligent.'

'How awful for her to lose her husband so soon after they were married.'

'Yes, a tragedy, heart-breaking. Miss Maud was never the same again.'

'In what way was that?'

'Never lost the sadness in her face. 'Course, they couldn't have a funeral. His body wasn't found and that made it worse, her never being sure if he'd come back or not.'

'Did she have a job, a profession?'

'Kept the books for her father's firms, had a head for commerce like him.'

'He must have been a very influential man around here.'

'He was that all right, until the Great Depression that is. He'd such debts then that his businesses went under and they said his death was brought about by all the strain.'

'So they had to sell this lovely old house?'

'And everything in it, antiques, carpets, pots and pans, the lot. I came back when it was empty and it was like I'd only ever dreamed I'd worked here for all those years.'

Zilla steered the conversation to the Provis & Barter auction and brought out the firm's catalogue with its picture of the Caernarfon Castle painting. Miss Pont pushed her wire-framed spectacles onto her head and held the page closer to her face.

'Oh, yes,' she said. 'I remember this one so well. Miss Maud's favourite, this was, hung opposite her bed so she could always see it.'

'Why was she so fond of it?'

'Why? Because that's where they went on honeymoon, her and Captain Huw, near Caernarfon. He was a Welshman, you see.'

Zilla described Joan's two prints but Gorsty House had so many pictures on its walls in those days that Miss Pont couldn't recall them.

'And what of the rest of the family? Did Miss Maud have brothers, sisters?'

'Just a sister.'

'What can you tell me about her?'

'Not a lot, I'm afraid.'

'Before your time in service here, was she?'

'I knew of her but what do you want to be asking questions about that one for?'

'Only to build a clearer picture of Miss Maud's upbringing and her family.'

'Well, there're some things they wouldn't want mentioned, I can tell you.'

'What sort of things do you mean?'

'Private matters, nothing to do with anyone else.'

'What in particular, though?'

'I wouldn't know, I'm sure.'

Miss Pont looked away, didn't want Zilla catching her eye. The old lady was raised to tell the truth and shame the devil. Zilla thought the witness needed to be led at this point.

'Maybe Miss Maud's sister getting pregnant out of wedlock?' she said. 'Might that be something they'd want to keep quiet?'

206

Miss Pont drew breath through her nose and sat up straight, bridling at such a wicked slander - or because this stranger had uncovered the family's secret.

'You must have heard about it, Miss Pont. Such a scandal would've surely caused gossip below stairs for years afterwards.'

'No good ever comes of gossip. I never heed it and you oughtn't to, either.'

Miss Pont's loyalties were offended. But sometimes, what isn't said reveals more than what is. She'd as good as confirmed John Henry's story about his disgraced mother. Challis's murder victim must have been Harriet Rose's sister.

Joan could have known Maud and been given the two prints as a gift. Zilla would phone Malcolm Feingold directly she got back to her hotel. He needed to judge if what she'd discovered helped Joan.

'I'm truly sorry if this is upsetting for you,' Zilla said. 'But just tell me why Maud went to live in Manchester when her sister was long dead by then?'

'How should I know?' she said. 'Anyway, the gong for afternoon tea will go shortly and I'm never one to be late.'

*

Uncle Jimmy was in his workshop when Spence got back; bent over an antique rosewood table, glasses on the tip of his nose, dust in his wiry grey eyebrows, repairing damage to a delicate inlay with satinwood and holly.

'Enjoyed yourself, kiddo?'

'Went to the marshes,' Spence said. 'I've never been anywhere like that before.'

'Be careful how far you go out, though. Treacherous, if you don't know them.'

His tools were oiled and sharp, arrayed by size and purpose above the bench. On the shelves by the lathe were mouldings and patterns and air-drying on a rack in the roof space, lengths of maple, mahogany, walnut, cherry, ebony.

Here was order and method. Spence was warming to him - if not his wife. He remembered Mum saying Evelyn conveniently forgot her own beginnings, steaming salted water by an open window so neighbours might think they'd money for a roast and two veg.

'All front, that Evelyn,' she'd said.

But Uncle Jimmy was open and honest and talked to Spence about the news and grown-up matters. Auntie Evelyn might stand for Fenbeach Council. Lutton Hall was in a poor state when they bought and renovated it just after the war. And they didn't just own all Zion Street but five houses in Rusholme, three in Withington and one in Didsbury. Fourteen properties and all that rent - but no children.

'Come on, kiddo. Fancy a spin in the old MG?'

Thirty minutes later and the little crimson car was barrelling down a ruler-straight fenland road at seventy miles an hour. Rooks flapped up from the fields as they passed and the wind made tails of Spence's hair.

He was too excited to be scared. Uncle Jimmy braked, turned round by a field gate and told Spence to sit on his lap.

'Put your hands on the wheel, I'll steer but you'll feel what it's like to drive fast.'

They headed home with Spence laughing and whooping and his uncle happier than he'd been for years, too.

*

Evelyn was flower arranging at Fenbeach church but had left them a cold ham and salad supper. Propped against a vase of flowers on the big kitchen table were two letters for Spence.

'Looks like you've got some news from the home front, kiddo.'

Spence recognised Auntie Kitty's handwriting - a bit chaotic and up and down like her. Inside the envelope was a postal order for five shillings and a note scribbled in pencil.

A little birdie gave me a dead cert on the gee-gees the other day so I put a few bob on for both of us and here's your share. You go to the Post Office and cash it and buy yourself some toffees and a treat. Take care of yourself and come back to us soon. All my love, Auntie Kit.

'Who's the other one from, Spence?'

'It's my Mum's writing so she must be home.'

Hello love, I'm settling in at 35 once more and everyone is being so kind as you would expect. Anyway, I'm well on the road to recovery so you mustn't worry about a thing. Uncle Edgar had a good journey back on the train and everyone here sends their love. They're all missing you but not as much as me. It's very kind of Evelyn and Jimmy to give you this little holiday so be good for them and keep out of trouble. Lots and lots of kisses from Mum.

'Well, that sounds like Joan's on the right track at last,' Uncle Jimmy said. 'Does she say anything else?'

Spence took a moment, pretending to re-read her last sentence. Then he smiled across the table at his uncle.

'She says my Dad is still working away on an important job but he'll be home before we know it and then everything will be back to how it was.'

Thirty-Five

Lady Barn Hotel, Fallowfield, Sunday 18th January 2015

Judge White woke from an uneasy doze on the settee in his room. A file of statements he'd been reading had slipped from his lap onto the carpet and the tea in his cup was cold.

Car headlights swept the slicked black road beyond the sealed window and passengers could be glimpsed briefly within the illuminated buses passing by, then were gone into the rainy night. White craved their anonymity, never more so now the media launch of *his* public inquiry was only eight days away.

Elspeth would expect a call but he had nothing he wanted to say. Absence wasn't guaranteed to make the heart grow fonder. It was almost seven o'clock. He ought to wash then go down for supper.

The face in the mirror above the bathroom sink was that of a prisoner clinging to the rail, soon to be condemned by the gods of hubris.

How could he have let conceit outbid caution? How could chairing a politically fraught inquiry in front of TV cameras, journalists and a hostile public, be comparable to judging a criminal case within the privacy and protocols of a crown court?

When he'd met the other panel members - a retired female chief constable, a solicitor of Asian heritage and a regional newspaper editor - they deferred to him as if he were some respected grey eminence from afar.

But he was drowning, not waving. Behind the practised charm was a re-occurrence of the same fever of self-doubt and insecurity he'd suffered in childhood and at Oxford. Only much later, in the theatrical disguises of the judiciary, did he find the assurance to play the role and say the lines. His was performance art. But it required the audience to remain in their seats and never to seek or audit the motives of the character within.

*

The Lady Barn was a discreet boutique hotel with a restaurant offering a half decent menu. White chose a first course of mousse au Camembert and a main of pintade chasseur with a bottle of Pinot Noir - anything to help him sleep.

The restaurant was busy for a Sunday evening though not full. A CD by Edith Piaf played but not intrusively. White finished the starter and a waiter poured him a second glass. His guinea fowl came with a dish of glazed carrots and cauliflower with apple.

He became conscious of other diners pausing to look up as a woman entered the room and spoke to the maitre d'hotel. She was svelte, early thirties, wearing jeans with a blue silk jacket and moved with the catwalk confidence of someone who knew she turned heads. It alarmed White that she was heading straight towards him.

'Judge White?'

He half stood up, napkin to his mouth. There was something familiar about her face but no one should have known where he was staying.

'I hope you don't mind if I join you for a minute or two.'

'I'm sorry, we haven't met before, have we?'

'No, I don't think so. I'm Sophie Bartells from Channel 4 News.'

That's where he'd seen her - and in photographs attached to the who-was-who briefing paper put together by Dan Luston. He should have remembered.

'Ah yes, I know of you,' White said. 'I'm sorry to appear rude but I can't possibly talk to you or any journalist at the moment for reasons I know you'll appreciate.'

'That's all right, I'll do most of the talking. It's off the record anyway, Lobby rules and all that.'

She sat herself down, elbows on the table between them, chin resting on her clasped hands, smiling and sure he wouldn't want to make a scene. The waiter came across and unasked, poured her a glass of White's Pinot Noir.

'Thank you,' she said. 'L'chayim.'

She touched her glass against his. White felt cornered - but registered the envious glances of men at tables nearby.

'How did you find out I was staying here?'

'Would you believe I rang your wife and she told me?'

'Yes... unfortunately, I would.'

'But hiding away in Fallowfield of all places? What's that about?'

'Only that I have a mass of papers to read so prefer somewhere quiet and out of the city centre so I can concentrate.'

'Understandably... your inquiry is vitally important. It's a story I've gone out on a limb to investigate so I suppose I've got a vested interest in you getting to the truth.'

'You mean you haven't got to the truth?'

'Journalists have no right of access to official documents and they can't compel witnesses to reveal what they know so without a whistle-blower, we're usually on the outside looking in.'

'And you believe people in my position always get the whole picture, do you?'

'I'd like to think so but is that naive of me?'

It was White's turn to smile. He refilled their glasses and waited for her next pitch.

'What I don't understand is why the Tories are having this inquiry in the run-up to the general election that's going to be bumpy enough for them as it is,' Bartells said.

'They must have their reasons.'

'Yes, but the three deaths you'll be looking at happened over a two year period but just in this last year alone, there were seventeen deaths in police custody nationally. Why haven't the authorities acted before now?'

'I can't answer for them, I'm afraid.'

'You must know that most of these victims were schizophrenics or otherwise mentally ill or they've had drug or alcohol problems yet they've been restrained to death by police officers and no-one's ever held responsible.'

'I'm sure this is something my inquiry will look into.'

'That and also all the official evasion and obstruction their families have faced when they've tried to find out what really happened?'

The waiter returned. White declined a dessert but asked for coffee for them both.

'And maybe a drop more of the Pinot Noir?' Bartells said. 'You don't mind, do you?'

White had little direct experience of journalists and their wiles and ways. But being shmoozed by one so rampantly ambitious yet effortlessly beguiling - and with chutzpah to spare - flattered the last bit of his male ego yet to die off. That apart, he was fully aware she was young enough to be the daughter he never had.

'The moment this inquiry's over, I'd really like to interview you for Channel 4 News.'

'I'm sure you would, but I'm not one for publicity.'

'It's a bit late for that now. You're going to get it whether you like it or not and if you don't mind me saying, the trick is to do just the one big interview with someone you can trust.'

'Like you, you mean?'

'Of course, and unlike the rest of them, I know the real significance of this story and the serious wrongs that your report and recommendations could put right.'

'You have to appreciate that I've never sought the limelight.'

'That much I know. I've hardly been able to uncover anything about you.'

'So you've tried, have you?'

Bartells laughed and refilled his glass.

'I know you got a first at Keble, defended rather than prosecuted, became a judge twenty years ago and lean Left if you lean any way at all. But no-one seems sure why you didn't chuck this hot potato right back where it came from.... so why was that?'

'I'm sorry, but we're crossing a line here. I've enjoyed meeting you and no doubt we'll see each other again in the course of the coming months but I simply can't enter into any sort of dialogue that would prejudice the inquiry. You see that, don't you?'

'Absolutely, of course I do,' Bartells said. 'Look, this is my card, all my contact information's on there and I've scribbled my home address and number on the back. You never know but there are times when we all need friends at court.'

*

Against expectations, Judge White had enjoyed the evening with his uninvited guest. He rarely met people who weren't stuffy or fawningly deferential. Lawyers charged by the minute - some by the word - so had little incentive to get to the point. Sophie Bartells knew what she wanted and from whom to get it. He looked again at her home address and could scarcely believe the coincidence. But he was tired and slightly tipsy. That night, he slept better than he had for a while... until he woke in the early hours, wondering why she'd toasted him in Hebrew and mentioned Fallowfield so pointedly. How deep had she *really* been digging?

Thirty-Six

Bootle Street Police Station, Manchester, Wednesday 2nd September 1955

It was migraine weather - oppressive, slate grey clouds dragging over the humid city like wet sacks. Mid-morning and it was dark enough for cars to need headlights. Thunder rolled in from the Pennines and with it, a deluge guttering off roofs and overwhelming drains as shoppers ran for cover.

Challis looked down from his office window. A flood, a screaming baby at home and a dyspeptic boss. The head of CID had just had him in to demand a sit-rep on what progress - if any - Challis was making with his wartime murder investigation.

'I've backed you this far,' the superintendent said. 'But our own legal people think you should wind your neck back in with the suspect's wife.'

'But she's the key to nabbing him.'

'No, Vincent. She's a very sick woman. I'm told on good authority that if we don't drop the charge on some sort of technicality, her brief is planning to crucify us in the Sunday papers when it's all over.'

'Believe me, Sir, John Henry White is a killer.'

'So you keep saying.'

'Just give me a little more time.'

'You've got a week, and if you ever catch this blighter, charge *him* with stealing the pictures. Meanwhile, I don't care how you do it but just get his wife off the hook - and me, for that matter.'

White had to be caught before Challis lost face completely. Some smart arse had already pinned up a cartoon in CID showing Hitler with the words *...wanted for murder. If seen, call Mr Challis urgently.*

He rang Gormley in Special Branch and fixed a meet in criminal records. There was nothing to report from Zilla Arbib's phone.

'It's been inactive for days, no calls in, no calls out.'

'That figures,' Challis said. 'She's not at work or at home and I'll bet the farm she's helping that bastard White in some way.'

'You've still no other leads?'

'No, someone's hiding him and if I don't find him soon, I'll be directing traffic in bloody Deansgate.'

'All right, I'll keep listening but if upstairs find out that I'm busting the rules for you, they'll have me back in a big hat, too.'

*

The chatelaine of Lutton Hall greeted Zilla with exuberant warmth.

'Hello, I'm Evelyn. You're most welcome, do come in.'

Zilla would've arrived two days earlier but the gearbox on her Sunbeam convertible developed a fault and the garage in Coleford had to send away for parts. She'd phoned Vron at work and was told Spence was missing his family.

'Evelyn felt he seemed quite introverted when I rang her,' Vron said.

'As soon as my car's fixed, I'll motor over there and try to reassure him that he'll be coming home before long.'

Lutton Hall was Georgian, three storeys, faced in ashlar with Virginia creeper twisting up its symmetrical frontage but neatly squared off around the sash windows. Evelyn delighted in showing Zilla some of the ground floor rooms. She had a good eye for period furniture - a pot board dresser with spice drawers, a chest in burr elm, a small marquetry kneehole desk decorated with flowers and floral sprays.

There were too many paintings to take in at a glance - oils and watercolours of landscapes, ships, portraits of plump girls and lean horses. On the floor, oriental carpets and kilims, all richly patterned. New money had bought old objects but Zilla never derided ambition. Evelyn deserved credit for having journeyed so far from the back streets wherein her brother and his family were still trapped.

'What a beautiful house, so tasteful,' Zilla said.

Evelyn smiled and guided Zilla into the cool of the drawing room. It was a hot, windless day. The fleshy pink creases of Evelyn's *décolletage* glistened slightly.

A plate of smoked salmon with slices of lemon and brown bread was laid out on a faded oak table. Evelyn offered Assam tea but Zilla preferred water.

'I'm afraid my husband won't be with us until later,' Evelyn said. 'He's taken Spence to Boston to collect some antique or other which needs restoring.'

'That's good. Spence will enjoy that. Is he any happier?'

'It's difficult for me to say because Jimmy and I don't really know him or how he is normally but he can seem remote, able to live within himself.'

'Yes, he can do that but witnessing his mother's deterioration up close has affected him badly. He's seen things no child should.'

'I gather from Edgar and Vron that she's not much better and she's living with them.'

'Yes, and that's involved more disruption for Spence and really hasn't helped.'

'How do you mean?'

'Well, he was due to start at Manchester Grammar School but it's felt that this should be put back for another term to give life at home a chance to get back to normal.'

'Manchester Grammar? That clever, is he?'

'Indeed he is. I teach at the university and I've students who aren't as mature or gifted as Spence. To have his understanding of concepts and ideas at that age is remarkable. Not only that, his written and verbal skills reflect an intuitive ability to analyse information so I haven't any doubt he's Oxbridge material.'

'Seems like you've rather taken him under your wing.'

'It'd be a crime not to encourage such talent, whether one is a teacher or a parent.'

'Joan's a good person, of course, but I think I know where Spence gets his brains from, even if my brother missed out on his share.'

'Have you any thoughts as to where he might be?'

'None whatsoever,' Evelyn said. 'Have you any idea why he's disappeared?'

Zilla shook her head. The truth - like any discussion of why she'd been in Coleford or of the uncomfortable facts she'd unearthed about Evelyn's family - was more wisely left for a day yet to dawn.

*

It was a struggle but Kitty finally persuaded Joan to have an outing to Platt Fields with her. Everyone at 35 feared Joan's retreat into herself, her excuses to not even sit in the back garden, her lack of interest in her appearance.

'We need a blow of fresh air, our Joan. A little treat for us both.'

They strolled arm in arm round the lake, not hurrying, just mingling with mothers and prams, watching couples in skiffs and kids playing in the sunshine.

Joan's doctor had prescribed tablets to ward off her depression. They worked to an extent but dulled her reactions. She found it hard to keep up with conversations and often just smiled in lieu of offering an opinion. But leaving the park, Joan asked the question uppermost in her mind.

'They'll be back soon, won't they, Auntie Kit?'

'Who, love?'

'Spence and John Henry.'

'Of course they will. Only gone for a few days. You just concentrate on getting better for when they come home.'

'They'll need feeding and I'll have beds to make and washing to do.'

'It's all taken care of. We're seeing to everything, don't you worry about a thing.'

They bought fish and chips and ate them from newspaper as they walked back into Fallowfield village then crossed over the main road to Estelle Modes.

'See anything you like, love?'

Joan looked at all the post-austerity fashions coming out of London and Paris, the flared skirts and bright, colourful tops which recalled the world before the war. She pointed to a plain cotton dress, red with white dots. Kitty led her inside. An assistant tried not to show she'd caught a waft of vinegar from their fingers.

'How might I help you ladies today?'

'We want that dress there,' Kitty said. 'It's got to be in a size to fit my niece.'

'You know it's nine guineas, do you?'

'That's all right, love. I've brought my purse.'

She set down the cash on the counter and smiled as the assistant wrapped Joan's present. Joan stood in a state of child-like grace and smiled, too.

'You're so kind, Auntie Kit.'

'Don't mention it. You've got to put your best side out in this life.'

'How did you come by all that money?'

'By picking a winner, love. Came home against all the odds, just like our Spence and John Henry will.'

*

'I want to go back, Miss Arbib. I want to be with Mum, to help her.'

'Of course you do, Spence. Everyone understands that but she's still not herself and if you go back too soon, she'll fret even more.'

'No she wouldn't, she'd be happy to see me.'

'Yes, but she'd want to look after you like she used to and she's really not well enough to do that yet which is why she's having to take it easy with your aunts at 35.'

They were a mile or so from Lutton Hall in a lane adrift with cow parsley and moon daisies. The sun was high and gave the lead-covered spire of Fenbeach parish church a look of cloudy silver. Away in the distance, the fields had seemingly turned to liquid in the shimmering heat.

For a boy with a bike, from there to the marshes was the freedom to roam from breakfast to bedtime. Yet this wasn't what Spence wanted - not that day. Zilla hated letting him down.

'I know it's hard, Spence, but it won't be for that long.'

'How long, then?'

'I don't know for sure.'

'Can I come back when my Dad gets back?'

'I'm sure you can, Spence. Just give us all a bit more time.'

Spence withdrew into himself and they walked back to the house in silence.

*

Zilla slipped beneath the warm water of Lutton Hall's baptismal iron bath. It was a moment of cleansing, of purification on a day when circumstances required the truth to hide its face.

She dried her hair and put on slacks and a fair isle sweater. Evelyn said it'd be a simple supper in the kitchen. Zilla went quietly into the attic room she was sharing with Spence. He was asleep but even in the half-light, she could see the tear stains on his unwashed face.

In the drawer of his bedside cabinet was the notebook in which she'd urged him to write stories or his thoughts while at Lutton Hall. The temptation to read his last entry was too great to resist.

My comics and films at the pictures make war look clean so there is no blood or pain and the soldiers die straight away but this is not the truth. Uncle Edgar says that war makes men lose their reason. He has always been very gentle to me but he has killed hundreds of men, worse than the worst murderer ever caught. But he would not have become a killer unless for the war and what he did all those years ago is still clear to him and because of this, I don't think he minds if he joins Auntie Frances soon. It makes me very sad because Uncle Edgar is the only person who makes me feel safe.

Spence would never lose his power to touch Zilla's soul. She went quietly downstairs and joined Evelyn and Jimmy.

'Gone off all right, has he?'

'Yes, he's well away. Must be tired from his day out.'

'It's a rotten time for a sensitive lad like Spence,' Jimmy said. 'But I'm enjoying his company so he can stay as long as he wants.'

Evelyn poured three glasses of her own elderflower cordial to complement the salad, cold chicken and buttered potatoes she'd prepared.

'Anyway, here's hoping Joan will soon be able to have her boy back,' he said.

Two floors above them, Spence would've agreed with his uncle's toast. But at that moment, he was on his knees rifling through Zilla's handbag and luggage for what he needed for his great escape back to Zion Street.

Thirty-Seven

Mercy Cottage could have been imagined and drawn by a child - four windows, green front door with a porch, smoking chimney and flowers in the garden. It was set in the black earth of land reclaimed from the sea centuries before and built with its gable end to the prevailing wind from the marsh.

Spence had sometimes seen a Bedford lorry parked in the yard. It belonged to the Fenbeach Farmers' Co-operative and took fruit and vegetables to markets north and south. The man who lived at Mercy Cottage did the run to Manchester. Uncle Jimmy said so. But the morning when Spence wanted the lorry to be there, it wasn't.

He still knocked on the door. There was no reply but he heard a baby crying inside. Spence went round to the back garden. A woman was hanging out nappies. She was younger than his Mum and wore her gingery hair tucked under a headscarf.

'Hello, are you lost?'

'No, I've come to see the man who drives for the Farmers' Co-op.'

'That's my husband but he's in hospital.'

'But he drives to Manchester, doesn't he?'

'When he's not having his appendix out, yes.'

'I'd like to go with him. I've got some money, I can pay him.'

'Do your parents know about what you want to do?'

'Yes, they live in Manchester and they want me back so I can start a new school.'

Spence had witnessed grown-ups dissembling so he knew the basics. The woman hoisted a prop under the line and her baby's nappies surrendered to the breeze.

'So what are you doing round here?'

'I've been on holiday.'

'Whereabouts are you staying?'

'In Fenbeach, with my auntie and uncle.'

'And do they know about this trip you're planning?'

'Not yet but they're always saying I must use my initiative so I'll tell them tonight.'

'Well, make sure you do and then you can come back next week and my husband should be here then.'

Spence rode off, disappointed at this delay but sure he'd be home soon. Once at Manchester market, he would catch a bus - or walk - to Grenville Road then watch his Mum's face light up. No one who wanted her to get better could say that wouldn't help.

He made for a part of the marsh where he'd not been before. It had that same emptiness and desolation he was going to miss but that morning, he sensed a difference, almost a shift in its mood.

Gulls cried through the air as they ever did and the turbid creeks still pretended no harm. But autumn was being carried in on a keener wind. Plumes of grey smoke rose on the horizon from burning stubble fields soon to be ploughed and re-sown. It wouldn't be long before leaves on the stunted trees along the drovers' lanes went yellow. Seasons turned on the passing of a day. Here, and in the sighing, dying reeds hung with the borted webs of spiders, were a thousand tiny worlds within a world. Spence could start to appreciate Miss Arbib's *true order of things,* the transient cycle of life and death, change and renewal.

'We are in a permanent state of *becoming*,' she'd said. 'It is a condition of living but nothing that occurs does so in isolation. We all exist subject to this natural law but remember, Spence, every action has a reaction and inescapable consequences.'

He had waved her off from Lutton Hall after breakfast. She told him to put on an extra jumper and that she was going to post his books and school exercises soon. 'That brain of yours needs feeding,' she said. 'Then it can work even harder.'

She'd stroked his hair and hugged him to her as a mother might. Yet he'd robbed her without a thought only a few hours before. He sat down on the grass with that which wasn't his - a pound note, a ten shilling note, three shillings and sixpence in change, a Players cigarette from a packet of twenty, and a box of matches.

What he'd done was wrong - stealing, going through her handbag, reading her private papers. It was a sin and he would have to confess it one day. Yet a greater good was being served. Miss Arbib would surely understand. He'd get a Saturday job and pay her back.

First, he would smoke her cigarette. He'd always wanted to know why adults liked smoking and even practised doing it with a pencil in front of a mirror. Now, he'd got the real thing between his fingers.

He struck a match but the wind blew it out. Only on the fourth attempt did he succeed and inhaled as he'd seen Uncle Edgar doing. And in that sea-salted, earthy air, each draw gave him a sensation of pleasure he'd never experienced before. It rolled through his head, relaxed his limbs and he forgot, if only for those moments, the guilt he felt for abusing Miss Arbib's trust.

He threw the stub into the creek by where he sat. The sun glinted off something metallic in the tall grasses beyond a creek thirty yards away. A man in camouflage fatigues, all browns, greens and yellows, was standing as still as a heron, as if he were of the marsh himself. Under his right arm was a shotgun with

226

two barrels - and he was staring across at Spence. Who was he? What had he seen?

Spence quickly pocketed the stolen money and ran. The man shouted for him to come back but he was in a panic. Rather than ride to Lutton Hall and be followed and identified, he left his bike where it was near the causeway. He made instead for a brick and concrete bunker out towards the sea. It looked like a wartime observation post and a safe place to hide.

He kept running, jumping across the tributaries between the endless islands of spongy grass and sedge. Only when he got closer to the building did he realise it was the other side of a seam of sinking mud and couldn't be reached.

Spence had never been out that far before and could even see the sleek grey heads of seals bobbing in the water. He might have turned back then - and should have done. But he chose to keep out of sight, to lie down and be soothed by the elemental music of the marsh - the shushing of the sea and the wind moving through the reeds which enclosed him.

Then did he sleep? Did he fly as if in a painting by Chagall and look down at his tortured mother or observe his uncle, sitting alone on a bench in Platt Fields, smoking and thinking? And where in all that world of dreams might he have searched for his father? But the tide was turning as the moon ordained it must. Right across that vast sweep of marsh, the narrow creeks Spence had leapt so easily began to fill and become wider and deeper with every minute that passed.

*

The boy's safety concerned Alfred Poucher. He had watched him several times before, wandering the marsh on his own with no particular purpose.

227

Poucher had recovered the bodies of many a one like him, awed by the bleak beauty of the place but unable to read the sea or the sky and understand what was foretold.

He returned to his shack to launch the punt in which he took wildfowlers shooting. The relentless current swirled up the main channel and it was an effort to paddle against it.

Poucher's worry - as always - was the weather. Autumn mist could roll in from the North Sea in a matter of minutes and if it did, he'd need more than good fortune to find the boy.

He listened for anyone shouting for help. Only the gulls replied so he began calling out himself. Still nothing. He steered along one of the smaller creeks. A movement in the reeds caught his eye but it was a duck or a rat, not a skinny kid in grey pants.

Poucher stood up to get a better view. And where the marsh met the sea, he saw something like a red flag being held aloft. It was the boy waving his jumper. It took another five minutes before Spence could clamber into the punt, shivering with fear and cold, his trousers and sandals wet and muddy.

'You've the luck of the devil, boy,' Poucher said. 'Another half hour and you'd be a gonna. This marsh will swallow man and beast alike so you'd best be mindful of that in future.'

Spence was ferried back to the man's shack. It was built of tarred boards, metal sheeting and patched here and there with tarpaulin. Inside, it was dark and smelled of seaweed and the remains of creatures Poucher killed, cooked and ate. He lit his paraffin stove to boil a kettle of water and to dry off Spence's clothes. Then he made a pot of tea and put plenty of sugar in a cup for Spence.

'This'll steady you, boy,' he said. 'Now, you wait here. I'm going to fetch someone.'

Spence had been sure he was going to die. How odd that he should owe his life to the old man who'd scared him.

He had eyes of the palest green as if the sea had washed out all their colour. His hands were the claws of a hunter, rough and powerful with nails like ivory talons, dirty underneath, yet they had pulled Spence from his grave.

The tea warmed him. He stopped shaking. His eyes adjusted to the dimness and he saw a table with an oil lamp and a Bible, two chairs, a camp bed and a few pots and pans on a shelf above a food safe in the corner.

But dominating all was an easel with a half-finished painting of a skein of geese flying across the marsh at first light. The old man was an artist.

He came back after twenty minutes with a woman carrying a baby in her arms. It was the lady whose husband drove the lorry to Manchester. She smiled at Spence and asked if he was all right. He nodded and thanked her.

'My goodness, but your guardian angel has been extra busy today,' she said. 'You must have been so terrified.'

Spence blinked through his silence and that was answer enough.

'Well, thank the Lord that Mr Poucher came along when he did.'

She put her baby on the bed and pulled up a chair close to Spence.

'Now, I know this has been a terrible ordeal for you but if you're feeling up to it, I'd like you to tell me your name and where you're from and where you're staying.'

Spence answered most of her questions but was wary enough to keep back the truth about why he was on holiday. Then she told him she was the district correspondent for the local paper.

'I send in stories and I want to write one about you being rescued,' she said.

'You'll be a celebrity, boy,' Mr Poucher said. 'Everyone reads the Free Press.'

'I'd also like to take your photograph with Mr Poucher in his punt. Can I do that?'

*

The following Tuesday's Free Press would carry a picture-story of Spence's great adventure on the front page under the headline *MARSH RESCUE DRAMA*.

A schoolboy was minutes away from drowning on Drove End marshes when local artist and wildfowling guide Alfred Poucher saved him from the incoming tide.

Spencer White, who will be eleven this week, is on holiday from Manchester and staying with his aunt and uncle, Mr and Mrs James McKillop of Lutton Hall, Fenbeach. He got into difficulties while exploring the marsh on his own.

Luckily, Mr Poucher, 75, had seen Spencer earlier and set off in his punt to search for him. He said: 'Visitors don't realise how dangerous these marshes can be.'

Spencer said: 'I've learned my lesson.'

Mr Poucher, of Curlew Cottage, Drove End, is in Holland this week, exhibiting his wildlife paintings as part of an exchange with Fenbeach's twin town, Zandvoort.

*

Alfred Poucher was right about the Lincolnshire Free Press's circulation. The paper went into twenty thousand homes every week. One such was that of 'Pep' Tomelty, a mechanic of Seas End Drove and a former army private.

Against the wishes of Mrs Tomelty, he was giving shelter to an old comrade in trouble. Had she known this friend was wanted for a possible murder, Mrs Tomelty would have gone to a phone box and told the police where he was.

Thirty-Eight

Police Museum, Newton Street, Manchester, Monday 26th January 2015

'Ladies and gentlemen, thank you for coming this morning. I'm Judge Spencer White and I hope you've all had a chance to read your press briefings regarding the purpose and scope of this inquiry into the deaths in police custody of three men here in Manchester. As far as today goes, I am content to answer general questions but I will not be giving any one-to-one interviews at this stage in the proceedings.'

White took a sip of water and eyed the opposition - four camera crews, two photographers and five newspaper reporters, one of whom wore a tie and looked like he wasn't sleeping rough.

Dan Luston stood at the back, silky fair hair, sober dark suit, waiting with arms folded for his big production to start. It was certainly not White's idea to stage the press conference in the reconstructed Victorian courtroom at the city's Police Museum.

'We have to make sure the TV people get interesting pictures,' Luston said. 'That'll give us a better chance of making it onto the one, six and ten o'clock bulletins.'

'This is a judicial inquiry, not an event for the benefit of the media.'

'With respect, Judge, you're right and you're wrong.'

'How so?'

'We're three months from the general election so we have to compete against any emerging political stories and anything else happening in the world today to get our message across to the public and the only way to do that is through the media.'

The journalists were on what would've been the old courtroom's uncomfortable wooden seats reserved for the public. Sophie Bartells was next to the panelled dock wearing a tailor-made trouser suit with black satin lapels.

The weak winter sunshine coming through the windows caught her glossy brown hair. White avoided eye contact. He was behind the magistrates' bench in a leather-covered armchair with his inquiry colleagues either side. They even had props like copies of Stone's Justice Manual, Archbold and other law books. It all felt contrived but as White knew only too well, courts were the ultimate theatre. He invited questions from his audience. The reporter with the tie stood up.

'Manchester Evening News. Sir, you've indicated a wish to publish your findings in the next twelve weeks. Do you anticipate any political interference in the meantime?'

'I'm not sure I see the connection you're trying to make.'

'Well, the deaths you're investigating sparked considerable public disorder which didn't look good for the government and as we're coming up to an election, won't they be anxious to avoid any more bad publicity from trouble on the streets if your report doesn't take the heat out of the situation?'

White weighed his answer carefully.

'My colleagues and I will follow the maxim of going where the evidence leads and whether or not that takes the heat out of the situation, as you put it, must remain to be seen. Next question, please.'

White shaded his eyes from the TV lights and noticed a man staring intently at him from the back of the room. He didn't look a media type - early sixties, sports jacket, pale brown trousers. White felt he'd seen his face before yet couldn't think where or when. But his attention quickly returned to the business in hand.

'Sophie Bartells, Channel 4 News. Given all the official denials of any wrong-doing in these men's deaths in the past, how much confidence can their families have that your report won't be the White Report but will be seen as the White Wash Report?'

The hacks tittered and White allowed himself a pained smile.

'Miss Bartells, I think it'd be helpful for everyone to wait until my colleagues and I have assessed the evidence, then they can read and comment on our report as they wish. To suggest on day one that we won't get to the truth is premature in the extreme.'

'So you mean you're confident of getting to the truth?'

'Your question implies that the truth has so far been covered up.'

'That's the belief of the men's families and those who campaign on their behalf.'

'At this precise moment, I cannot say if it has or it has not,' White said.

'But if it has been, you'll say so without fear or favour?'

'As I have indicated, it's in the interests of everyone that we interview all the witnesses, read the documentation, official and otherwise, then publish an interim report by the end of April. The families and the police of this city and the wider public deserve nothing less than a prompt and impartial inquiry into these events.'

Bartells pointed to the panelled enclosure where prisoners would once have stood as her cameraman filmed her lobbing the next question.

'Is it not the police themselves who will be in the dock?'

'Miss Bartells, you surely don't expect me to prejudice my own inquiry, do you?'

More questions were asked, photographers crouched this way and that to get their pictures until White tapped the glass of the pendulum clock behind him.

'Ladies and gentlemen, I know you'll appreciate that we have a job of work to do so if you'll allow us, we must make a start. Thank you once again for your attendance.'

The man White thought he recognised was the first to turn and leave the room.

*

The mother of the third man to die in police custody, Luke North, kept her distance from the families of the other two when White's inquiry opened in the Police Museum's lecture hall.

Like the parents of Michael Clancy and shoplifter Adrian Kelly, she had buried a son. But these families had a lawyer to represent them. He knew their grief came with a price. For Mrs North, nothing would ever compensate for the loss of the tortured, schizophrenic boy she couldn't save from himself. She sat looking neither angry nor vengeful, just uncomprehendingly sad and old before her time.

White made sure she had water and kept her in sight as Sergeant Timothy Healey told counsel for the inquiry how Clancy turned violent when being detained in the street.

'He was powerfully built and young,' he said. 'He'd jumped bail for dealing heroin and knew he'd be facing a long stretch. It took four of us to restrain him because he fought like a wild man.'

As would happen with the arrests of Kelly and North months later, Michael Clancy lost consciousness under the weight of officers trying to handcuff him.

'So your prisoner was crushed to death?' counsel said. 'Hardly a text book outcome.'

'My squad did everything we reasonably could to arrest these men,' Healey said. 'It was us who tried to resuscitate them, to save their lives in situations which were not of our making or our choosing.'

Counsel moved on to the death of eighteen-year-old Luke North. Healey, late thirties, six foot and built like a prop forward, said Luke had been shouting aggressively at passers-by in Albert Square.

'We tried to calm him down, find out what his problem was, then he lashed out at us so we'd no choice but to take him in and as we did, he struck me in the mouth and knocked out two of my teeth.'

'Had you any understanding of why he was behaving in this way?'

'He seemed off his head, Sir... drink, drugs, he was just crazy.'

At this point, Mrs North stood up, a slight figure in black whose mourning would never end. The hall became hushed as she left her seat to confront Sergeant Healey.

'Please sit down,' counsel said. 'You will be heard in due course.'

'No, let this lady speak,' White said.

'I'm sorry my son hit you,' she said. 'He'd not been taking his tablets... he wouldn't have been shouting at you, just at the voices in his head, lots of voices all talking at once. That's what was driving him mad. Luke was a good boy, not aggressive, not really. I'm sorry for what happened... so sorry.'

White called a fifteen-minute adjournment. But Mrs North caught a bus home. She'd said her piece. No words, not hers or anyone else's, could ever ease the pain she felt.

The inquiry saw CCTV footage from the custody suite at Bootle Street Police Station showing Luke, limp and over-powered, being put into a cell. Soon after, Healey went in on his own but came out less than a minute later.

In Mrs North's absence, White questioned him for her. 'Why did you need to go into that cell when I'd have thought you'd have been with the dentist?'

'I wanted to make sure he was OK, Sir.'

'But that was the custody sergeant's responsibility, not yours.'

'I could see how distressed the boy was.'

'Or were you going to pay him back for knocking out your teeth?'

'No, definitely not. When I got in the cell, he was already lying on the floor. I tried to resuscitate him then I called for help. You can see that on the CCTV.'

'But we only have your word for what happened inside the cell.'

'I'm telling the truth, Sir.'

'So the marks on his face weren't caused by your fists?'

'Absolutely not and the medical evidence confirms that those injuries and those to his body were caused during his arrest and by the physical efforts I made to revive him.'

Dan Luston frowned at the tone and accusatory line of White's questioning. Counsel for the inquiry wasn't best pleased at being usurped, either. White seemed not to have read their script.

'Forgive me, Sergeant Healey,' he said. 'But to lose one prisoner is unfortunate, to lose two could be seen as careless so what are we to make of you losing three?'

'I do my job to the best of my ability, Sir. I have told you the truth.'

*

Luston took White's arm and said he needed a quiet word. He steered the judge downstairs and said one of the forthcoming witnesses would like to talk to him.

'Is this really appropriate?'

'It's Rose Lingard,' Luston said. 'She was the Police and Crime Commissioner when the three men died but resigned so she could go back to being an MP. She's standing in the election and if the Conservatives win, she's tipped for the Ministry of Justice.'

'You think that allows her special privileges?'

'Sometimes, Judge, not everything can be done by the book.'

Luston led him along a corridor of five preserved Victorian police cells with thick iron doors painted brown and sheets of metal in the brickwork to foil escapes. Sitting on a slatted wooden bed in the last cell was the lady herself. She stood, smiled engagingly and shook White's hand.

'I'll leave you to it,' Luston said. 'I'll be back in ten.'

'This is all very novel, not to say secretive,' White said.

She patted the bench beside her as if summoning a swain but White didn't move. He'd never lost a childhood terror of enclosed spaces. The cell was a virtual tomb and he'd no intention of having its heavy door close on him, not even for a would-be minister of the Crown.

'What is it that you want to discuss?'

She got up and faced him. There was a force about her as with all who are close to power. But hers was primitively feminine, too. Here was a woman with

238

brains and ambition but who also deployed her attractions as a general might his snipers.

'I want to ask you how you see your inquiry panning out.'

'With respect, that really is none of your business. You are a witness to whom we will listen at the right time and whose testimony will be treated seriously.'

'I'm sure it will, but you personally intervened in proceedings earlier and you seemed to be gunning for the police as if in your mind, they're already guilty.'

'How I run my inquiry is a matter for me, now if you'll excuse me - '

'Before you go, let me remind you that two previous inquiries into this matter both found that no officer was to blame for what happened.'

'And you'd prefer me to reach that same conclusion?'

'Oh, I think you will, Judge... I really think you will. Some evidence is going to be put before you soon that is absolutely compelling. Just you wait and see.'

Rose Lingard smiled once more then pushed past him, leaving only the perfumed fragrance of lilies in the dank air. White's unease about this assignment suddenly surfaced again.

A parallel drama must be playing out behind his back. He went and sat in the semi-darkness of the cell, overwhelmed by some amorphous fear greater than claustrophobia.

It was then that the identity of the man in the press conference came to him. He was the chauffeur, the one who'd driven him to the marsh on the day he cast his father's wartime letters into the creek... the day he said a final farewell to a man he'd loved and loathed in equal measure but who would never allow himself to be known.

If Rose Lingard unnerved White, something about the chauffeur's inexplicable presence, his relentless gaze, carried a sort of implied but real threat.

This had no context that he could determine yet was tangible. White shivered. Someone was walking over his grave. He had to get out of that cell.

Thirty-Nine

Lutton Hall, Fenbeach, Tuesday 8th September 1955

Spence went down with a heavy cold after his soaking in the sea. Auntie Evelyn insisted he stay in bed. It was Uncle Jimmy who took him trays of food - and Beechams Powders - for she'd no wish to catch any germs. He also brought up books and puzzles and began teaching him the rules of chess. But that morning, Uncle Jimmy had news, too.

'You're famous round here now, kiddo,' he said. 'Your picture's in the Free Press and you've even got fan mail downstairs.'

'Fan mail?'

'All right then, birthday cards.'

'But my birthday's not till tomorrow.'

'Doesn't matter. They're here in good time. Anyway, eat your toast, have a wash and get dressed then you should get out on your bike and have a blow of fresh air.'

Auntie Evelyn had gone shopping to King's Lynn and Uncle Jimmy was about to leave for an auction of antiques in Newark.

Spence felt odd reading about himself in a paper, as if what was reported had happened to someone else... maybe to the stranger whose face was represented by hundreds of tiny black and grey dots on the newsprint. But he could see the fear in that face and knew it was still in his head. He pushed the paper away and picked up his birthday cards instead. He should have left opening them till next day. But they were from home, from what - and those - he missed most.

Auntie Kitty sent a ten-shilling postal order, Auntie Emily one for five shillings and Auntie Vron enclosed a pound note. He need not have stolen a penny from Miss Arbib and for that, he already had a conscience. Uncle Edgar's card simply said *to the best lad in the world*. Spence saved his mother's till last. Inside was a letter.

My dearest son

I think about you and miss you every day. I'm starting to feel better because everyone here is being kindness itself. Auntie Kitty has bought me a lovely dress from Estelle Modes. Uncle Edgar is going in for an operation next week and that can't come soon enough as he doesn't look well and we're all worried about him. Promise me that you are looking after yourself. Miss Arbib comes to see me most days and is being a great help with lots of things.

I must close now if I am to catch the post because I don't want to miss your birthday. Don't worry, love, it won't be long before we'll have a big family party for you with lots of presents.

All our love, Mum and Dad.

He read that last line several times. *All our love, Mum and Dad*. If his Dad had come back, why couldn't he? This was not fair. He would ride to Mercy Cottage as soon as it stopped raining. Maybe the lorry driver was out of hospital and could take Spence home in time for his birthday. That was the only present he wanted.

*

Malcolm Feingold's secretary told Zilla to go straight into his office the moment she arrived. He'd rung earlier and said he had discovered something sensitive linked to Miss Tester's death, which he wouldn't speak about on an open line.

'Based on your conversation with her cleaner, Mrs Turner, I've been to her house to take a formal statement.'

'And did she confirm what she told me?'

'She did indeed but I got something else from her, too. She remembered someone trying to break into Miss Tester's house very shortly before she died.'

'That's interesting.'

'It gets better,' Feingold said. 'Mrs Turner contacted the police and a detective went to investigate. He saw all her valuables and that she'd thousands of pounds in cash so he advised her to put it back in the bank after Christmas.'

'She obviously didn't.'

'No, but that's not the point. Mrs Turner came up with the name of the detective - and without being led by me, either.'

'Go on – surprise me.'

'It was our friend, Challis.'

*

The weather did not improve. Rain spilled out of the blocked gutter above Spence's bedroom window to cascade onto the yard below. He set out his birthday cards on the mantelpiece above a tiny hob grate. But he took them down a moment later. Like him, they'd only look right in Zion Street. He couldn't settle, not to a book or a game. But Lutton Hall was his to explore.

The dusty attic room across from his was like a museum of old furniture and junk - a tin bath, ladder-back chairs, a cockerel in a glass case. There were framed paintings of horses and houses and people long dead, heaps of blue and white plates, a birdcage, even a stuffed fox.

Spence had no need to be quiet but crept downstairs to the first floor landing. Uncle Jimmy's many clocks passed the time of day but not together. The room where he and Auntie Evelyn slept had peacock wallpaper and an ancient four poster bed, dark and carved and with curtains over the top and side. Necklaces of silver and pearls dangled from the outstretched arms of an art nouveau figurine on the dressing table.

The smaller room next-door was what Auntie Evelyn called her study and kept locked. But the key was in the dish of china fruit on a narrow side table nearby. He'd seen her take it from there.

Beneath the window was a desk with a tooled leather top in green and gold. Her personalised notepaper lay in a box by an open diary listing church and parish council meetings. There were shelves of worthy books which looked new and unread and one wall hung with paintings of country scenes in oils and watercolours.

But Spence was uncomfortable enough about being a thief without turning spy. He re-locked Auntie Evelyn's study and went downstairs. It'd stopped raining. He raided the biscuit barrel for his lunch, took an apple from the bowl on the dresser and got his bike. Mercy Cottage beckoned.

He had barely ridden out of Lutton Hall's gate when a man in oily brown overalls and standing by a parked van flagged him down.

'You're young Spencer White, aren't you?'

Spence nodded but kept his distance. The man smiled.

'I read about you in the paper today - '

Spence said nothing.

' - and so did your Dad.'

'He can't have done. My Dad's in Manchester.'

'No he isn't, son.'

'I got a letter from my Mum this morning. She told me.'

'No, your Dad's less than two miles from here.'

'I don't believe you. You're tricking me.'

'I promise I'm not. I'm your Dad's pal from the army and he's desperate to see you.'

Forty

The farmhouse where John Henry waited for Spence had been derelict for years. It was home now only to sparrows and bats and abandoned implements rusting in the cobbled yard.

Doors hung off hinges and weeds grew in those gutters that hadn't already collapsed. Roof spars had gone grey in the salty wind and showed through where some of the pantiles had crashed into the bedrooms below.

Spence often rode by this ruin on his way to the marsh but never stopped to look around. Yet somewhere behind one of its blind windows or in the shadowed corners of the empty brick barns, was the stranger who'd given him life.

How like him to be absent when needed. The more Spence started to understand the ways of the world and those who ran it, so respect for his father diminished. And yet he hated that this was so.

'Spence, over here. Quick.'

His Dad beckoned him into the house. He took Spence's hands in his and squatted down, face-to-face and close enough to hug. But they didn't.

'It's grand to see you, son. I've only just found out you're at Evelyn's.'

John Henry looked drawn, unshaven, even hunted. He smiled as if such a meeting was somehow normal.

Part of Spence wanted to scream and bash his fists into that inadequate, selfish face. But he just stared. The resentment and anger he harboured against his father began giving way to compassion at the pity of it all, at a life so unfulfilled and without meaning.

'What are you doing here, Dad?'

'I've been staying with my pal from my regiment, old Pep.'

'But why aren't you with Mum?'

'It's a long story, son... complicated, not easy to tell.'

'But she needs you. She's been in hospital and she's in trouble with the police and the hangman came to lock her up. You should have been there to stop him.'

'You haven't seen the reports in the Evening News, have you?'

'What reports?'

'About some pictures, Spence... some pictures that were supposed to be stolen.'

'I don't understand what you're talking about.'

'The two in our front room in Zion Street, they were stolen.'

'But they're Mum's pictures. How could she steal what was hers?'

'Serious things are going on here, son... things I can't tell you about, not now.'

His Dad looked trapped. He kept checking out of a window obscured by mealy spiders' webs and the remains of dead flies tightly bound in silk.

'But I want to do something to help, I want you and Mum home again, like it was before.'

'I know,' John Henry said. 'All right, there is something you can do. I'm going to give you Miss Arbib's phone number and I want you to ring her as soon as you can and tell her that the pictures belonged to my Dad, your Granddad Freddie, and he gave them to Mum for looking after him during the war. Have you got that?'

'Yes, I can do that but why can't you tell her, or tell the police?'

'Because I'd be asked all sorts of questions I don't want to answer. You do this for me and it'll help Mum because she might not be in a state to remember who she got the pictures from.'

'What are you going to do now, then?'

'I've got to find somewhere else to kip till all this is sorted out. I can't stay at Pep's any longer.'

'Why can't you stay at Auntie Evelyn's?'

'Because we never got on and you mustn't say anything to her or Uncle Jimmy about meeting me. You understand, don't you?'

'Yes, I understand,' Spence said.

His Dad then went to a corner of the room and picked up a rucksack as if to leave. He also took hold of a long canvas bag.

'What's in there, Dad?'

'Something Pep's given me to shoot my food with. It'll be like being back in the army and living off the land.'

Spence wanted to delay their parting, for this rare sense of closeness not to end. He told him about Mr Poucher's remote shack on the marsh and how he could shelter there for a few days.

'I'll show you where it is and bring you something to eat and some smokes and you'd be warm and dry.'

'My, my, but you're a bright kid... a bloody sight brighter son than I'm a father.'

'No, don't say that.'

'It's true enough, Spence. I've made a mess of everything.'

'You always try your best, Dad.'

'But it's never good enough, never has been and never will be. Look at me... who'd be proud of a man like me?'

The pity in Spence's heart turned to sadness. Everything his father said was true and could not be denied. He put his arms - the strong one and the weak one - around his fallen hero's neck and kissed the face he had so often hated and feared.

When Zilla heard the phone, she worried it would be her head of department again, dropping more unsubtle hints about her absences from work. She thought about not answering but it kept ringing. It was Spence and he was in a great hurry to get all his words out.

'I've got a message for you from my Dad. He says the pictures were from his Dad, my Granddad Freddie, and he gave them to Mum for looking after him in the war so she hasn't stolen anything.'

'Slow down, Spence. You're saying you've met your father, you've seen him?'

'Yes, my photograph's been in the paper and he saw it and sent his friend for me.'

'So you know where he is?'

'Yes, I showed him a place where he can hide till everything is sorted out.'

'You must tell me where this is, Spence. It's so important.'

'Will you come here, then?'

'Of course I will, I'll drive over tomorrow.'

'Then I can tell you about the other painting.'

'What other painting?'

'The one of the castle, the one in Wales.'

'How on earth do you know I'm interested in that?'

'If I tell you, you must promise not to shout but I've seen it, I know where it is.'

'Spence, listen to me. This is all very serious. First of all, is your father all right?'

'Yes, he can look after himself. He's got a gun - sorry, got to go. Someone's coming.'

The phone went dead. Zilla closed her eyes in a state of confusion and dread but knew she had to act quickly.

Those with an ear on Zilla Arbib's phone to monitor her bankrolling of communist subversives, traced the call to the home of James and Evelyn McKillop of Fenbeach, Lincolnshire. This intelligence was immediately flagged up to Inspector Gormley of Manchester Special Branch.

He rang CID and was told Challis had gone down to the pub next door for a stiffener before heading home to a baby who didn't sleep. Gormley joined him at the bar a few minutes later.

'Mine's a single malt, old man.'

'Celebrating something, are we?' Challis said.

'No, but you will be.'

He slipped him the Telex message he'd received. Challis read it quickly and handed it back with a hint of a smile.

'I knew that bastard would surface before long.'

'Cut it fine though, didn't he? Another twenty four hours and the boss would've had you helping old ladies across the street.'

Challis returned to the nick and put his head round the superintendent's door.

'I've got him, Sir, got a fix on John Henry White.'

'Not before time, Vincent. Where is he?'

'Hiding in the back of beyond in Lincolnshire,' Challis said. 'I want to put a job together and get off early tomorrow.'

'Right, give me an outline soonest and I'll make a call to get some local help for you.'

'One other thing, Sir. We've every reason to believe that White's armed so I need your permission to draw a firearm for myself.'

The head of CID nodded and Challis backed out of his office. He'd run his prey to earth and now scented blood.

Forty-One

John Henry was in that slippage between sleep and waking, unsure if what he saw in the dim light was a trick of his half-conscious mind or bleak reality.

He lay under fusty blankets on a camp bed in a shed with an earthen floor and walls of wood and corrugated iron. Spence had taken him there the previous night and for that - and the provisions he'd brought round later - he was grateful. Yet though the door wasn't locked and the window not barred, it was a prison. He was free to leave - but to where and to what?

'I'll be back after breakfast,' Spence said. 'Then I'll bring some treats for us.'

John Henry stood outside and peed in the rushes. The first pinkish lights of day appeared over the marsh. How fast life can unravel. Pull a thread hard enough and everything begins to fall apart.

And all this for a moment of anger in a time of war and killing. How heavy had been the guilt he'd carried. It might even be a relief to set down his burden and atone.

For now, he lit the paraffin stove to warm his hands then ate the last of Spence's cheese and bread which he broke off in hunks. The milk he drank from the bottle. He'd become a tramp, an unwashed, foul-smelling itinerant. Little wonder Pep's wife wanted him gone.

But he would have to collect his motorbike once Pep had fixed the brakes. Maybe Spence could take a message to say where he was hiding. But making his son and best army pal accessories to murder wouldn't do either any favours.

Spence arrived good as his word, soon after eight o'clock. In his saddlebag were sausage rolls, a meat pie, cakes, more milk, two bars of chocolate and cigarettes bought from the village shop.

'Here's a feast and no mistake.'

'Well, it is my birthday, isn't it?'

'Spence... 'course it is. I'm so sorry, son. I'm a rotten Dad, aren't I?'

'Doesn't matter. We'll have a proper party another day.'

John Henry tried to smile but looked like a fugitive in the films, hollow-eyed and afraid of something he knew was there but couldn't quite see. Spence told him about phoning Miss Arbib.

'Good, she'll know what to do for the best.'

'Dad, if Granddad Freddie gave the pictures to Mum and they were stolen, where did he get them from?'

'There's a question. He was always buying and selling pictures to make a few bob.'

'You didn't like him, did you?'

'No, not much.'

'Why was that? Was he horrible to you?'

'You're better off not knowing about those days, son... they're over now, anyway.'

Spence took this as confirmation of what he already thought - that if no one had made his Dad happy as a boy, how could he know what to do when he had one of his own? He had need to believe this for then it made forgiving his father's behaviour and many sins that bit easier.

*

A few minutes after Spence had rung her the previous evening, Zilla phoned Lutton Hall. She spoke to Evelyn, ostensibly to check Spence's well-being before talking to him herself. Zilla said he mustn't mention this to his aunt, uncle or father but she'd be in Fenbeach next day.

'This is our secret,' she said. 'I'll meet you about one o'clock outside the Bull Hotel in Market Street and you can take me to your father and we'll try and make things right again.'

Zilla collected Edgar before seven o'clock then began the long trek through the midlands to south Lincolnshire. Her Sunbeam was a classy, distinctive coupé, apple green and easy for Challis to keep in sight. He'd plotted her likely route to Fenbeach and kept a few cars behind. But he had not anticipated Edgar Sydenham being with her.

Special Branch had a thin file on him as a known associate of communist agitators at the Dunlop factory where he was a machinist. From his own inquiries, Challis knew he'd been wounded at Passchendaele, was de facto guardian to Joan White and would soon retire.

His presence was a complication but he had looked old and stooped as he got into the Sunbeam. If he had any sense, he would keep out of the way when White was lifted.

Challis's personal firearm was in the glove compartment. He'd advised the Lincolnshire bobby meeting him to draw a weapon, too. John Henry White had killed once, was now armed and might well resist arrest.

But whatever happened in the coming hours, he'd be taken back north in handcuffs or a wooden box. Challis wasn't fussed which. If he had to choose, the headlines from a shoot-out would be more gratifying than those of a court case.

Forty-Two

Zilla and Edgar took Spence into the lounge of the Bull Hotel and ordered tea and sandwiches. Edgar held out his closed hands for Spence to pick whichever contained his birthday present. Each concealed a folded ten-shilling note so he was on a winner either way. He then pretended to twist off Spence's nose and they both smiled at this remembered routine from happier days.

Zilla thought Spence thinner and nervier and saw that he still screwed up his eyes every few minutes. He couldn't keep still, either. But he was excited and wanted to tell them how he'd found his father.

'You eat something first,' Zilla said.

'I will but you've got to let me know what's really going on,' Spence said. 'You always say I must be truthful but you've not been truthful with me.'

'I'm sorry we've not given you the whole story,' she said. 'But we haven't got it all ourselves and sometimes, a fib can be less hurtful than the truth.'

'But why's Mum been in the Evening News and why's Dad hiding from everyone?'

Zilla told him about Miss Tester, how she'd been his father's aunt but was robbed of pictures and other possessions when she died in an air raid.

'Are those the pictures that were in our front room?'

'Two of them, yes, and now you say you've seen the third one, the castle picture.'

'Is this why the hangman took my Mum away?'

'Yes, and that's why we've got to talk to your Dad,' Edgar said.

'Did he take these pictures from the lady's house?'

'We don't know what happened but we need to find out so we can help your Mum.'

Spence thought for a moment then told them about his photograph appearing in the local paper and the coincidence of John Henry seeing it and arranging to meet.

'He wanted somewhere to stay so I showed him this shack on the marsh.'

'And you'll take us there?' Zilla said.

'Yes, it'll be a big surprise for him.'

Zilla then asked how he knew about the castle picture. At this, Spence looked down at his shuffling feet and took a shamefaced moment before starting his confession.

'Because I went through your handbag when you came here last time - '

'You did what?'

' - and I saw that old catalogue you had and you'd drawn a big ring around a picture and a question mark and I knew I'd seen it, the real one.'

'That's very observant but what made you look in my handbag in the first place?'

Spence took another breath before answering.

'I wanted to get some money to pay a lorry driver to take me home.'

'So you stole from me?'

'I'm sorry, Miss Arbib. I know I shouldn't.'

Zilla saw how close to breaking down he was. She went to him and took him in her arms. He didn't shy away and she stroked his hair.

'I only wanted to see if Mum was all right.'

'Of course you did, we understand.'

'I'm sorry, you can have all my birthday money.'

'Don't be silly. All you have to do to make amends is to take us to your father and show us where the picture of the castle is.'

*

255

Challis and the local detective constable assigned to assist kept watch on the Bull Hotel from the saloon bar of the Market Tavern opposite.

'Dangerous sod, this man White,' Challis said.

'Was he a suspect back then during the war, Sir?'

'Never got that far. My boss over-ruled the pathologist, wouldn't listen to me and wouldn't have it that the old lady had been murdered so no further action was taken.'

'What's your new evidence against White, then?'

'A couple of pictures that were nicked from her house have turned up in his.'

'Couldn't he say he'd bought them from a third party, all innocent like?'

'He can say what he likes but he had motive, opportunity and was in possession of her stolen property.'

'But without a witness statement or a confession, how will these pictures put him at the scene of the crime?'

'I don't know how many murderers you've collared in your time, son, but the ones I bring in usually see reason and cough in the end.'

As this discussion took place, Spence was leading Zilla out of the Bull Hotel's back entrance for the short walk back to Lutton Hall. Her car remained parked - and under surveillance - at the front while Edgar stayed in an armchair in the lounge, dosing his unsettled guts with kaolin and morphine.

*

'Auntie Evelyn's doing her flower-arranging at the church,' Spence said.

'And where's your Uncle Jimmy?'

'Stamford, I think.'

Spence unlocked the door to Evelyn's study. Hanging on the chimney breast in a scalloped gilt frame was the third picture stolen from Miss Tester - the watercolour of Caernarfon Castle by Alex Lawson. It showed a woman walking by three waterside cottages in the lee of the castle's dark stone towers. Smoke curled out from the chimneys and Zilla could see how this simple Victorian depiction of hearth and home would have captivated Miss Tester's sad and romantic heart. Here was a widow's memory of all she had lost and could never get back.

Zilla, emboldened now, went to Evelyn's desk and began opening the drawers.

'What are you after, Miss Arbib?'

'I'm looking for anything else of Miss Tester's.'

From the third drawer down she lifted out a stamp collection then several felt-covered trays of old coins. Even as she did, a noise came from the landing outside. The door opened and there stood Evelyn, her face as red as the roses on her dress.

'What in God's name do you think you're doing?'

*

Challis was getting anxious. Arbib and Sydenham weren't leading him anywhere. The local detective went across to the Bull Hotel for a discreet look-see. He ran back with news Challis didn't want to hear.

'The woman and the kid have scarpered.'

'Christ Almighty.'

'Went out the back way apparently.'

'So where's old Sydenham?'

'Asleep in the lounge.'

'So if White's in walking distance of here, why hasn't he gone with them?'

'The girl on reception thinks he's not well. She's seen him taking medicine.'

'He'll need bloody medicine when I've done with him. Come on, gloves off or my next shit's a hedgehog.'

Challis strode into the empty lounge and shook Edgar awake.

'Edgar Sydenham? You know who I am and what I'm investigating.'

'You're that bastard who's crucifying our Joan.'

'She's not the one I'm after,' Challis said. 'I've reason to believe you know where John Henry White is hiding and unless you take me to him, I shall arrest you for obstructing my inquiries.'

'I served under little upstarts like you in my war.'

'Then you'll know where your duty lies now.'

Edgar lit a Park Drive and made no attempt to move. Challis sensed the eyes of the younger cop on him. He reached inside his jacket for the Webley he'd drawn from the police arsenal.

'Get up, get up now.'

'You think that scares me? I had machine guns parting my hair once and still kept walking towards them so I suggest you bugger off and leave me be.'

'Listen, Edgar, you'd not be doing it for me, you'd be doing it for your Joan. You know White's a no-hoper and the sooner we sort this mess out, the better for her and the lad.'

'You leave him out of this or I swear to God I'll swing for you.'

'Threaten me all you like but I'd say I know where your true loyalties lie so come on, Edgar, let's get going.'

*

Evelyn was breathless with anger. Zilla stared her out then took down the Caernarfon Castle picture and laid it on Evelyn's desk.

'This painting is stolen,' she said.

'Are you insane? That was left to me by my father.'

Zilla then put the coin and stamp collections on top of the picture.

'These are stolen, too.'

'This is outrageous. I'm going to call the police.'

'Before you do, look at this then maybe you'll begin to understand what's really been going on and why Joan's in the terrible state she is.'

She handed Evelyn the newspaper account of Joan's court appearance headlined MURDER MYSTERY IN ART THEFT CASE. As she read it, the only sound to be heard came from Jimmy's asthmatic clocks. Evelyn sat down and let the cutting fall to the floor.

'Joan's pictures and yours were stolen from a house in Hulme,' Zilla said. 'They belonged to a Mrs Bethel who went by her maiden name... Maud Elizabeth Tester.'

At this, Evelyn looked up and there was recognition in her eyes.

'She was your mother's sister, wasn't she? So how did you come by these things that were stolen from her?'

Suddenly, Evelyn was a woman of little substance, bombast gone, hard-fought membership of the landlord class in jeopardy.

'The police will want the truth, Evelyn...'

She began wringing her hands, visualising social disgrace and the loss of all she'd striven to achieve.

'They came from my father's house,' she said. 'It all did, the picture, the coins, the stamps, everything. I'll give it all back, I don't want any of it.'

'So you cleared out his house after he was killed?'

'Yes.'

'Just you, not your brothers?'

'No, just me.'

'And what else did you find that wasn't your father's?'

'Some silver cutlery, books, a few household things, nothing of any great value.'

'But what about the money you found there, Evelyn?'

'Money? What money?'

'Well over five thousand pounds in cash, wasn't there?'

'No - '

'That was all Miss Tester's savings... set you up nicely, didn't it?'

'No, no - '

'You could buy those properties up north, live off the rents and play the lady of the manor in this grand country house.'

If Evelyn owed much to a German bomb, another which had lain unexploded for years beneath a life so carefully constructed was about to destroy it with no warning.

She gave out a howl of pent-up rage and erupted from her chair. The collections of stamps and coins were hurled against the wall. For that moment, the air seemed filled with spinning silver and squares of coloured paper. Then Evelyn lifted the castle painting and smashed it against her desk. Blades of glass showered across the room. Spence cowered in a corner, terrified by such fury.

Evelyn slapped Zilla across the face. She'd cut her hand for spatters of blood made a perfect arc across the chimney breast where the castle picture had hung.

'Yes, I took the money - and why shouldn't I?'

'Because it wasn't yours, Evelyn. You were stealing.'

'And what had been stolen from me as a girl by that monster of a father I had? Tell me that. What price would you put on my violation night after damned night - '

Spence couldn't bear any more screaming and hitting. He ran down the stairs, through the kitchen and out into the yard where he'd left his bike.

In his hand was the newspaper story saying his mother was a thief and his father a murderer and in his eyes, the tears he'd held back till then.

But Uncle Edgar would know what to do. He had to find him. And as Spence got near the Bull Hotel, there he was... being helped into a car by the hangman.

Forty-Three

Evelyn sat at Lutton Hall's kitchen table smoking - a habit she abhorred - her future blown apart by her past. She was becalmed by shock, unable to think beyond her hurts and the bewildering speed of her downfall.

An hour before, she'd been with the wives of a magistrate and a solicitor from the Townswomen's Guilds, arranging flowers at the altar of Fenbeach's glorious medieval church.

Yet her own edifice of respectability, so carefully built over so many years, could now be shown to rest on sand... sand and theft, maybe even murder.

Exposure and scandal must surely follow. Yet for all Evelyn's deceit and avarice, Zilla felt sympathy for her. She had taken revenge of sorts on a predatory father. But the Fates have a sense of natural justice, too. Cruel and summary though it might be, it was applied only when they saw fit.

'Look, Evelyn, there's nothing here that's broken beyond repair,' Zilla said.

'You can't know that any more than you can know what's at stake for me.'

'No, but what's crucial is to have established that your brother did not kill Miss Tester. The police have got her death wrong and it's disgraceful how they've hounded him and Joan, a real miscarriage of justice if ever there was one.'

Evelyn, her anguished face pink and blotchy, saw nothing in this - or in the wreckage of her own designs - to which she might cling.

'And how do you think I'll ever hold my head up again when my friends and the people round here read of these sordid details? They're bound to come out.'

'That depends how you and I play our next moves, Evelyn - '

Before Zilla could set down her terms, Spence panted into the kitchen, shouting for her to come immediately.

'What is it, Spence? What's wrong?'

'It's the hangman. I've just seen him by the hotel.'

'Calm yourself. Who do you mean?'

'The policeman who took my Mum away, the hangman and he's with another man and they've got Uncle Edgar and they've just driven off.'

Evelyn let out a despairing cry and banged the table with both fists.

'See what I mean? The police are here already. God, the disgrace of it all.'

'It's all right, Evelyn,' Zilla said. 'This man is interested in me not you and I know exactly why. Look, we haven't much time but I need to borrow your car.'

'Why, what for?'

'Because he must have followed me so he knows what my car looks like and it's vital I get to John Henry before he does.'

'Then take it... take it like you've taken everything else from me, you witch.'

*

A sea mist closed over the marsh, chill and damp. It diffused the sour yellow headlights of Evelyn's Riley and forced Zilla to go slow through the featureless lanes.

She and Spence could barely see where they were heading. It took a while then he made out the cottage where Mr Poucher lived. His shack wasn't too far away. For Zilla, the fog was a gift. Spence had told them roughly where John Henry's hideout was but even on a clear day, Edgar hadn't the local knowledge to find it quickly - and neither had Challis.

She parked well off the causeway. Spence led her onto the marsh, through spikes of reeds and grasses which snagged at her stockings as they jumped the soupy brown creeks slithering out to the sea. Zilla's heeled shoes kept coming off in the soft ground and her feet were soaked.

'I'm not dressed for a cross country hike, Spence - and such a dangerous one, too.'

'It's not dangerous if you know what you're doing.'

The shack slowly materialised through the mist - wind-bitten planks, rusting tin roof weighted down with baulks of timber, a punt laid across wooden blocks. Zilla took Spence's hand and paused before this refuge from a storm. Gulls screamed in the mist like lost souls, unseen and unsettling.

'This is *it*? Your father's here? Dear God, what a place to end up.'

*

Challis was losing what little patience the Lord had bestowed upon him. Sydenham couldn't have deliberately misdirected him more if he'd tried and the plod assigned to help hadn't the wit to find soap in a sink.

'For Christ's sake, there's a killer on the loose and we're farting about in the fog. Where is this bloody shack?'

'Our Spence just said it was on the marshes,' Edgar said. 'I've never been here in my life so I don't know.'

'But what about you, Constable? Isn't this supposed to be your patch?'

'No, I'm from Lincoln but the uniform bobby in Fenbeach said something about a place called Drove

End. He thinks there're sheds and such like on the marshes there.'

'Then why the hell didn't you say so first off? Isn't my day rat shit enough for you?'

*

Zilla hoped John Henry didn't register her shock at the sight and stink of him. He couldn't have bathed for a week, had slept in his demob suit and his eyes were dark-ringed and full of suspicion in the fetid hut in which he hid.

Spence gave his father a grin. He began to return it but ruffled his son's hair instead. Zilla winced at these moments, imprinting themselves photographically in Spence's memory like black and white stills, impossible to erase, impossible to forget.

'Mr White, we all have to get out of here quickly,' she said. 'You need to come back north with us now.'

John Henry shook his head and turned to peer out of the one small window he had onto the desolation outside.

'If I go back there, I'm done for.'

'But if you don't then Joan will suffer even more and she's in a terrible state already.'

'I know, I've been told what's been in the Evening News.'

'Then you'll realise her solicitor needs you to make a full statement about your father having these stolen pictures and giving them to Joan.'

'Miss Arbib, you haven't any idea of what happened back then.'

'No, that's not true. I've unearthed a lot of new information that'll help her.'

'But how will it help me?'

'That's blindingly obvious. It'll go to demonstrate that you didn't kill Miss Tester.'

265

'Miss Tester? Who's she?'

'Your mother's sister... the old lady in Hulme who originally owned Joan's pictures.'

'And I'm supposed to have killed her?'

'Yes, the police say you murdered her. It's what this tragic business is all about. That's why the police put poor Joan in court on a trumped-up charge in order to get at you for Miss Tester's murder.'

John Henry stopped pacing the cell-like room and stared at Zilla in disbelief. He sat on the bed. Its metal frame creaked as he rocked back and forth. The implications of what she said were profound. Should he tell her... should he share the secret he'd kept down the years? Or could he still maintain his silence, let the police do their mistaken worst while he continued to live - but with the lie which shamed and shackled him?

'Dear Christ, what a bloody mess it all is.'

'But we can get you out of it, Mr White - and Joan, too.'

'I doubt it, no-one can relieve me of this.'

'Relieve you of what?'

'Of what's in my head.'

'And what's that?'

'The burden of guilt, Miss Arbib, that's what... the burden of guilt.'

'You'll have to explain. I thought I was bringing you excellent news.'

John Henry looked up at her with a trace of a smile at her naiveté yet one which couldn't disguise the defeat in his tired face. But he had come to a decision.

'I didn't kill this woman, whoever she is.'

'But you went on the run when Edgar told you the police were looking for you.'

'And there was good reason to.'

'But it wasn't the action of an innocent man, was it?'

266

'No, because I'm not innocent. I ran away because I was afraid... no, I was terrified that at long last, I had been found out and was being called to account for the death of someone at my hand.'

'You mean that you *have* killed someone?'

'The police have got the right man but for the wrong murder,' John Henry said. 'The person I killed was my father.'

*

Spence was sent to the Riley to get more cigarettes from Zilla's handbag - and to save him from the details of what John Henry was about to confess. Spence only pretended to run to the car and crouched by the upturned punt instead. He listened at the shack's rotting plank wall, forgetting his mother's warning that eavesdroppers only ever heard bad things.

'I was on leave, seventy two hour pass,' John Henry said. 'Came home and found Joan in a state. She wouldn't say why at first but it came out, little by little and wouldn't you know, my father was the cause of it.'

'Why, what'd he done?'

'Same as he'd done to Evelyn when we were kids.'

'He'd not raped her, had he?'

'While Joan was taking care of him, yes... nursing him, making him meals.'

'That's absolutely dreadful.'

'She never got over it mentally. It was years before we were man and wife again and had our Spence.'

'So what did you do?'

'Searched for him that night but there's an air raid going on and I'm in uniform and a copper says a bomb's fallen two streets away. The civil defence men need help so I go and the bomb's hit the side of a terrace and it's about to collapse and the gas main's on fire. It's chaos and there's my Dad, doing his bit like a hero.'

'Were you still angry at him?'

'Angry? You bet I was still angry. I told him someone was trapped in the cellar then I got him by the throat and for the first time in my life, I'm not afraid of him. I tell him what he's done to Joan and he starts claiming she led him on which was a wicked lie and the biggest mistake he could make.'

'Why, what did you do?'

'I hit him, hit him in the head with a brick or a lump of rubble, I don't know which but I watched him go down, watched the blood come out of his senseless head then I dragged him to where the fire was starting to take hold.'

'What... you left him, got out yourself?'

'Yes, just before the gable end came down and do you know something, that old bastard might have had it coming but I've never known a day's peace since.'

Forty-Four

Spence had never heard his father speak at length before. But when had he ever had such a need for another to see inside his soul? A calmness gathered around Spence, relief that his mother was safe from the hangman. Yet this realisation came with guilt, as if having her escape the rope equated to wishing his Dad hanged.

Only in the past hours had Spence truly come to appreciate how weak and fallible his father had always been, trapped by birth and circumstance, unable to struggle free from all that had gone before. Yet even then, the boy who would be a judge knew that pity provided only context, not mitigation. It was admirable for Miss Arbib to have political sympathy for his parents as victims of a class system loaded against working people. But how could this save a son who had murdered his father?

These concepts and contradictions troubled Spence as he retraced his steps and ran towards where Miss Arbib had parked Auntie Evelyn's car.

The mist began to lift almost as quickly as it had come, burned off by a sun still low in the sky as if this were that day's second dawn. The turning tide in the creeks caught its light, spinning in their eddies and whirlpools all the way to the shining sea, out by the wartime bunker near where Spence almost drowned.

He paused and on the wind which carried the sighs of the waves he heard voices. Men were talking. He crouched in the tall grasses on the marsh side of the causeway and slowly raised his head.

And there, looking into the Riley, was the hangman. A second man stood nearby, smoking with Uncle Edgar.

But what made Spence double over and want to vomit was the gun in the hangman's hand.

*

'You must think carefully about what you've just revealed, Mr White,' Zilla said. 'I urge you to come back and talk to Joan's lawyer. I'm sure he'd advise you to sit tight and let the police investigation into Miss Tester's death fizzle out. Your father's death isn't an issue, officially it's just a terrible consequence of war and all but forgotten. There's no need to risk your future by saying or doing anything about it.'

John Henry lit a cigarette from the stub of the last one. He looked over to the corner where he'd left the shotgun Pep had loaned him to shoot for the pot. On a shelf above were two boxes of cartridges.

'But I want it over with, Miss Arbib. It eats away at me, I'll never be free of it.'

'You've a boy to make you proud in Spence... a wife who loves you and needs you. Please think of them, fight for them, don't wreck their lives.'

The door of the shack was pushed open roughly. Spence stood before them, panting and barely able to get his warning out.

'The hangman's found us... got a gun, coming now.'

John Henry, his face pale beneath its ingrained dirt, turned to Spence and fell to his knees. He took him in his arms as Uncle Edgar had once done, stroked his hair, kissed his forehead and looked into his eyes but without saying anything.

The embrace took a matter of moments. What could be said in such a silence? What words of atonement might be summoned from such a depth of remorse? But the son saw and the son understood and would take the memory into his own dying day.

*

'There's the bugger we want,' Challis said. 'He's got the kid with him.'

Challis and the other detective were two hundred yards behind John Henry, splashing over the smaller rills and jumping banks of glistening mud. Edgar, pained in body and spirit, stumbled after them. John Henry ran on blindly through the sedge, making for the bunker which Spence knew was a dangerous dead end.

'Dad! Dad! Not that way! Come back!'

Zilla caught up with Edgar. He leaned against her to get his breath. Both Zilla's shoes were lost and Edgar already looked close to collapse. Then they saw Challis raise his gun and fire. The sound carried across the marsh. Ducks rose out of the reeds in a panic. Edgar screamed at Challis.

'He's not armed, for Christ's sake! There's no need to shoot.'

Spence hurled a lump of earth at the hangman. He threw another but that missed, too. Challis aimed and fired at John Henry again.

'Stop, Dad! Stop!'

But John Henry either didn't hear or didn't want to. He careered on to where the sea made a moat around the island of slightly higher ground on which the bunker was built.

Challis fired a third shot. John Henry turned and looked upon the man who would have him dead, then to Spence, not thirty yards distant and like his father, seemingly beyond help.

The bunker offered only an illusion of sanctuary. He must have known this yet began to move towards it. But the narrow beach of mud couldn't take a man's weight. It sucked him in, sucked him down so he flailed at the edge of the water, trying to wrestle himself out of the grey-brown sludge. It stopped up his

271

eyes and ears and his mouth and as each second passed, choked off whatever strangled gulps for air he tried to take.

They watched him, powerless... the two cops with guns, his would-be saviour, Zilla, and Edgar, the man who was more father than uncle to the boy at his side. Then the tide carried John Henry away, his head bobbing up and down like those of the seals which fed and basked in that same place. And in a moment he was no more. The sun shone, the gulls screamed and the marsh returned to itself.

Challis made to leave but Edgar barred his way.

'Satisfied with your day's work, are you?'

'He could've surrendered,' Challis said.

'I didn't hear you offer him the option.'

'That's because you're old and deaf.'

'But not daft. A corpse suited you better than a court case, didn't it?'

'My colleague here heard me shout a warning plain enough.'

'Not only are you a bastard, Challis, but you're a lying bastard,' Edgar said. 'But listen to my words, friend... there will be a day of reckoning and you will pay for what you have done to my family and to this lad.'

'Don't threaten me, Sydenham. I am the law and it's on my side, not the likes of you.'

At this, Edgar spat between Challis's feet. He went back to Spence who hadn't moved and still stared into the water as if willing his father to be returned to him.

'Come on, son, let's get you away from here.'

With a last supreme physical effort, Edgar picked him up. Spence didn't weigh much. He felt the beat of his heart against his own. Edgar had carried many a burden like this once... young fellows who'd seen sights they ought not to have done, weeping like lost boys for that was all they were.

As Edgar and Spence moved away, so they looked down at the footprints of a man who only ever trod lightly upon the earth. And even these few marks would disappear with the next tide. John Henry White might never have been there at all.

Forty-Five

Southern Cemetery, Manchester, Thursday morning 2nd April 2015

Judge White paid off his cab and began a long walk through a landscape of leafless, bone-grey trees dripping rain on the dead and the sooty stone monuments which marked their time on earth.

It was a day purged of colour save for a few roses and cornflowers, laid at the feet of cherubs or by carved crosses like that above the remains of the north's great artist, L.S. Lowry. He would have known many a morning like that, dank and dour and not without a hint of menace.

White went first to the Jewish section and located the pale marble monument to his friend, Zilla Arbib. He'd had it inscribed *Teacher and Guide, 1912 - 1972* below a Star of David.

He stood bareheaded, hands clasped, still grateful. From the pocket of his ulster, he took a pebble and placed it on top of the headstone as tradition required. It would not wilt or blow away like a flower but show that he had been there, that his regard extended beyond death. His was the only pebble.

White turned and left. He put up his umbrella to shelter, if not to hide. In the distance, anonymous figures moved between the trees and through the gauzy drizzle just as Lowry might have depicted them, their stories unknown.

It took White several minutes to find the plot where his own family's memorials were grouped together. He took away weeds and litter and scraped moss from names cut as deep in stone as in his heart. All the occupants of 35 lay together, never again to be parted - Frances, Emily, Kitty, Edgar, Vron and his mother,

Joan, dead in her fifties from a heart attack. At least, that's what it said on her death certificate.

But for John Henry, there was no resting place. His son had nowhere to kneel, only on that seam of mud where the sea stole what could never be replaced. Here, he'd offered back his father's love letters in a symbolic act of closure. But even then, he'd still felt what Germans call *atterszoren* - the rage of age - at what he'd lost. White had always known of the alien boy within, the one shaking with envenomed temper and wanting to kill a playmate. And the time came when this stranger took over and the night that it did - and those days after - could never be erased.

*

Edgar heard the front doorbell and rose stiffly from his easy chair to answer it. Away from the fire, the wounds of war reminded him how cold it was getting. More snow was threatened - and the hardest of winters. Not everyone would get through it.

He opened the door and for the second time in his life, was handed a telegram. If the first had brought only grief, this would be the cause of great happiness.

Joan's face appeared over the banister on the landing above.

'That wasn't John Henry, was it, Uncle Edgar?'

'No, love. It's a telegram for Spence.'

'From his Dad, is it?'

'No, just tell him to put his books away and come down and join us for some tea.'

Edgar smiled and waved the official piece of paper at Kitty and Emily. There was tension and excitement in the living room as Spence ripped it open.

'What does it say, love?' Joan said.

'It says, Ma, that I've got a place at Oxford.'

Edgar's damp old eyes conveyed more than words and sentiment ever could. He'd met a few Oxford men once and observed that behind an accent and in front of the guns, all were equal. Joan smiled with pride.

'My boy, off to university to be a lawyer,' Joan said. 'Your Dad will be so pleased.'

No one sought to alter her reality. It had been kinder during those past seven years to let her believe John Henry was working away, that he'd be home before long.

Miss Arbib argued for Joan to be sheltered from the truth. If not, her nature would be to assume blame for everything - for being raped, for John Henry's murderous revenge on his father then his tragic death on the marsh. And all because she'd tried to sell two stolen pictures - a charge police later dropped.

Joan hadn't the mental strength to understand how or why she'd been widowed. She kept vigil for her husband's return, setting his place at table, watching at the window, and all this sustained by the kindness of others and the tablets of doctors.

Spence went into the hall to ring Miss Arbib with his news. They'd put a phone in at 35 after Evelyn signed over all five of her properties in Zion Street to Joan in a private settlement negotiated by Malcolm Feingold. It was blood money by any other name but gave Joan - and Spence - the security they'd never had and left Evelyn's reputation unsullied by scandal.

All went quiet when Spence left the room. Edgar shovelled more coal on the fire. Kitty poured fresh tea for Joan and Emily. Spence would go to London next month to work with a barrister friend of Zilla's and gain experience of life in chambers until he went up to Oxford in October the following year. Their central roles in his life were almost over. His new beginnings were their endings. They would drink to his success that evening but with sadness behind their smiles.

*

They called a cab to take them through the snow from 35 to the Friendship Inn. Edgar ordered Champagne and stood to toast Spence.

'Here's to the lad who brings credit to us all,' he said. 'To Spencer William White, to all he will achieve at Oxford and in later life.'

Others listened from the bar and raised their glasses, vicariously proud that one of their own was going up in the world. A few were old soldiers like Edgar and came across to shake Spence's hand and buy him a beer.

'Drink up, professor,' one said. 'Plenty more where that came from.'

Spence, eighteen and reserved, wore the pin stripe Burton suit and white shirt bought for his Oxford interview. But now he was in the company of men, drinking and smoking with them as if comrades home from the Front. Nothing else mattered for they'd be going back up the line come the dawn.

'Grown into quite a handsome young man, hasn't he?' Zilla said.

Edgar nodded and waved the waiter over to order another round.

'Does he ever talk to you about his father, about what happened?'

'No, locks everything inside himself, does Spence.'

'He's never said a word to me about it, either. I sometimes fear that he threw himself into studying with such intensity simply so he didn't have to confront his loss.'

'You'll never know what's in that lad's head unless he chooses to tell you and more often than not, he won't be doing that.'

Kitty, in a suit of mustard check and hair dyed brick-dust red, was being urged to play the pub's well-scuffed Broadwood. The audience applauded music hall favourites like *If You Were The Only Girl In The World* and *You Always Hurt The One You Love*.

Everyone joined in, people whose hardships showed in their faces like the marks of masons on old stones. Men who hammered metal, carried coal, dug roads, laid pipes and battled through wars, laughed and sang with their wives in this brief interlude between toil, their cheeks redder than the poppies of Passchendaele from the beer which raised their spirits.

But the same was making Spence maudlin. More than once he thought he glimpsed his Dad in a fug of cigarette smoke or saw the back of him, going to the bar. How he wished he was with him that night, wished that sentimental, useless sod of a father was there, singing daft arias in made-up Italian... just one last time.

Don't you want a kiss from your old Dad...

Yes, but never more, never more.

Spence's grief, so long suppressed, wasn't the time-healed scar he pretended. He understood now how an amputee could feel pain from a limb which was no longer there.

His Ma stood by Kitty at the piano in one of Vron's two-piece outfits, navy blue with a white blouse. Spence saw the loneliness in her eyes, the disconnect between her, where she was and what was happening. A couple nearby sniggered because she looked and sounded drunk. Spence would have taken her away

278

from this ridicule but she began talking, as if to herself.

'My husband... John Henry, he's on an important job but he's coming home to me soon. He promised he would... and this is our song, the song that made us happy.'

Through the hubbub came the opening words of *You Are My Heart's Delight* and all that Joan thought cultured and romantic became a slurred and bittersweet lament for what she still didn't realise was gone forever.

It was embarrassing. People turned away and began talking. Kitty stopped playing and Edgar guided Joan to her seat. Vron and Emily put their arms around her for she'd started to weep. Spence stayed where he was, consumed by the vengeful rage that was his inheritance. His Ma had been broken on the wheel of one individual's crusading justice and that same man had hunted his father to death like a wild animal.

The Friendship Inn had a public phone in the entrance lobby. Spence rang Bootle Street Police Station and asked for Detective Inspector Challis. When Challis answered, Spence said he had information about a murder for him.

'Really? Who am I talking to?'

'My name doesn't matter.'

'So why should I waste my time on someone who might be a crank?'

'Because I know the identity of a killer... I was there when he killed another man.'

'If you're having me on, you'll be eating your Christmas dinner through a straw.'

For all this, they agreed to meet an hour later near the police station. Spence returned to the pub's best room and found Miss Arbib.

'I need a big favour from you,' he said. 'I have to get into town right away.'

'But why, Spence? All your family's here, this is your party.'

'We'll be back well before closing time but there's a debt I must settle tonight.'

*

Judge White was due to meet Dan Luston for lunch at The Bank, a gastro-pub beneath the elegant Portico Library in town. All but one key witness to the inquiry - Rose Lingard, the former Police and Crime Commissioner - had now been heard. Luston's minister would want to know White's preliminary thoughts before anything became public ahead of the general election in five weeks.

White's mobile rang as he neared the cemetery exit. It was a woman with a confident manner and a northern accent.

'Hope you're not getting too wet standing there, Judge. At least you've got a brolly.'

'Who is this? Are you watching me?'

''Fraid so, but I have to do it this way. It's safer.'

'Why? What do you want?'

He looked across the sweep of graves either side of him and saw only a young mother pushing a pram, an elderly couple carrying flowers and various cemetery employees with tools and wheelbarrows, preparing flower beds for summer.

'Listen, I haven't much time. There's a bench, fifty yards in front of you. I've left something on it so go and open it and I'll stay on the line.'

White was suddenly uncomfortable. Whoever - and whatever - she was, this woman knew his private mobile number and had the ability to surveil him for a purpose he couldn't know.

A brown A4 envelope lay where she said. Inside were five photographs, black and white, covertly taken with a long lens. Each showed a woman in the front seat of a Mercedes, kissing a man whose face was partly obscured. They could have been pictures from a divorce case or a Sunday tabloid's exposé, tacky and salacious. But the lady was Rose Lingard. Yet again, White felt himself being manipulated around a chessboard. But whose - and why?

'What's your motive in giving me these pictures... to discredit my inquiry somehow?'

'The inquiry that's never meant to get to the truth, you mean?'

'You need to explain yourself,' White said. 'If you really can see me, make yourself known. Walk towards me, let us talk in confidence.'

'Don't be naive, Judge.'

'Then there's nothing more to say. On their own and without context, these photographs have little or no evidential value.'

'Not unless you also get hold of Rose Lingard's emails, not her office emails but those from her private account.'

'And what will they tell me - that she's having an affair?'

'Of course but more than that, her lover's identity.'

'And who is that?'

'A police officer with kids who's already appeared before you, the one who killed that young lad in the cells, the one Rose Lingard has to protect at all costs because if he goes down, so does she and her political career. It's not an inquiry you're chairing, it's a cover-up.'

*

Snow fell soft and silent through the halo of the streetlight beyond Challis's window and deadened the echo of the town hall clock striking eight. Apart from a Salvation Army band playing carols alongside the spangled Christmas tree in Albert Square, the city was strangely quiet. Shoppers and office workers had already caught buses home and hardly any traffic was moving.

Challis had paperwork to sign off before attending the usual Friday night session in the Abercromby with his team. He would give his mystery caller a spin first just in case there was a job in it. This wasn't likely, though. Challis knew of no unsolved murders in the city.

He rang his wife and promised they'd spend next day together as a family. Their young son had written a wish list of the presents he hoped Santa Claus would bring him in a fortnight.

'Don't let the boy down again,' Mrs Challis said. 'He hardly ever sees you and he needs his father around.'

'Stop trying to make me feel guilty. You know what police work is like.'

'You don't have to tell me. I've had years of it.'

Challis booked off and walked down towards the Nag's Head on Jackson's Row where he'd left his new Cortina. It'd been bought on the drip, a car with speed and panache to match its owner's image of himself. He locked his briefcase in the boot then walked back the hundred yards or so to the pawnbroker's shop doorway where he'd told his new informant to meet him. Parked further up the street under the electric menorah of Jackson's Row Synagogue was a Sunbeam convertible.

It was covered in snow and unrecognisable as the car Challis had followed across England in his search for a man who had got away with murder.

But watching unseen from the shadows opposite was someone who felt Challis had done exactly the same.

*

Zilla agreed to drive Spence into town partly to save him from himself. Getting drunk was a rite of passage for a young man but ill advised on that night, in that company. His mother was distressed enough. What began as a celebration party quickly became a wake for a husband whose wife still believed him to be alive.

Zilla asked Spence about the debt he had to settle so urgently. But he blanked her, took refuge within himself. He stared instead into the dancing snow as it transmuted the meanest back-to-back terraces into homesteads of magic and memory so venerated by Chagall.

Windows shone yellow and sparks rose like stars in the coal smoke of a thousand kitchen chimneys. Here was safety and certainty, the remembered world of childhood and happier times in Zion Street, glimpsed for a moment but gone now, gone forever.

'Where is it you want me to take you, Spence?'

'Just off Deansgate, a street called Jackson's Row.'

'There's a shul there. It's Shabbes, I'll go to the service and wait for you.'

Spence was only in his subfusc suit so she insisted he kept warm in her long navy-coloured duffel coat with a hood. From a distance, he could have been a monk. He didn't look back and quickly disappeared behind the curtains of swirling snow.

Zilla entered the synagogue, felt its warmth and welcome and heard the evening prayers of the observant. Yet she somehow knew all was not well that night, something was wrong. It was as if even the angels which blessed a good Sabbath were afraid of what the coming hours would bring.

*

There he stood... the hangman who had brought about the death of Spence's father, consigned his body to the maw of the sea, robbed him of all that might have been and condemned his Ma to wander some twilight path between sanity and madness. What did he want from this man - an apology, a good act of contrition, a promise not to do it again?

Challis hadn't broken the law. He had done his blameless duty in the office of constable yet caused suffering without end. It was held that vengeance was the Lord's. But Spence, the nascent lawyer in his cups and in his loss, wanted to speak truth to power himself. He crossed the street, his heart occluded with hate yet with no weapons but words.

'Inspector Challis?'

'I'm Challis. You the one who rang about a murder?'

'I did. I saw a man murdered.'

'Fancy a pint? The Nag's Head's just down the street and it's a bit chilly out here.'

'No, I don't want a drink,' Spence said. 'You don't remember me, do you?'

'Should I remember you?'

'No, maybe not. I was only a kid when you saw me last.'

'I see a lot of people, son. Listen, my bollocks are near freezing off so are you going to tell me what you know or not?'

Spence looked into the face that had looked into his father's as the sea closed over his mouth and the undertow took him down and out of this life.

'I'll tell you who the murderer is... it's you, Vincent Challis. You murdered my Dad as surely as if you'd put a bullet in his head.'

'Who are you? Take that fucking hood off and let me see you.'

Challis made a grab for the lapels of Spence's coat. Spence tried to push him back with his one strong arm but the cop was heavy and built like a boxer. As a fight, it was a cruel mismatch. Challis trapped him in the doorway, punched him in the stomach. Spence doubled over. Challis followed with an upper cut and burst Spence's nose.

'I'm taking you in, you bastard.'

He put Spence in a headlock to drag him to Bootle Street Police Station. This left Spence's hands free. He grabbed Challis's testicles and squeezed them violently and wouldn't let go. Challis dropped to the ground, screaming in agony.

Spence ran down Jackson's Row, half blinded by snow and tears - tears of pain from his bleeding nose and anger that he'd not got the better of Challis on any level. He reached Challis's car and felt a child-like urge to do something - anything - to avenge himself.

'Stop, you little shit!' Challis said. 'I know you. I know who you are, now.'

Without thinking, Spence unscrewed the Cortina's petrol filler cap. He snapped open the Zippo lighter Uncle Edgar had given him last birthday, flicked the wheel to light the wick and dropped it into the tank.

Challis came hobbling towards him, roaring threats and holding his crotch. Spence made it away just before the car exploded. Challis didn't. He was caught in the blast and hurled against a wall on the opposite side of the street.

285

Flames and black smoke poured from the wreckage. Nearby windows cracked in the intense heat. Drinkers came from the Nag's Head. Worshippers hurried down from the synagogue and police officers from Bootle Street, too. Someone brought a blanket to put over Challis. He was barely conscious.

Spence re-appeared from the direction of Deansgate with a scarf covering his nose and mouth. Zilla saw him mingling with the crowd and edged nearer. She didn't have to be told that Spence had settled his debt.

'Get clear of here before anyone starts asking questions,' she said. 'I'll pick you up outside Kendal Milne. Go... just go.'

The next day's Evening News carried a front-page story and a picture of Challis's burnt-out Cortina.

A leading Manchester detective was critically injured last night in a mystery blast which destroyed his parked car near Bootle Street Police Station where he worked.

Detective Inspector Vincent Challis, 49, a veteran murder investigator with 32 years' service, sustained serious head injuries in the explosion which police say is currently unexplained.

Parts of Jackson's Row and Deansgate were sealed off as detectives looked for clues in what could have been a revenge attack by one of the many criminals Inspector Challis has put behind bars.

A police spokesman appealed for anyone who was in that area between eight and nine o'clock last night to come forward. Inspector Challis, who is married with a 7-year-old son, was rushed by ambulance to Withington Hospital and underwent emergency surgery. His condition was described as critical this morning.

The Evening News was unable to report that Challis had suffered irreversible brain damage, nor could it be known then that he would live in a vegetative state for another decade.

In all that time, he would only ever utter the words *snow* and *white*. He would often say them together, over and over again... *snow white, snow white, snow white*. It was not until many years later that this made any sense to his family.

Forty-Six

The Bank, Mosley Street, Manchester, Thursday afternoon, 2nd April 2015

'Forgive me, Your Honour, but you don't seem quite yourself,' Luston said. 'Anything on your mind about the inquiry, any problem I can help with?'

Judge White looked across the table at Luston, not a callow man, just too young to know self-doubt, too evangelical. He was doing God's work for his was the power and the glory, forever and ever. But life and the law had caused White to be suspicious of those with such certainties.

That being so, he wondered how far, if at all, he might trust this emissary of those he couldn't see but feared were stitching him into their conspiracy.

'I would like some additional time to be allocated to the inquiry,' White said. 'I want certain new matters to be researched thoroughly.'

'Matters such as what, Sir?'

'Some allegations have been made which, if true, are both serious and central to what my inquiry is concerned with.'

'Sorry, but I'm not aware of anything of this nature which has been raised in open session or submitted in written form.'

'These allegations were conveyed to me privately but deserve examination.'

'With respect, Sir, you might be exceeding your terms of reference,' Luston said. 'The minister wants your preliminary report out before the election so this whole sorry business is put to bed quickly and we don't have any more public disorder.'

White had anticipated this response. He returned to his mushroom risotto to consider options. Ideally, he'd have Rose Lingard's appearance delayed - and efforts made to obtain her private emails.

Luston's reaction was enough for White to realise he'd probably not get the go-ahead for either. But he could play politics, too. He struck the ball back over the net, hard and low and into Luston's private parts.

'Let me show you some photographs,' he said. 'Our last remaining witness, Mrs Lingard, is visible in them and with a man, believed to be a married police officer and with whom she is allegedly intimate. What's more, it is alleged that this same officer is implicated in the killing of our third prisoner, Luke North.'

Luston appeared to have been hit and in pain. He examined each of the five pictures and wanted to know what proof White had to back up these allegations.

'This is what I want researched. But be aware, Mr Luston, the allegation is that the former Police and Crime Commissioner for this city and who is also a potential minister in the government of this country has, at the very least, a damaging conflict of interest here. If that is not worthy of consideration by my inquiry, I do not know what is.'

Luston immediately computed the political implications and asked White how he'd come by the photographs.

'I will not say yet nor do I know the motive of the person who gave them to me.'

'Doesn't that cast doubt on the wisdom of raising this matter at this late stage, even if what is being claimed here were admissible, which I would doubt?'

'That is why I want extra time for it to be inquired into.'

'If this doesn't happen, what do you propose doing next?'

'Well, before Mrs Lingard's appearance tomorrow, I shall brief counsel for the inquiry to ask her such questions as may help to bring further clarity to her role in the affair.'

'Sir, if I may, I would advise against that course of action in the strongest terms. The media will read between the lines and blow it out of all proportion. It'll take the focus off the important business of your inquiry and become a tabloid circus with no benefit to anyone because the situation will be completely out of control.'

'And so will I be if you block what is a perfectly reasonable request.'

'I'm sorry, Your Honour, but you must excuse me. There are calls I must now make.'

Luston left his eggs Benedict half eaten and hurried into the street, speed-dialling those who needed to know that their tame judge had just got out of his cage.

*

Next morning, White arrived early in the lecture hall where his inquiry heard testimony. He'd rung his counsel and other panel members wanting to arrange a private session to tell them of the allegations against Mrs Lingard.

Each call went to voicemail. White didn't think this odd until Sir Patrick Prentice made an unscheduled entry, his mandarin's face longer than the lid of a coffin.

'I won't say good morning, Judge White, because it isn't. I gather you're planning to piss in the well from which you drink. Please tell me this is not the case and I can get the next train back to London.'

'If you mean do I want to establish if there's been a cover-up regarding the deaths of any of the three men in police custody, then yes, that's my intention.'

'Oh, dear. I hope the strain of chairing this inquiry isn't becoming too much for you.'

Sir Patrick had the sorrow-not-anger look of a headmaster about to thrash a promising pupil for a breach of school etiquette.

'Judge, before you embarrass yourself by having any uncorroborated and scandalous allegations put to Mrs Lingard, there is someone you need to hear first, someone with what we humble civil servants call evidence.'

'Who are you talking about?'

'One of Mrs Lingard's relatives, actually.'

'What on earth have they got to do with this inquiry?'

'I think it's best that he answers your questions, not me.'

At that point, an internal door opened behind White. He turned and saw the chauffeur who'd driven him to the marshes coming towards him in a dark navy suit, pale blue shirt, sober tie and carrying a briefcase.

'Judge White, may I introduce Vincent Challis,' Sir Patrick said. 'He was a policeman once, like his late father. By one of life's little quirks, this Mr Challis also happens to be the father of Mrs Lingard. Anyway, I shall leave you two together. I don't doubt that you'll have much to talk about.'

Forty-Seven

White and Challis faced each other across the table. Each stared at the other. Not a word was uttered. White knew he was no longer on the bench but in the dock. Guilt had leached down the generations - from Freddie White to John Henry, from John Henry to Spencer White. And Spencer had added to their old sins with a deadly one of his own.

The Fates were now calling him to account for all this wickedness. Someone had to pay, someone had to atone.

Challis reached into his briefcase and began to lay out the exhibits in the case for the prosecution. First came the letter he'd palmed from the creek behind White's back. It was curled over from being wet then dried out. But Joan White's name and address in Zion Street was clear to read.

Next came a black police notebook. It had belonged to Detective Inspector Challis and detailed why John Henry was wanted for Miss Tester's suspicious death, the theft of her pictures and the officer's version of what happened on the marshes.

White's hands shook. Had he have eaten breakfast, he would've been sick. Challis then produced a newspaper cutting about his father sustaining critical injuries when his car exploded.

'What a way to get your own back,' Challis said. 'Condemned my father to ten years of life that wasn't worth living, you did. I'll never forget it but in case you have, you might care to inspect this.'

He held up a creamy-coloured shirt with light brown staining across the front.

'My father wore this that evening in December 1962,' Challis said. 'The blood was assumed to be his but with modern science and access to a person's DNA, let's say from the hair in a brush, we can identify his attacker without a shadow of a doubt.'

He let his words hang in the air. Challis could only guess at how White's blood came to be on the shirt. White offered no defence. But Challis had a final *coup de théatre*.

'My father was reduced to communicating by pointing and grunting but in all his confusion, he could still say two words again and again... snow white, snow white.'

He paused once more for effect, to allow White to take in what seemed obvious now but then appeared like a madman's ravings.

'Only all those years later, when I drove you to the marsh and wondered what the hell a man in your position was doing so I snaffled one of your letters and saw the names, only then could I begin to join up the dots which led us here today.'

With that, Vincent Challis returned each piece of evidence to his briefcase and waited for a response. But this was a brief White wouldn't ever master. Vengeance could never be used as mitigation. He remained silent, damning himself for allowing a stranger to see what should've been the most private of moments on the marsh.

Lightning struck itself that day. Challis the chauffeur still had the curiosity of a police officer but was also burdened with the riddle of his father's tragic death. But in solving it, he faced a tantalising dilemma. If he sought the prosecution of the man responsible, his own daughter would inevitably be engulfed in the sex scandal she covered up. Those who promised political glory for her would run for the hills and she'd be ruined.

It was then that Sir Patrick returned and took charge once more.

'Gentlemen, this is how I see things,' he said. 'If you, Judge White, question Mrs Lingard as you propose, I cannot prevent Mr Challis from going to the police or the media with what he's just shown you. In that event, the mutual destruction of both parties is assured. Is that a fair summary?'

White hardly needed telling that he'd not just lose his liberty but his name, reputation and everything else it had taken him a lifetime to achieve. Resignation was his best option.

'But I don't wish for that to happen,' Sir Patrick said. 'I'd much prefer that I take possession of Mr Challis's material and the photographs of Mrs Lingard. You, Judge White, will publish your preliminary findings showing no one was guilty of anything. Your reward will be in the post and Mr Challis can look forward to his daughter achieving great things on the political stage. If we all agree, let us all put the past behind us and move forward for the greater good.'

*

White's final meeting with Sir Patrick took place in late April after another press conference in the Police Museum's reconstructed Victorian courtroom. A local paper reporter attended but no one from radio or TV, certainly not Sophie Bartells of Channel 4. But no news was good news for some.

'I'd call that a great success,' Sir Patrick said. 'A job well done by one and all.'

They walked downstairs, past the dank, dark cells where prisoners once awaited their fate, then through the old crime room and its forensic exhibits towards the exit.

'You knew about me all along, didn't you?' White said.

'I'd not put it as strongly as that, no. We knew your father died a wanted murderer but that little bit of grit didn't become a pearl until friend Challis saw your odd behaviour on the marsh, stole one of those letters and told his daughter about you.'

'But why have you gone to such lengths to protect her?'

'Rose is our filly in the race. She's going places, high up places.'

'But you must have known she was having an affair with that sergeant.'

'Must I?'

'And he had to be under suspicion for at least one of those men's deaths.'

'Well, we all have skeletons in our cupboards, don't we?'

'And what about the person who contacted me? How will you keep them quiet?'

'Don't worry about her, scorned wives can be taken care of.'

At no point had White ever mentioned the gender of his source to anyone.

'So I was only ever a spear-carrier in your little play, a stooge, someone to see things your way, like Mrs Lingard will be obliged to do from now on.'

'You're a man of our world now, *Sir* Spencer... what do you think?'

They passed beneath a row of sepia photographs of officers with mutton chop whiskers, men who cracked heads with their batons, clipped kids round the ear and sent killers to the gallows for that was their duty and it had to be done.

Sir Patrick, his duty also done, stepped into the sunshine with White then they went their different ways. Standing watching them from across Newton Street was Vincent Challis.

Forty-Eight

The River Great Ouse near Ely, Wednesday, 13th May 2015

White allowed himself a grimly ironic smile, searching for Arcadia on a boat called *Zion* but knowing both destinations were illusions and could never be found.

The contrails of jets cut across the intense blue sky between shifting clouds and swallows feeding on the wing, diving and scything just above *Zion's* wake. It stirred the weeping branches of willows on both banks and set coots and grebes bobbing about. But even as White sailed through this tranquillity, by water meadows where cattle grazed and poplars shook, he remained troubled and ill at ease.

Elspeth had wanted to know when he might be knighted for services rendered.

'I have no idea,' he said. 'The officials who decide such things do so in private and their ways are a mystery to all, not least to me.'

But White had no intention of accepting an honour for putting his name to a politically expedient whitewash of a report. His blackmailers had forced him to bend the knee or they would ruin him. He'd agreed under duress and in shock but realised he'd never be free of their threats or whatever new demands they might yet make.

The past, which gave them power over his present, had to be exorcised. He had to atone for the lie he had lived - and let the truth be known. For this, a great sacrifice was called for.

Elspeth had watched him loading *Zion* with stores and equipment for the expedition to Ely. He asked if she wanted to go with him but in a way which conveyed his desire to be on his own.

'Just try to unwind and relax a little, dear,' she said. 'I don't know why but you've been very tense these last few weeks.'

They embraced with what passed for affection between them. Elspeth waited for him to start *Zion's* engine and cast off. Only then did she turn back to the house and wonder how long it would be before she saw him again.

*

Ely was in sight, the tiny fen city of red-roofed houses, antique shops and tea rooms buttressed around a gem of a cathedral, rising high above the pan-flat fields where once there was only wild marsh.

White made another phone call from his mobile to a private number in Manchester but again got no answer. He berthed *Zion* on the waterfront. Passers-by stopped to admire her and White returned their smiles and pleasantries.

But his mind was elsewhere. He returned to the cabin and began writing a letter. For days, he'd mentally rehearsed the arguments for and against what he planned to do. Elspeth would be devastated but White wished for an honourable end to the situation he himself had authored. His conscience, so biddable for so long, demanded no less from a man who'd judged others for crimes far less wicked than his own.

If he'd any doubts, they were dispelled by Rose Lingard's television appearance during the election six days before, smug and smiling, being lionised for increasing the Conservative majority. On Monday, she'd been shown walking into 10 Downing Street for David Cameron to reward her with a minister's job in Justice.

White's own deceit and hypocrisy had played midwife to hers.

He waited for the ink to dry on his letter then picked up the brown paper package he'd stowed aboard *Zion* before Elspeth could ask any questions.

Anyone watching him walking into town would have seen a pensioner with silver hair, slightly built and using a walking stick, in a creamy-white Aran sweater, dark cord pants and blue deck shoes.

White went first to the Post Office counter in the Costcutter convenience store in Market Street and bought a stamp. He stood for a moment before the post box, letter in hand. If he dropped it in, there could be no turning back. This was a moment like no other. He drew a breath and did what he had to.

Nearby was a café with outdoor tables, blue gingham cloths and vases of cut flowers. Women were drinking coffee and eating pastries they ought not to but laughing and doing so all the same. He took a seat among them and ordered Earl Grey tea. Bits of gossip about husbands and neighbours came and went on the warm air. Not for the first time, he thought about the secrets and lives of others, people we pass but do not see and cannot know, each as invisible as White was to those around him now. Maybe that was fortunate.

He unwrapped the paper around his package and looked at his mother's two pictures one last time - at the fisherman on the beach and the men in a boat by a windmill. They were wrongly come by, ill fated and maybe even cursed as their unfortunate original owner and two widows might once have testified.

For all their connections to home and family, he wanted rid of them just as he had his father's letters. They could go to the first charity shop he came across. It happened to be in Coronation Parade and run by Scope, an organisation that helped the disabled. His mother would've approved.

'Are these any use to you?' White said.

'I'm sure they will be,' the assistant said. 'Prints, aren't they?'

'Yes, nothing special but they're nice frames and might brighten up someone's wall.'

White walked back to *Zion* past the cathedral, a place of worship for fourteen hundred years and where, had he been religious, he might have sat quiet and reflected on what was in front of him.

But he didn't stop. He was tired and wanted only to lie down.

*

Around mid-day next morning, an official from East Cambridgeshire District Council carrying out a survey of boaters regarding proposed new mooring charges, went onboard *Zion* to speak to the owner. The door was open and Classic FM played on the radio. Someone was at home.

'Hello? Anyone there? I'm from the council.'

There was an odd smell, not of cooking or fuel... something almost animal. He went towards the galley, calling out as he did.

The man's body was fully dressed and slumped face down over a table. Blood had run from a wound in his right temple, staining his grey hair and pale cheek then into a dark, almost oily pool on the table's laminated surface.

Some had also dripped onto the floor. The right arm was crooked and the fingers of that hand still gripped the gun. The council official began to shake. He had never seen the stillness of death before, never smelt it. Now it stared up at him and he couldn't stop staring back.

*

Channel 4 News only got confirmation of Spencer White's death thirty minutes before they went on air. Jon Snow did a live two-way with Sophie Bartells in Washington where she'd just become the station's North America correspondent.

'You covered Judge White's inquiry into those three deaths in police custody, Sophie. What have you been able to find out?'

'Jon, as you might imagine, there's disbelief among the people I've managed to reach by phone. He was highly regarded and chosen to head what was a politically sensitive inquiry because he was seen as tough and independently-minded.'

'And yet he was criticised in some quarters for a report which cleared everyone.'

'Well, I talked to him privately and he assured me he would go wherever the evidence led. I don't doubt that if he'd have found blame, he would've apportioned it.'

'Sophie, it's being reported locally that a World War One handgun, a Browning, was found on Judge White's narrow boat. Can you confirm that?'

'No, not officially but interestingly enough someone who'd worked in his chambers once told me that he was fascinated by the Great War because a relative of his had fought in many of the battles with great distinction.'

'And has the Ministry of Justice made any comment yet?'

'Yes, Rose Lingard, a minister there who was also a witness at Judge White's inquiry and the Police and Crime Commissioner when the prisoners died, says she is profoundly upset at his death and her thoughts are with his family and friends.'

*

Just before the Scope shop closed that evening, a man entered in black motorcycle leathers and a helmet, which he didn't take off. He pushed up the visor so only his eyes and nose were visible.

'I was looking around in here yesterday and saw a couple of pictures brought in but I didn't have any cash on me. Have you still got them?'

'People bring in stuff all the time. What were they like?'

'Gold frames, picture of a beach and another like a Dutch scene with a windmill.'

'Oh, them. They're in the back, not been priced up yet.'

'Doesn't matter, they're only prints but I'll give you twenty pounds for them.'

'You liked them that much, did you?'

'Only for sentimental reasons.'

She fetched the pictures and put them in bubble wrap for protection then took his money and rang up the sale on the till.

'That's most generous of you, Mr - '

'Vincent.'

'Mr Vincent?'

'That's right.'

And so the pictures changed hands again and in the swells and rhythms of life which no-one can foretell, another man who thought he'd avenged his father might yet come to know their curse.

Epilogue

Arundel, Egerton Road, Fallowfield, Monday 18th May 2015

Anna Wozniak cleaned houses for the estate agency which let and managed _Arundel_. It was never a grand house but retained its Edwardian features - cast iron fireplaces tiled with birds and flowers, elm floorboards, elegant staircase. It had three bedrooms, a sitting room with a large bay window and a modern fitted kitchen.

Anna now took a break from vacuuming and washing to make herself an instant coffee at its breakfast bar.

Arundel was let furnished. Its previous tenant had moved out three weeks before. Anna had to push hard to open the front door against a drift of circulars and newspapers. This rubbish went into a black plastic sack, but not the letter which took her eye.

Someone with old fashioned, copperplate handwriting which Anna admired, had addressed the envelope in ink. She should have disposed of it.

But something about the letter intrigued her, fed a peasant nosiness and a need to imagine lives less mundane than hers. It might be from a lover - or a wife who'd found out about an affair. Against her better judgement, Anna opened it and began to read, following each word with her finger.

Dear Miss Bartells

I have tried telephoning you several times but you have been out. How extraordinary that you should live in a house I once knew well as a child. It was owned then by the woman to whom I owe my career and so much else.

I saw it written once that we are all prisoners of our past, that we are pinned like butterflies to a board by *what has gone before. Well, in my time, I have fluttered my wings but only ever created the illusion of flight.*

I have borne a great sin for many years which so weighted me down that the freedom I sought was unattainable and in my more optimistic moments, I knew that only my death would bring about a release from these burdens.

Sins, as we all know, come with a price and I was required to pay that price during the public inquiry you so rightly saw as a further cover-up of how three men came to lose their lives in police custody.

People with power found out about my sin and the price of their silence was the anodyne report you criticised even before it was published. I was blackmailed in what was a politically motivated conspiracy to hide the truth. But in allowing myself to be manipulated, I have come to feel even more tarnished.

The sin I committed has been compounded by my cowardice and instead of finding the redemption I need, I have begun to loathe myself.

I now wish to take up your offer of a television interview. I have much to tell you which I think you will find interesting.

I believe I know the reason for at least one death being covered up. There is a photograph to substantiate this allegation.

I also have notes of my conversations with the senior civil servant who, for political purposes, has connived to keep the matter secret. I hope the process of confessing to you in this public fashion will finally liberate me from the burdens I carry. Might I suggest we meet this coming weekend?

I have a narrow boat called Zion which is berthed in Ely in Cambridgeshire and will be for another ten

days. But I should warn you that certain people will, I am sure, go to great lengths to stop you making this public. Anyway, let us meet and discuss the best way forward.
Warmest regards,
Spencer White.

Anna finished her coffee, slightly alarmed. She didn't fully understand all that was written. Yet despite her imperfect English, she knew what she'd just read about political conspiracies and deaths being covered up was serious.

But if she showed it to her employer, she could be dismissed for opening a client's private correspondence. Her husband would tell her to throw it away. They were newly arrived from Bialystok. It was bad for a family's health to ever get involved with police anywhere. But Anna, good Catholic that she was, sensed the letter was a confession so too important to be ignored.

She knew two people who would know what to do for the best. The first was the friendly Evening News reporter who exposed the Wozniaks' crooked landlord when he raised their rent illegally. The other was the candidate who took time out of her election campaign to get them rehoused.

She was now their Member of Parliament and the papers said she was a minister in the government. That made her a very important person. Anna had both their cards at home. Tomorrow was her day off. She would phone one of them in the morning.

THE END

Acknowledgements

I am hugely indebted to Patrick Prentice, a veteran of foreign news coverage at The Daily Telegraph and The Times who, along with publisher-editor, Anne Loader, subbed and corrected my efforts. Without their wise counsel, I would have spun off into many a fenland ditch.

Sincere thanks are due to my mentor, the actor Patrick Malahide, for his invaluable and constructive criticism of the manuscript, ditto to CP Lee, his wife, Pam, for theirs.

My research was greatly aided by Katie Brown of the Greater Manchester Police Museum, Rachael Kneale of Manchester Grammar School and Andy Tighe of the Home Office.

Jeanette Wilson, a former Lady Mayoress of Manchester, was unstinting in her willingness to help and so, too, was Andy Sherwill, Editor of The Forester, Coleford.

John Barrance, Adrian Bradshaw, John Cooper-Smith, Danielle Davayat, my daughter, Dr Kitty Farooq, David Fowler, Tonie Gibson, Lawrence Greenberg, Toni Hyams, Josephine Jones, Sophie Linden, Kearn Malin, Declan Ryan, Malcolm Scott, Laurie Sherwood, Rex Sly and John Thorne all assisted and I am most grateful to them.

Three judges were also most helpful to me but convention requires that they remain anonymous. If there are mistakes in the manuscript, they are mine and not anyone mentioned above.

Finally, I acknowledge the input of ideas - and the saintly patience - of my wife, Ann de Stratford who, despite many reasons not to, continues to support me.

* The verse in Chapter 9 is taken from Apologia Pro Poemate Meo by Wilfred Owen.
* The verse in Chapter 15 is from To My Mother by Robert Louis Stevenson.

An Afterword

Childhood is a credit bank for authors. Riches lie in its vault of half-remembered family secrets, within the silence around a scandal or the anguish on a face full of tears.

But the grown-ups of then are the dead of now. They cannot be questioned by our older, wiser selves. We have neither context nor corroboration for what we have always believed to be true about events and people all those years ago.

Thus innocence skewed our reality and can continue to deceive, for recollections from those formative times remain vivid and powerful, often more so in later life.

Would-be scribblers are always advised to write about what they know. My first two novels featured a hack caught up in a search for identity - and in the darker aspects of journalism, espionage and allied trades.

Long before they were published, I had attempted to fictionalise my beginnings in the bombed-out streets of post-war Manchester. But I hadn't the wit then to think it through properly or get the plot and structure right. The project was a failure and I genuinely forgot about it.

Early in 2015, I accidentally found the manuscript in a drawer. Only then did I see how it could be brought up to date, made to live and breathe and bleed.

Before me once more was the repertory company of characters in what had been my extended family - a wounded Great War uncle, an eccentric lesbian aunt who gambled and her sister, still grieving for the child she lost in the 1930s.

These and other memorable relatives I called back from the grave or bid the wind return their ashes to me. It will not be long before I am as old as they were then. Their hurts and hardships are no longer unknown to me.

And what of my parents? Were they not central to who I was and might become? Indeed they were. But here it got difficult, too close to the bone for comfort.

I found it painful to audit what I knew of their strengths and many weaknesses. Therein lay the reasons why they were condemned to lives they could never escape but which, through chance and circumstance, I managed to do.

These familial truths - albeit they were mine alone - had to be confronted if the characters they would inspire were to engage the reader. So...

My mother was loving, generous, trusting and unworldly, a woman without a trace of guile to whom misfortune came as clouds before rain. I mourn her to this day.

My father was emotionally absent, an angry, unfulfilled man full of hopeless dreams and schemes, unable to understand why the system would always win and he would always lose. We were never close.

But now I had my actors. We could all go back to the sooty terraced house where I first lived, to its remembered smells of Woodbines and coal smoke and where the talk was still of Hitler's bombers and the glow in the night sky as Manchester burned.

This - and more - a child absorbs. And all these years later, my spectral cast can perform in a political drama of my imagining, bearing burdens even greater than those which troubled their real lives.

But in the end and after so much soul-searching, it is only a story, an "entertainment" as Graham Greene called his brilliantly observed books.

I am afraid that the American reviewer who generously suggested I was in the line of successors to John le Carré was much mistaken. All we have in common are weak and terminally selfish fathers.

But at least we got novels out of their frailties - le Carré with *A Perfect Spy* and me - infinitely more modestly - with *The Boy From Zion Street*.

Whatever misgivings I had about my old man, I must accept that had he worked in an office, played golf and could afford a mortgage, I would have struggled to find anything remotely intriguing in so mundane an upbringing.

I hope with all sincerity that readers will recognise his character is ultimately treated with compassion. His fictional son wanted only to love him, however hard that might be.

It is a matter of consuming sadness for the boy that such sentiments were never expressed by either side.

But there's art aping life again and that's the pity of it all.

Geoffrey Seed, Powys, Summer 2016

19873179R00183

Printed in Great Britain
by Amazon